# A Beautiful FUNERAL

# ALSO BY JAMIE MCGUIRE

## THE PROVIDENCE SERIES

*Providence*
*Requiem*
*Eden*
*Sins of the Innocent: A Novella*

## THE BEAUTIFUL SERIES

*Beautiful Disaster*
*Walking Disaster*
*A Beautiful Wedding: A Novella*
*Something Beautiful: A Novella*

## THE MADDOX BROTHERS BOOKS

*Beautiful Oblivion*
*Beautiful Redemption*
*Beautiful Sacrifice*
*Beautiful Burn*

## RED HILL SERIES

*Among Monsters: A Novella*

*Apolonia*

*Happenstance: A Novella Series (Books 1-3)*

*Sweet Nothing*

# *A Beautiful* FUNERAL

JAMIE McGUIRE

Visit my website at www.jamiemcguire.com

Cover Designer: By Hang Le, www.byhangle.com

Editors: Fiona Lorne and Jenny Sims

Proofreader: Pam Huff

Interior Designer: Jovana Shirley, Unforeseen Editing, www.unforeseenediting.com



ISBN: 978-1534623576

*To Lisa Hadley,*
*Your smiling face and generous spirit remind me why I do what I do.*

# CONTENTS

# CHAPTER ONE

## THOMAS

I SAT ON THE SMALL, cold loveseat in Liis's hospital room. The brown and blue color-blocked walls and minimalist décor reminded me more of an Aloft hotel than a maternity ward. My future wife looked cozy and beautiful, holding Stella's tiny, curled body against her chest in the same bed she'd birthed our daughter. For the first time in seventeen hours, I rested. My shoulders sagged, and I blew out a long puff of air. Little to no sleep had never bothered me, but watching the woman I loved more than anything suffer so much pain for that long had taken its toll.

Liis was visibly exhausted. I could see the purple half-moons under her eyes, and although she was the most beautiful I'd seen her, I felt torn between offering to take Stella and waiting for her to request it.

Stella was sleeping in her mother's arms just feet away. Seeing them serenely holding each other was both comforting and jarring. Stella was a new life that we'd created, a perfect combination of two people who had once been strangers. Now, she would have her own thoughts, feelings, and—because she's our daughter—strong opinions. I wondered about her entire life as she lay sleepily suckling at Liis's breast.

Finally, my impatience won out. "Liis," I began.

As if she knew, Stella stopped nursing, and her head fell back, her mouth open. Liis smiled and carefully positioned the baby onto her shoulder.

"I can do it," I said.

Liis smiled, patting Stella's tiny back gently and rubbing after every third tap or so. Stella's body jerked as an almost inaudible burp broke the silence of the dark hospital room.

My shoulders fell. Liis smiled, breathed out a quiet laugh, and then touched her lips to the dark, soft wisps of hair on Stella's head.

"You've got to give her up sometime," I said softly. I had held my daughter for just a few short minutes before they took her away to record her weight, measurements, and footprints. After that, they returned her to Liis for another half-hour before whisking her away for her first bath.

"It'll get easier, right? To share?" Liis asked, only half kidding.

"I hope not," I said with a tired grin. "I realize you just got her back, but I can change her and rock her back to sleep."

Liis thought about my offer and then nodded. Always the negotiator.

I stood up again, walking across the room to reclaim my daughter. As I carried our daughter to her clear bassinet, Liis's breathing evened out. Even her FBI personnel file had stated she'd always had a knack for grabbing shut-eye when she could, especially just a few hours before a raid. Her head fell to the side. She had sunk into oblivion just seconds after she'd finally agreed to let me take over.

Liis was most comfortable when in control, but as hard as she resisted, I knew she trusted me. I was the only one she would trust with her heart, especially now that it was living outside of her body in the form of the perfect being who'd just completed our family. It had taken nearly ten years of hints and coaxing to get her to agree to even consider a proposal. Liis had been happily married to the Bureau, and until she learned Stella was on the way, she wasn't open to infidelity.

Stella gazed up at me, her blue eyes watching me with wonder. She'd woken up when I'd lifted her into my arms, and she scanned my face with curiosity while I cleaned her up and wrapped her in a dry diaper. Trying not to wrinkle my nose, I spoke to her tenderly while I swaddled her in a soft, ivory blanket, telling her how glad we were that she'd finally arrived. For a perfect being, Stella could certainly leave a disgusting mess.

She stretched her neck, and I smiled, cradling her in my bare arms. My sports jacket, white button-down, and tie were hanging over the recliner. A white undershirt and slacks weren't appropriate for the office, but taking care of someone smaller than I was made me feel eleven years old again, wiping faces and asses and everything in between, barely able to keep my own T-shirt and holey jeans clean. I couldn't wait to get home to shower and snuggle with my two favorite women in the world, wearing three days of scruff, gray sweatpants, and my favorite Rolling Stones T-shirt.

In the hall, I heard a short scuffle, and then a light commotion just outside the door. Whispered voices hissed, unhappy and persistent. I took a step to stand between Liis and the door and then turned, positioning my body between whoever was outside and my daughter.

A nurse pushed through, looking disheveled and a bit shaken.

"Everything okay?" I asked, remaining alert. From the corner of my eye, I could see that Liis was awake and ready to react.

"Um, sure," the nurse said, pausing when she noticed our posture. "Is everything okay in here?"

"What was the noise outside?" Liis asked.

"Oh," the nurse said, pulling on a pair of gloves as she stood by Liis's bedside. "It's a fight to get into your room. Those agents outside don't play around."

Liis relaxed, and I walked over to the rocking recliner just a few feet away from her, pulling back Stella's blanket to check that she was fine.

"The director just wants me back at work ASAP," Liis said, settling back against her pillow.

"Not happening," I said.

In truth, if the director had his way, Liis would have given birth at the office. We were at the end of our largest case, and Liis was the most trusted translator and analyst at Quantico. I'd been the case lead for eleven years, which was more than half of my time in the Bureau. My youngest brother, Travis, had been undercover, but when the shit hit the fan and his wife was threatened, Travis executed Benny and a few of his men. Abby handed over all the info she had on her father, Mick—another one of Benny's pawns—getting us closer than we had ever been to finally wrapping up the case. Benny's underboss and eldest son, Angelo Carlisi, was just about to go down, and everyone wanted the investigation locked down tight.

Liis and I had spent hours in the director's office explaining to him our position on our new family. The risk was so much higher, making us all the more eager for a conclusion.

"I'll just bring her to work. The director can change diapers," Liis joked.

"He might take you up on that," I said with a smirk.

The nurse wasn't amused. "Is there a chance the agents could … I don't know … look at my face and remember it an hour later? The pat downs are getting old."

Liis and I traded glances but didn't respond. We understood her frustration, but more than just the director knew that Liis and I were responsible for bringing half of the Vegas organized crime families to justice. Benny's death had made everyone nervous. We were the FBI's top agents on the case with a baby on the way, and one of Benny's men was in custody and very close to testifying. They had already targeted us twice, so the Bureau wasn't taking any chances. We'd had agents shadowing our every move as soon as Liis's baby bump became prominent.

"Stella might as well get used to having two special agents for parents," I said, pushing off my toes. The rocker swept back and then forward, a gentle motion highlighted by something creaking with sleepy rhythm in the base of the chair. Memories of rocking Travis when he was a toddler, still in diapers, came to the forefront of my mind. His shaggy hair, chicken legs, and the sticky ring around his mouth—a telltale sign Grandpa had been over. He'd bring over five suckers in his pocket and always leave with one. Children ate candy, and Dad was passed out drunk in the bedroom while I was keeping the boys from playing in traffic. I'd stopped being a child when Mom died.

The nurse nodded, but I could see by her expression she still didn't understand. Before leaving, she glanced at Stella with pity reflecting in her eyes. I planted my feet on the floor, stopping the chair. Stella fussed, and I patted her back while deep in thought. Stella was loved before she was even born, a shiny new nursery and a full bookshelf waiting for her at home. That someone would feel sympathy for our daughter had never crossed my mind. We were fully capable of surviving whatever the Bureau put in our paths, but now I wondered how it would affect Stella.

"Did you call your dad?" Liis asked.

"Earlier."

"Everybody else?"

"I asked Dad to give it a day. I don't want to spend all day on the phone."

Liis sat back and closed her eyes. "I guess as an only child, I don't think about things like that," she murmured before drifting off.

I draped a thick cloth over my shoulder and then supported Stella's head while I positioned her against my chest. I pushed off on my feet again, and the recliner swayed back and forth. The rhythmic squeaking made my eyes feel heavier, and I noticed Liis breathing more deeply.

I touched my cheek to Stella's soft hair. She was so innocent and vulnerable, and Liis knew as well as I did just how much evil was in the world we'd brought her in to. It was our responsibility to keep her safe.

I looked over at my sleeping girlfriend and then over at my sports jacket that covered my shoulder holster. Two standard-issue Sig Sauer 9mms were snugly hidden away, ready for anything. I knew Liis had one tucked into Stella's baby bag, too. I swayed back and forth, resting my head and trying to let the tight muscles in my neck relax. Even after Stella had settled down and I had lain her in the bassinet, I couldn't stop my ears from cataloging every sound from the hall—the soda machine, the elevators, the nurses checking on patients in the other rooms. Babies crying, the agents murmuring, and the vent kicking on. Unlike Liis, even when I wanted to sleep, I couldn't.

I reached for Liis's pitcher of water and poured myself a cup. I would sleep when she woke. Too much was at stake. Not even the agents outside would protect Stella as fiercely, so one of us had to be awake at all times.

Raindrops spattered against the window as I triple checked the baby's bag and readied the car seat while Liis signed the discharge papers. The nurse watched us with careful curiosity, likely hearing gossip about the armed agents standing guard outside our room all night and the fresh pair of agents assigned to escort us home that morning.

Liis cradled Stella in one arm while signing the various documents. She'd been a mother for less than forty-eight hours and was already an expert. I smiled at her until she motioned for me to take Stella. I walked over, trying not to show my excitement at my turn to hold the tiny, soft human we'd created.

I lifted Stella into my arms and then walked the few steps to the car seat that sat on the floor. "Shit," I hissed, trying to maneuver the baby under the handlebar and into the small space like a puzzle piece. Stella didn't stir while I struggled with the five-point harness and fussed over the padding that covered the shoulder straps and the pillow around her head.

"Thomas," Liis said with a small laugh. "It's perfect. If she wasn't comfortable, she would tell you."

"You sure?" I asked, glancing back at Liis. With every milestone of our relationship, I continued to be in awe that just when I thought she couldn't be more beautiful, she was. The day we moved in together in San Diego, the day she told me we were having Stella, the day I finally moved to Virginia, and every day I noticed her belly was a little bit rounder and her cheeks a little fuller—I felt like a con for somehow misleading her into marrying me. While she labored, and then when she gave birth, and now, sitting up and looking tired but gloriously happy in the morning sun, the mother of my child was once again the most beautiful I'd ever seen her.

Liis breathed out a laugh. "What?"

"You know what." I stood, carefully bringing the car seat with me. "Ready?"

Once Liis nodded, the nurse pushed the wheelchair next to her bed. Liis stood, unhappy about being fussed over while she moved over to her next mode of transport, but it was hospital policy, and Liis had always liked to pick her battles.

Wearing a blue button-down and gray maternity pants, Liis let the nurse push her toward the door. I opened it and nodded to the agents, Brubaker and Hyde.

Liis couldn't restrain her smug smile, recognizing both agents were female. "You know what I'm thinking, right?" she asked me.

"That women are better drivers and better with a gun, so you're happy about our escorts?"

"Correct," Liis said.

Brubaker smiled too.

After I secured Stella into her car seat and helped Liis into the backseat of our Suburban, I slid behind the wheel, signaling to the agents to move forward. Brubaker was ahead of us in a black Tahoe, and Hyde was behind in an identical vehicle. I rolled my eyes. "Are they trying to announce our exit, or do they think the mafia is stupid?"

"I don't know," Liis said, leaning forward to see into the side mirror.

"All clear?" I asked.

"So far."

"What is it?" I asked, seeing the concern in Liis's eyes.

"I don't know that yet, either."

I reached back to pat her knee. "It's going to be okay, Mommy."

She craned her neck. "Please let's not be that couple who calls each other Daddy and Mommy."

I frowned. "How else will Stella learn what to call us?"

Liis sighed, a rare concession. "Fine. Just … only do it around her, but not in public."

"Yes, ma'am," I said with an amused grin.

Liis leaned back, appearing relaxed, but I knew better. She continued to periodically lean over to glance in the rearview mirror and then down at Stella.

"How's she doing?" I asked.

"We need one of those mirrors that sits above the car seat so you can see her in the rearview," Liis said. "What if one of us is in the car with her alone? We'll need some way to check on her."

"Making a mental note now," I assured her.

She closed her eyes for half a second before they popped open again to look at the side mirror. She gave it a second glance and instantly metamorphosed from tired new mother to FBI agent. "White sedan, four back. Left lane."

I glanced back. "Got it." I touched the radio on my lapel. "We've got a tail. White sedan. Left lane."

"Copy that," Hyde said.

Brubaker radioed in, and we barely drove two miles before receiving word that more vehicles were on the way. Just before they arrived on-scene, the sedan took an exit.

"Make sure someone follows," Liis said.

"Don't worry," I said, trying to remain calm. "They're all over it."

Liis swallowed, struggling to keep her cool. Being parents was an added security issue we couldn't plan for. I knew part of her wanted to follow the sedan, to catch them and question them, and lock them away from our fragile new family. As urgent as her commitment was to being an agent, her need to protect our daughter was stronger.

We drove the remaining fifteen minutes home without event but were unable to enjoy our trip with our new addition as other new parents would. As we unhitched the car seat, the agents stood guard. Hyde and Brubaker glanced around, occasionally speaking into the small radios in their ears while Liis and I took our daughter to the porch. We waved to the neighbors and then walked up the stairs to the front door. Under the shade of the porch, I dug for my keys and then touched one to the lock.

Hyde gently touched my forearm. "Sir, I'd like to take a look around first, if you don't mind."

"Of course," I said, stepping aside.

Just two days ago, I would have been the one to sweep the house. I would have left Liis with the agents while I checked each room, closet, behind every door, and under every bed before I let my pregnant girlfriend enter. But now, my place was to stand next to her, protecting our daughter. Everything had changed in less than forty-eight hours.

Hyde unlocked the door and then drew her weapon. She held her Glock like it was an extension of her arm, walking through the front room so stealthily I couldn't hear her footsteps.

"Was I that good?" Liis asked.

"Better," I said.

"Don't bullshit me, Maddox."

"Never, Agent Lindy."

After a few minutes, Hyde returned, holstering her sidearm. "All clear, sir."

"Thank you," I said, following Liis inside.

Liis took a deep breath as she crossed the threshold, already feeling more at ease. I carried Stella's car seat into the nursery, setting it gently on the floor. Liis had decorated in grays, blue-grays, tans, and coral with not a bow or ballerina in sight. Liis was determined to keep Stella as gender-neutral as possible, even before she was born. An ivory upholstered rocking chair was in the corner next to the crib, a square pillow of a fox outlined in blue in the center.

I unbuckled Stella, lifted her limp body into my arms, and then lay her on her back in the crib. She looked so tiny within the walls of her brand-new bed.

Everything was new—the carpet, the Santa Fe-style rug, the five-by-seven portrait of a cartoon fox on the side table, the curtains, the paint on the walls. Until that moment, the room had been beautiful and pristine but empty. Now, it was filled with our love for the brand-new baby for whom the room belonged.

After staring at Stella for a moment, Liis and I traded glances.

"Now what?" she whispered.

I adjusted the nursery camera and signaled for Liis to follow me out into the hall. I shrugged.

She shrugged too. "What does"—she shrugged again—"this mean?"

"It means I don't know. I was expecting chaos and crying when we got home. You know … all the horrible things you see in the movies."

Liis smiled and leaned against the doorjamb. "She's perfect, isn't she?"

"I'll reserve judgment until two o'clock this morning, or the first time she shits in my hand."

Liis playfully elbowed me. I kissed her temple.

"I think I'll lie down for a bit," Liis said, reaching for the monitor.

I swiped it off the dresser first. "I've got it. You rest."

She pushed up on the balls of her feet, kissed the corner of my mouth, and then touched my cheek. "I'm so happy, Thomas. I never thought I could feel like this. It's hard to explain."

I smiled down at her. "You don't have to. I know just how you feel."

Liis ambled down the hall to our bedroom, leaving the door cracked open about three inches.

I chuckled to myself as I headed to the kitchen, opening the dishwasher to unload the dishes Liis had just started when her water broke.

My cell phone buzzed in my pants pocket, and I fished it out, holding it to my ear. "Maddox." I listened, walked over to the window, and moved the curtains to the side. My heart sank.

"You're not serious," I said. I listened as the director gave me instructions that made my blood run cold. "The plan is to let them shoot at me?"

"They've already taken a shot at Travis."

"What? Is he okay?" I asked, the hairs on the back of my neck standing on end.

"Just grazed his shoulder and he's a little banged up. They ran his car off the road." The director cleared his throat, uncomfortable having to say his next words. "It was meant for Abby."

I swallowed the bile that rose in my throat. "How do you know?"

"Travis was driving her SUV. Surveillance of all soft targets was in the shooter's vehicle, including Abby."

"By soft targets, you mean …"

"The members of your family, Thomas. I'm very sorry."

I blew out a breath, trying to remain calm. If they had surveillance photos, the Carlisis had Travis figured out for a while. They'd been watching my family; close enough to photograph. That explained Travis's interrogation in Vegas. What we thought was Travis somehow blowing his cover leading to an impromptu kidnapping and beating while they tried to get more intel was actually planned. "Have they been located?"

The director paused. "Travis's SUV hit a tree at a high rate of speed. They came back to finish it, but they didn't walk away. The Carlisi family is now three made men down. Bobby the Fish. Nikko the Mule. Vito Carlisi."

"Benny's son. That means the Carlisis only have two possible successors left." Benny had seven children but only three sons. The oldest, Angelo, was the underboss, with the other two in line for the job. Benny was old school, and he'd passed onto his children and his crime family that only men could inherit his illicit empire. I was hopeful that if their attempts left them without a Carlisi underboss, everything Benny built would fall apart.

"Travis took care of it," the director said.

"Of course, he did." My muscles relaxed. What could have been a huge clusterfuck was actually falling in our favor. I should have known. Once someone takes a swing at Travis, he always made sure they wouldn't do it again. Even if they were three of the Carlisi family's best hitmen.

"The youngest of the Carlisi boys, Vincenzo, and two soldiers have been traced to a silver Nissan Altima. They're headed your way now. They are likely aware of Vito's death by now."

"Coming here? Now?" I asked, looking back toward Stella's nursery. "What about stray bullets? Ricochets? We're going to let them do a drive-by in front of my home with my wife and daughter inside? This seems sloppy, sir."

"Can you think of another plan in the next eight minutes?"

I frowned. "No, sir."

"Hyde will have Liis and Stella secured in the back of the home with vests. This is our one chance. It's up to you, of course, but—"

"Understood, sir."

"You're sure?"

"You're right. It has to happen this way. It'll buy us time."

"Thank you, Agent Maddox."

"Thank you, Director."

The bedroom door cracked open, and from my peripheral, I could see Liis leaning against the doorjamb, holding her cell phone to her ear. They had called her, too.

"But we just … they can't possibly know—" She sighed. "I understand. Of course, and I agree, but … yes, sir. I understand, sir." She looked at me with tears in her eyes, clearing her throat before speaking again. "Consider it done, sir."

The phone fell from her hand to the floor, and her eyes lost focus. I rushed across the room to cradle her in my arms. I meant to be gentle, but I knew I was holding her too tight.

"I can't believe this is happening," she said, her voice muffled against my chest. Her fingers dug into my back.

"If there was any other way," I began.

"Travis is okay?" she asked. She had already been briefed, I was sure, but she needed to hear it from me. I wouldn't sugarcoat it just because she was a new mother, and she knew it.

"He's a little banged up. They're three goons short."

She breathed out a laugh and then lifted her chin, her eyes wide and glossing over with realization. "I'm going to have to tell them, aren't I? It will have to be me."

I hesitated, conflicted feelings swirling inside me. I didn't want to put her through that. My eyebrows pulled in. "The Carlisis will just send more, Liis. I know it's a long shot … but you have to."

She shook her head. "I can't. I …."

I clenched my teeth, trying to keep it together and stay strong for her. I cupped her jaw in my hands. "It'll be okay. You can do it."

Her chest caved, and she puffed out a breath. "How can I do that to them?" She touched her forehead, shaking her head in disbelief.

"We do what we have to do. Like we always have."

Liis glanced back toward the nursery. "But this time, even more is at stake."

I checked my watch and sighed. "I have to pack and make some calls."

She pressed her lips together and nodded. "I'll help you."

Stella began to fuss, and I nearly lost it. "This is too much. This isn't right, leaving you alone with her. She's barely a day old, and you here, alone …"

She hugged me. "I won't be alone."

I squeezed my arms around her, breathing in her hair, memorizing the softness of her skin. "I can't … I can't tell her goodbye," I said. I'd had my heart broken more than once, but this was torture. I was already in love with the tiny girl in the crib, and leaving her would be the hardest thing I would ever do.

"So don't."

I nodded and then crept into the nursery, watching Stella breathe easily, swaddled and happily dreaming of whatever newborns dreamed of—Liis's heartbeat; my muffled voice. I leaned down and pressed my lips to her thick, dark hair. "I'll see you soon, my love. Daddy loves you."

I walked across the room and reached down for my vest, slipping it on as she watched with a pained expression, then I stuffed some clothes and toiletries into a bag and raised my phone, tapping out Trenton's number. I tried to keep my voice casual while telling him to expect us sooner than originally planned. In less than five minutes, I'd done everything I could do to prepare.

"Who's out there?" Liis asked when I hung up with Trenton.

"Dustin Johns and Canton," I said, putting on a light jacket.

"Brent Canton?" she confirmed. When I nodded, she sighed, relieved. They were the best snipers in the Bureau.

"They'd better not miss," she snapped.

"They won't," I said. I hoped not. I was putting my life in their hands. I took Liis into my arms, holding her tight, and then pressed my lips against hers, hoping it wasn't for the last time. "I'm going to ask you to marry me when we see each other again, and this time, you're going to say yes."

"Make sure we see each other again," she said.

Hyde opened the front door. "Thirty seconds, sir."

I nodded to her, grabbed my car keys, and glanced back at Liis, taking one last look before closing the door behind me.

# CHAPTER TWO

## TAYLOR

"CHEER UP, BUD. I bet she'll be at the house by shift's end," Jubal said, watching me fold laundry.

"You've said that every shift since she left," I grumbled, shaking out a pair of standard-issue navy blue cargo pants. The color was fading.

When Falyn did the laundry, she somehow kept them looking brand new for months. I cooked dinner and took out the trash; she'd do the laundry and the dishes. We tag-teamed taking care of the kids. Having Hollis and Hadley four months apart was a lot like having twins. One of us held down flailing legs and pulled out baby wipes while the other cleaned and re-diapered. I'd take Hollis to soccer, and she would take Hadley to volleyball. For nine years, we'd worked like a well-oiled machine. We'd even perfected fighting. Anger, negotiation, make-up sex. Now that she was gone, I had no one to compromise with, no kids to juggle, no dinner for four. I'd been doing my own laundry for two months—since she'd moved back to Colorado Springs with the kids—and my pants were already looking like shit. One more reason to miss her.

I folded the cargos over a hanger and hooked it on the rod inside my armoire. I hadn't been on the mountain digging firebreaks in four years. Only being home for six months out of the year had taken its toll on our marriage, so I hung up my pulaski and took a full-time job with the city fire department.

In the end, it didn't matter what I did. Falyn wasn't happy.

"How are the kids liking the new school?" Jubal asked.

"They're not."

Jubal sighed. "I wondered if it would be tough for Hollis. I'm surprised you let her take him."

"Split 'em up? No," I said, shaking my head. "Besides, she's his mother. She always has been. It wouldn't be right to pull the biological card now."

Jubal nodded. "True." He patted my shoulder. "You're a good man, Taylor."

My brow furrowed. "Not good enough."

My cell phone rang. I held the receiver to my ear, and Jubal nodded, already knowing I needed privacy. He walked back into the living area, and I swiped my thumb across the display, holding the phone to my ear.

"Hi, honey," I said.

"Hi." Falyn was uncomfortable with terms of endearment now—as if I shouldn't care about her because she'd left me.

The truth was I'd tried yelling. I'd tried being angry. I begged and pleaded and even threw tantrums, but all that did was push her further away. Now, I listened more and lost my temper less. Something my brothers had all learned early on. They still had their wives.

"I was just thinking about you," I said.

"Oh, yeah?" she asked. "I was calling because … Hollis isn't doing well. He got in a fight today."

"A fistfight? Is he okay?"

"Of course, he's okay. You taught him how to defend himself. But he's different. He's angry. Thank God it was the last day before summer break or he would have been suspended. He still might. Taylor, I think …" She sighed. She sounded as lost as I did, and it was both painful and a relief not to be alone in that. "I think I made a mistake."

I held my breath, hoping she would finally say she was coming home. It didn't matter why. Once Falyn came back, I could make things right.

"I was hoping … maybe …"

"Yeah? I mean, yeah. Whatever it is."

She paused again. Those in-between moments felt like dying a thousand times. Her voice said it all. She knew when she'd called she'd be getting my hopes up, but this conversation was about the kids, not me. Not us. "I was hoping you wouldn't mind helping me find a rent house in Estes. You have more connections there for housing than I do. It's going to be hard to find a three-bedroom apartment. The kids are too old to share."

I sat down on my bed, feeling like the air had been knocked out of me. "Couldn't you just … move back in? The kids' rooms are all set up. It's familiar. I'd love for you to come back. I want you to. It doesn't have to mean anything more than if you got your own place. I'll sleep on the couch."

The other end of the line was quiet for a long time. "I can't, Taylor." She sounded tired. Her voice was deeper than usual; ragged.

I'd begged before. It would only start another fight. This was about our children. I had to put us aside. "Falyn … move back into the house with the kids. I'll find an apartment."

"No. I'm the one who left. I'll find a place."

"Baby," I began. I could feel her discomfort through the phone. "Falyn. The house is yours. I'll let the school know they'll be back next year."

"Really?" she asked, her voice breaking.

"Yeah," I said, rubbing the back of my neck. "It doesn't make sense for me to live in that big house alone and you and the kids crammed into an apartment."

"Thank you." She sniffed. "The kids will be so happy."

"Good," I said, forcing a smile. I wasn't sure why. She couldn't see me. "Good, I'm glad."

She puffed out a breath of relief, and scuffing sounds against the phone had me imagining she was wiping away tears. "Okay, then. I'll, um … I'll start packing."

"Need help? Let me help you." The apartment she'd found in Colorado Springs was furnished, so there wouldn't be much heavy furniture, but I was desperate to return to our well-oiled machine.

"No, we can do it. We don't have much. There's nothing too heavy."

"Falyn. At least let me help pack up the kids. I haven't seen them in two weeks."

She thought about it for a moment, sniffing again. I imagined her weighing the pros and cons. She had to think about her choices longer these days, her decisions made only after having more information—something I had to start doing, too. I half-expected her to say she would think about it and call back, but she answered. "Okay."

"Okay?"

"I was considering telling the kids tonight. Do you want to be here when I do? I'm not sure if that would be confusing for them …"

"I'll be there," I said without hesitation. Some things required less thinking than others.

We hung up, and I swallowed the lump that had formed in my throat. I didn't dare say to her what I wanted. I'd held in the hope that once she was back we could really start to work on what went wrong. This time, I would promise not to push too hard or move too fast—I would show her I had changed.

I gripped the phone with both hands and held it to my forehead, silently chanting to keep it together and not ruin it this time. Nothing was more frightening than being your own worst enemy. Even when I wanted to do the right thing, it was a struggle. I had always lived by my emotions, and those close to me experienced the blowback. They saw the pressure build and the discharge, even if it only lasted for a few seconds in the form of rage. After years went by—and I hadn't learned or grown or made an effort to overcome it—the forgiveness came less easily for Falyn, and I couldn't blame her.

"You off the phone?" Jubal asked. I lifted my head and nodded, working hard to keep the suffering off my face. "The commander wants a word."

I wiped my nose with my wrist and stood, taking a deep breath. My muscles were tense. I knew what was coming. The commander had been in meetings all morning with the other shift commanders, the chief, and the city council—all about me.

"Taylor?" Jubal said as I passed him.

"Yeah?" I turned around to face him, annoyed. He'd interrupted my emotional preparation for what would go down in the commander's office.

"You need to take that temper and dial it down a few notches before walking in there. You're in enough trouble as it is. You're definitely not going to get her back without a job."

"It doesn't matter. Nothing has gone right for me since she left."

Jubal made a face, unimpressed with my shameless self-pity. "If you'd stop spending so much time placing blame, you might free up your head and your heart to think of a solution."

I thought about his words and nodded, taking a deep breath. Jubal was right, as usual.

The commander was on the phone when I knocked and came in. He lifted his index finger, and then directed me to sit in one of the two orange chairs positioned in front of his desk.

I did as he instructed, lacing my fingers together on top of my stomach and bobbing my knee. That office hadn't changed much since he'd taken over; the same pictures hung from the walls and tacks on various corkboards held informational posters around the room. The paneling gave away the building's age, as did the stained carpet and worn furniture. The only things different were a framed picture on the desk, the man sitting on the other side of it, and the nameplate in front of him.

COMMANDER TYLER MADDOX

"You rang?" I asked when he hung up the phone on its cradle. I grabbed the picture of us with Dad, all standing side by side, our arms around each other and happy. Thomas almost looked out of place, without tattoos and longer, lighter hair, and hazel green eyes as opposed to shit brown like the rest of us.

"Anyone else looking at this picture must think Tommy belongs to the milkman. Only people who know us recognize that he looks like Mom."

Tyler grimaced. "I know you've already told me once, but tell me again, Taylor. Tell me you didn't know who he was when you swung."

I tried not to get defensive, but holding back was hard when he was asking me to explain why I'd knocked out the mayor's son for touching my wife's ass at a bar. Tyler knew as well as I did that he would have done the same thing. Maddox boys didn't stop to ask the importance of someone before putting them in their place.

"The mayor just moved here a couple of years ago," I said. "How was I supposed to know who his douchebag son is?"

Tyler's frown didn't budge. "This isn't just a fuck up, Taylor. I don't know how I'm going to get you out of it this time."

I leaned forward, resting my elbows on my knees. "This time? You act like you've been bailing me out my entire life. I think it's been a give and take."

Tyler's shoulders fell. "Okay then, it's my turn, and you've fucked me out of it. My hands are tied."

"Maybe that cocksucker shouldn't have grabbed my wife's ass."

Tyler leaned back, huffing his impatience. "He tripped."

I clenched my teeth and white-knuckled the arms of my chair, trying to keep from leaping across the desk at my brother. "Don't repeat his fucking lies to me, Tyler. I saw it with my own eyes and so did half the crew. Jubal, Zeke, Sugar, Jew, Cat, and Porter all put their jobs on the line to vouch for me. They knew the mayor wanted them to say different in their statements."

Tyler glared at me for a minute, but his expression melted away. "I know. I'm sorry."

"So … what? I'm done?" I asked.

"We both are."

My brows pulled together. "What do you mean? They can't fucking do that. How can they do that?"

"*They* didn't. I handed in my resignation this morning. Looks like it's the last day for both of us."

My chest felt heavy, and I puffed out a breath in disbelief. "Are you fucking with me?"

Tyler shook his head. "We started out together. We go out together, right?"

I shook my head, feeling tears burn my eyes. I remembered how proud Tyler was when he received word of his promotion, how proud Ellie was, and how happy we all were when we celebrated that night. He was the best man for the job. He took care of the guys like he took care of me. "You don't deserve this. You worked hard for that desk."

Tyler stood up and walked around the table. He held out his hand, and when I grabbed it, he yanked me to my feet. "It's just a desk. You're my brother."

He hugged me, and my forehead fell against his shoulder. I tensed, keeping all the hurt and pain I'd felt since Falyn left and for losing my job—in addition to my guilt for Tyler losing his job, too—from flooding out of me in an uncontrollable release of emotion.

"I guess we can quit lying to Dad and really be insurance salesmen now." He hooked his arm around my neck and rubbed his knuckles on the top of my head with his free hand. "C'mon. We're going to be okay. Let's go break it to the guys."

"Hey, uh …" I began. "I'm going to have to find something else quick."

"Why?"

"Falyn's moving back with the kids."

Tyler's mouth fell open, and he stepped back, socking my arm with the side of his fist. "Are you serious, brother? That's awesome!"

I shifted my weight, crossing my arms across my middle. "The kids aren't happy in the springs. I told her to take the house."

"Oh."

"So I'm on the hunt for an apartment."

He made a face. "That's not as good of news as I thought."

"Me neither."

Tyler put his hand on my shoulder. "You want to stay with Ellie and me?"

"Nah," I said. "Thanks, though."

"You guys love each other. You'll work it out."

I looked down, chills running over my entire body. "If she loves me, then why did she leave me?"

That gave Tyler pause, and he squeezed his fingers into my skin. "We're crazy as fuck. It takes balls for those women to love us. And … sometimes it takes losing someone to finally have the courage to grow into the person they deserve."

My chest concaved, and I puffed out a breath as if Tyler had just punched me. Taking that kind of truth felt like falling on my own sword.

"Just … don't tell anyone she's coming back," I said. "I want to try to have a few good conversations with her before the mayor's son finds out. Arrogant prick."

"He can't steal your wife, Taylor. She doesn't want him."

I made a face. "She doesn't want me, either."

"That's bullshit, and you know it. We've all reevaluated at some point and realized our wives are getting tired of our crap. We straightened up, and it's all good. You were just a day too late."

"Something like that," I grumbled as we walked into the living quarters.

We stopped just short of the closest row of recliners. Every seat was taken by the guys from our shift. All of them were former hotshots like us, waiting for the alarm to sound so we could get a taste of the adrenaline and power that came with fighting something unstoppable and inhuman—and winning.

Tyler glanced at me and nodded toward the crew. I clenched my teeth and looked to the floor; shame and the feeling of letting my firehouse family down were unbearable.

Jubal sat up, recognition in his eyes. "Baloney. I don't believe it."

"I—" Before I could finish, the alarm bleated through every speaker in the building. We waited for the dispatcher, Sonja, to tell us the location and nature of the fire we were about to be called to.

"Box alarm at the Hickory Warehouse, 200 North Lincoln Avenue. Possible occupants."

"Inside?" I asked. "It's been vacant for years."

"Fuckity," Jubal said. "No, it's not. The Hickory family sublet it to Marquis Furniture five or so years ago. It's full of their inventory."

"We'll need the ladder and the two larger engines. Tender on standby!" Tyler said. He backhanded my shoulder. "Ride with me. Last one."

My eyebrows pulled in. "I told Falyn I would meet her in the springs tonight to help her pack up the kids."

Tyler grinned in understanding. "No problem. Patch that shit up so you'll stop whining, would ya?"

I half-heartedly smiled, watching my twin brother grab his commander's hat, jacket, and keys before jogging to the ambulance bay where his truck was parked.

The rest of the guys followed behind him to the fire trucks and ambulance, and I stood alone, feeling my jaw tense. Something didn't feel right.

"Goddammit, Tyler," I said under my breath, running out to put on my gear. I stepped into my bunker gear, grabbed my hat, and yanked open the door just as Tyler was backing out.

Tyler frowned at me as I pulled on my seat belt. "What are you doing, fuckstick? Go get your wife."

"Last time," I said, sitting back and putting on my game face.

He stepped on the gas, leading the crew to the outskirts of town so fast the haunting sound of our sirens trailed behind. He was already on the radio, speaking to the other brass who would arrive and communicating with dispatch about shutting down any way in or out to the public. We all knew the warehouse would be one hellacious fire, but I could see a flicker of nervousness in my brother's eyes. He had the same bad feeling I did.

The brakes of Tyler's truck screeched, and the tires dug into the gravel as he slowed in front of the warehouse. The south side of the looming three-story structure was nearly engulfed in flames. I rolled down the passenger side window, and even from a hundred feet away, I could feel the heat on my face. The flames whipped up into the sky, reaching with their glowing, misshapen fingers as they devoured and digested the steel and lumber that had withstood five generations of grueling Colorado weather.

Tyler leaned forward, pressing his chest against the steering wheel to get a better look. He had to yell over the roaring orange monster. "That's one big bitch!" He radioed into dispatch, requesting a shutdown of the roads leading to the warehouse. Consistent water pressure would already be a problem. We didn't need traffic running over the hoses, too.

For the first time before a fire, an ominous feeling came over me. "I gotta bad feeling, Tyler."

He puffed out a breath. "Gimme a break, big brother. You're too fucking mean to die."

I looked up at the fire. "I hope so. I haven't held my wife in three months."

# CHAPTER THREE

## TYLER

"IT'LL BURN FOR DAYS," I said, tugging once on my door handle.

"I'd better call Falyn," Taylor said. "Let her know I'm not coming tonight after all."

We had both climbed out of the truck, standing on opposite sides of the hood. I point at him. "Don't you fucking dare. We're going to restrain this hungry whore, and then you're going to pack up my niece and nephews and bring your family home."

Taylor glanced at his watch while jogging to Engine Nine. "I've got two hours!"

I glanced at the warehouse and yelled back to my brother, "She won't be out, but we can beat her back!"

Jubal and Sugar were already on fire attack, dragging a hose on the main floor, while Zeke and Cat were outside as their backup. Jubal had carried in a TIC—a thermal imaging camera—to locate the fire and any possible people inside.

"Hold off, Ladder Two," Tyler said into his radio. "Let's clear the building before we start throwin' steam."

Jew's voice came through the speaker, "Copy that."

"We're going to need ventilation," Jubal called over the frequency.

I gestured for Taylor to oblige Jubal's request. "Copy, Jubal." I lowered my radio. "Give me vertical ventilation, Taylor. With all that furniture in there as fuel …" I trailed off, troubled.

"We're at a high risk for a flashover," Taylor said, finishing my sentence.

"Then let's make sure we ventilate her right," I said. Fire fuel, whether it was hydrocarbons or natural vegetation like wood, released gasses at a certain temperature. Once those gasses ignited from super-heated air from the fire, an area could spontaneously combust, a phenomenon that would mean death for any firefighters in the vicinity. Other than a warehouse full of explosives or tires, thousands of pieces of furniture were a formidable rival for any fire department, and I knew my last fire was going to be my biggest challenge as commander.

I watched my brother walk away and felt my stomach sink. "Taylor!" He stopped. "Hold up. Keep an eye out down here. I'll do it."

"But," Taylor began.

"I said I'll do it!" I growled. I grabbed an ax off Engine Nine before heading for the aerial ladder to cut a hole in the roof. I signaled to Porter to follow me to the ladder truck. "Grab a saw!" I yelled to him.

He frowned, confused that a shift commander was running toward a ladder instead of remaining on the ground to keep watch.

We climbed onto the platform, and I waved at the operator, letting him know we were ready. Gears whined as the aerial ladder surged upward nearly fifty feet. As the wind whipped, heat pelted my face and glowing embers floated all around us. A nostalgic pang in my chest urged me to remember this moment because I was going to miss it. I had loved fire trucks since I was a boy, and I wasn't sure how life would be without feeling the rush of running into a burning building when everyone else was running out.

Porter closed his eyes and swallowed. Even under his bulky bunker gear, I could see that he was breathing hard.

"You ain't afraid of heights, are ya, Porter?"

He shook his head, his cheeks still fattened by youth. Straight out of school, he'd just joined Estes Park's Station four months ago. We hadn't even thought of a nickname for him yet.

"No, sir," he said. "I mean, yes, sir, but I'm going to do the job."

I slammed my hand down on the top of his helmet. "I just thought of a nickname for you, Porter."

His face brightened. "Yeah?"

"Honey badger."

Porter looked confused.

"You know what a honey badger is, Porter? They eat cobras. They don't give a fuck."

A wide grin spread across his face, but he quickly sobered when the ladder came to an abrupt stop.

"This is us," I said, hopping onto the edge of the rooftop. I tapped the butt of my ax down before putting all of my weight in one spot, making sure the roof wasn't spongey.

"How does it feel?" Porter asked.

"Stable," I said, carefully stepping down. After a few more tests with my ax, I waved Porter over, drawing an imaginary circle in the air above the spot I wanted him to cut. "Here!"

Porter nodded and then yanked on the chain of his saw. The flames were already licking the edges of the roof, and the heat was nearly unbearable.

"We don't have much time," I barked. "Get it done."

Porter carved through the thin top layer of the composite and the next layer of insulation. Just minutes after Porter began, smoke billowed from the hole he'd cut, and he took a step away from the intense heat.

I called Taylor over the radio. "She's opened up. We're headed down."

"Good work," Taylor said.

Porter and I returned to the platform, and I radioed for the operator to lower us down. Just as we reached the halfway point, the roof popped with a *crack* so loud it was like the building was snapping in two. A puff of thick, black smoke and some embers exploded from the opening we'd just created.

Taylor came over the radio again. "Back off, everyone. We've got … yep, it's spalling! Get the hell out of there!"

With more than six feet left to go, I jumped from the platform, running away from the crumbling warehouse toward my brother. I yelled into the radio. "Move! It's coming down!"

Jubal and Sugar burst from the main entry just before the brick's mortar joints began to give way. A large part of the front wall collapsed, pushing out a plume of dust, smoke, and debris.

I grabbed Taylor by the jacket. "You don't have time for this. Take my truck."

"You sure?" he asked.

I patted the side of his helmet. "Get outta here. We got this."

I scanned his face, watching Taylor war between staying to protect his little brother or save his family.

After several seconds, he ran to my truck, peeling off his gear and throwing it in the back before sliding behind the steering wheel. I'd left the keys in the ignition, knowing he'd be bailing early.

My focus alternated between Taylor leaving and the burning rubble. I pointed at different areas, barking orders to my men and talking into the radio. The fire was burning hotter, the smoke getting darker. We weren't anywhere close to having it under control. I could see Taylor sitting conflicted in the driver's seat. I knew he felt it was wrong to leave me alone, but just before he grabbed the door handle to rejoin us, I pointed at him, and he paused. "Get the fuck outta here! Now!"

## TAYLOR

SWEAT DRIPPED FROM MY FOREHEAD, and I wiped it away with my wrist. I could still feel the heat from the fire on my face and the heaviness in my lungs from the smoke. I made a fist and coughed into my hand once before reaching down to twist the keys in the ignition. It took everything I had to pull the gear into reverse and back away from my brother, but he was right. Falyn and the kids came first.

Driving the commander's truck proved advantageous as I passed two police cruisers exceeding the speed limit by at least fifteen miles per hour. When I finally reached the station, I ran in long enough to drop Tyler's keys on his desk and to grab my truck keys, wallet, and phone before getting back on the road for Colorado Springs. The plume of smoke from the warehouse loomed in my rearview mirror as I left Estes Park. I dialed Tyler's number, but it rang four times before the voice mail picked up. I couldn't shake the same ominous feeling I'd had while watching my brother leave for the warehouse fire without me. We'd fought fires separately before, but this felt different. That feeling had made me jump in the truck with Tyler before, and the farther away I drove, the more wrong it felt.

I concentrated on Falyn and the kids. The thought of Hollis and Hadley's excited reaction was an easy distraction. The combination of thinking about having my family back together and my gut feeling about the fire put the night Falyn left in the forefront of my mind.

We almost didn't go. *Fuck, I wish we hadn't gone.* The babysitter had backed out, and if Ellie hadn't called Falyn last minute, we would have just stayed home. What we thought was a stroke of good luck ended up being the worst night of my life. It had been over a year since we'd even gone on a date; it had been even longer since I'd seen Falyn interact with any other men besides my shift partners. My jealousy had never really been under control, so when a younger man approached my wife, swaying from a day of drinking and smiling at her like he knew he was taking her home, there was no thought process. Falyn tried to talk some sense into me, which only made me angrier. By the time he stumbled over and grabbed her ass, I was already beyond reason. I attacked. I beat the hell out of him. He went to the ER, and I went to jail.

The mayor made sure I spent all weekend in a cell. Tyler and the guys tried to bail me out several times without success. Falyn wouldn't answer my phone calls, and by the time I'd finally gotten home, she had packed up the kids and left.

I gripped the steering wheel. It whined under the pressure of my fingers, bringing me back to the present. The dread and utter fucking despair I felt coming home to an empty house were still fresh. The panic I felt after our first phone call, upon recognizing I couldn't beg, demand, or guilt her into coming home resurfaced. Love was fucking terrifying, laying your heart out in the open for someone else to protect or trample. My happiness depended on Falyn's forgiveness, and I still didn't know if she was willing.

My phone rang, and I pressed the button on my steering wheel. The display already told me who it was, but I was caught off guard, worried she would tell me she'd changed her mind. "Falyn?"

"Dad?" Hadley said.

"Hi, pumpkin! How was the last day of school?"

"It sucked."

"Again?"

"I got in trouble." She sounded disappointed in herself, and I imagined hot tears running over her chubby cheeks. She would start middle school next year, and I knew she was going to sprout up three or four inches at any moment. She was already taller than Hollis was, but he would overtake her in high school. I wasn't happy that she was growing up so fast, but at least she would be back in Estes with her friends.

She sniffed. "Hollis got into a fight today."

"Don't worry, Hadley. It's going to get better. I promise, okay? Very, very soon. Daddy's going to make sure of that."

"How?"

"You'll see. Put Mom on the phone."

"Hello?" Falyn said. I was sure the conversation with the school about both kids hadn't been easy.

"I'll be there in less than an hour," I said.

"Really?" she said, already sounding perkier.

I smiled. "Yes, really. I told you I'd be there, didn't I?"

"Yes, but … I saw on the news about the fire. I assumed you'd be there."

I thought about telling her there would be no more fires but decided it wasn't the right time. "I was. I left."

"Before it was controlled?"

"Close enough." I could practically hear Falyn smiling, and warmth ran through my body. I'd won big points for putting her first, even though I thought I always had by working hard and making a good living. She'd clearly needed me to prove it.

"I … thank you, Taylor. That really … means a lot."

I frowned, wondering why she was trying so hard not to love me. The things she'd said while I was being arrested cut me so deep I wasn't sure I could recover, when just her leaving was agony enough. She could have tied me to the bed and lit the house on fire, and I would have loved her still. I didn't understand the point of pretending, but maybe she wasn't. Maybe she *didn't* love me anymore. I cleared the emotion from my voice before I spoke. "Are you packing yet?"

"What I can without the kids noticing. I didn't want to give away the surprise before you got here."

"Good. I'll be there soon, ba—Falyn," I said, correcting myself.

"See you then," she said. No emotion in her voice, no disdain or sentiment. Nothing.

I wasn't sure what I would do if we couldn't work things out. She was it for me. Falyn had been my life since we were practically kids. She was the only life I wanted. When she left, I was miserable, but there was still hope. That hope motivated me. The dashboard lights switched on just after the last bit of daylight slipped behind the mountains. A sign on my right read *Welcome to Colorado Springs*, and I shifted nervously in my seat. I still held on to the hope that this weekend was going to be our point of turnaround instead of the point of no return.

# CHAPTER FOUR

## TRENTON

I WAITED OUTSIDE THE DOOR, listening to Camille trying not to cry. Every month was an endless cycle of hope and devastation, and almost eight years into our marriage, she was getting desperate.

The lights were dim. She liked it dark when her soul felt black, so I'd pulled the curtains when the three minutes was up, and she didn't say anything. Now, nothing was left to do but wait, listen, and hold her.

We lived in a small two-bedroom, just six blocks from Dad and Olive. The bedroom, like the rest of the house, was bright and minimally decorated with interesting art or my drawings. We'd repainted and laid new carpet, but the house was older than we were. Even though at the time of purchase it was a steal, the fixer-upper had turned into a money pit. The central heat and air and much of the plumbing system were new. At one point, we had to peel back the new—but wet—carpet to jackhammer the foundation to get to the pipes and replace them. The last ten years had been a long haul, but now we lived in a like-new home, even if we did have to deplete our savings four times to do it. We were in a good place, finally, and neither of us knew what to do with it but move to the next step. Infertility wasn't something we could fix, and that made Camille feel broken.

"Baby," I said, tapping on the door with my knuckles. "Let me come in."

"Just … just give me a second," she said, sniffing.

I leaned my forehead against the door. "You can't keep doing this to yourself. I think maybe it's …"

"I'm not giving up!" she snapped.

"No. Maybe try a different avenue."

"We can't afford a different avenue," she said. Her voice was even quieter than it had been. She didn't want to make me feel worse than I already did.

"I'll figure something out."

After a few moments of silence, the door clicked, and Camille opened the door. Her red-rimmed eyes were glossed over, and red blotches dotted her face. She was never more beautiful, and all I wanted to do was hold her, but she wouldn't let me. She would pretend her heart wasn't broken to keep me from hurting as she always did—no matter how many times I'd told her it was okay to cry.

I touched her cheek, but she pulled away, her painted smile fading just long enough to kiss my palm. "I know you will. I just needed to grieve."

"You can grieve out here, baby doll."

She shook her head. "No, I can't. I needed to take a moment for myself."

"Because otherwise, you're worried about me," I scolded.

She shrugged, her feigned smile turning into a real one. "I've tried to change. I can't."

I brought her into my chest, holding her tight. "I wouldn't want you to. I love my wife just the way she is."

"Camille?" Olive said, holding one side of the of the doorjamb. Her waist-length, platinum blond hair cascaded in waves from her center part down each side of her face, making her sadness seem to weigh her down even more. Her round, green eyes glistened, feeling every disappointment, every setback as deeply as we did because she was family, too. By chance and by blood, whether she knew it or not.

As I watched her lean the delicate features of her oval face against the wooden trim, I remembered being blown away by the truth: Olive, my neighbor and little buddy since she could walk, was adopted, and somehow, her biological mother had fallen in love with my older brother Taylor almost a thousand miles away in Colorado Springs. By chance, I'd helped raise my niece—involved in her life even more than my brother or sister-in-law.

Camille looked at Olive and breathed out a small laugh, pulling away from me while simultaneously licking her thumbs and then wiping away the smudged mascara from beneath her eyes. Her hair was longer than it had been since she was a girl, grazing the middle of her back and the same hue as Olive's, with a shaved patch just above her ear to keep it 'edgy.' I'd just redone the tat on her fingers—the first tattoo I'd ever done for her, and her first tattoo ever. It read *Baby Doll*, the nickname I'd given her early in our relationship, and it had somehow stuck. As hard as she tried not to fit in, Camille was a classic beauty. The name fit her then just as it did now.

"I'm okay," Camille said, following with a cleansing sigh. "We're okay."

She walked over to the doorway to give Olive a quick hug and then tightened the folded navy blue handkerchief she was using as a headband. She sniffed, the pain visibly fading away and disappearing. My wife was a badass.

"Cami," I began.

"I'm good. We'll try again next month. How's Dad?"

"He's good. Talking my ear off. It's getting harder to get him to come out with me. Tommy and Liis are bringing the new baby …" I trailed off, waiting for the inevitable hurt in Camille's eyes.

She walked over, cupped my cheeks, and then kissed me. "Why are you looking at me like that? Do you really think it bothers me?"

"Maybe … maybe if you'd married him … you'd have one of your own by now."

"I don't want one of my own. I want *our* baby. Yours and mine. If not that, then nothing."

I smiled, feeling a lump rise in my throat. "Yeah?"

"Yeah." She smiled, her voice sounding relaxed and happy. She still had hope.

I touched the small scar at her hairline, the one that never let me forget just how close I was to losing her. She closed her eyes, and I kissed the jagged white line.

My phone rang, so I left her long enough to grab my cell phone from the nightstand. "Hey, Dad."

"Did you hear?" he asked, his voice a bit hoarse.

"What? That you sound like hell? Did you get sick within the last two hours?"

He cleared his throat a few times then chuckled. "No, no … every inch of me is just older than dirt. How's Cami? Pregnant?"

"No," I said, rubbing the back of my neck.

"Yet. It'll happen. Why don't you two come over for dinner? Bring Olive."

I looked at my girls, and they were already nodding their heads. "Yeah. We'd love to, Dad. Thanks."

"Fried chicken tonight."

"Tell him not to start without me," Camille said.

"Dad—"

"I heard her. I'll just get 'em battered and seasoned and get the potatoes in the oven."

Camille made a face.

"Okay. We'll be over in a bit."

Camille rushed around, trying to get out the door to beat Dad to the oven. He'd left the stove on more than once, fallen more than once, and didn't seem fazed when he did. Camille spent nearly all of her spare time trying to help him avoid accidents.

"Can I drive?" Olive asked.

I cringed.

She smiled mischievously. I groaned, already knowing what she was about to say.

"Pwease, Twent?" she whined.

I winced. I'd promised Olive when she first got her license that I'd let her drive me when she turned eighteen, and her birthday was months ago. It was second nature to say no. I'd never had an accident, even as a teen. The two I'd been involved in were horrific, and both were with women I deeply cared about behind the wheel.

"Goddammit, fine," I swore.

Camille held out her fist, and Olive bumped it with hers.

"Did you bring your license?" Camille asked.

Olive answered by holding up a small brown leather wristlet. "My new Eastern State student ID is in there, too."

"Yay!" Camille said, clapping. "How exciting!" She looked at me with a fake apology in her eyes. "You promised."

"Don't say I didn't warn you," I grumbled, tossing Olive the keys.

Olive clasped the metal in both hands and then giggled, running for the door and out to the driveway where Camille's truck sat. As I walked down the flagstone walkway, I noticed Olive hop in and pull the seatbelt across her chest, buckling in and grabbing the wheel with both hands.

"Oh, stop. You're not bad luck." Camille opened the passenger door of her Toyota Tacoma quad cab and then pulled open the backward-facing rear door. She clicked her seat belt as I sat next to Olive. She immediately connected the Bluetooth on her phone to the truck, carefully choosing a song. Once the music began to play, Olive twisted the ignition and backed up. A new energy settled all around us. Camille rubbed my shoulders for a second to the beat thumping through the speakers.

"Maybe we should turn off the noise and let Olive concentrate," I said.

Camille's massage turned into a playful karate chop. "Noise?"

If hadn't experienced it, I would have never known she was crying in our bathroom ten minutes before. She was recovering quicker each time, but part of me wondered if it was real, or if she was just getting better at hiding it.

Just as we pulled into Dad's drive, I noticed thunderheads building in the sky just west of town. Thomas and Liis were flying in with their new baby sometime soon, so I checked my phone for the seven-day forecast—something that wouldn't have occurred to me to do ten years ago. Funny how time and experience completely rewired your brain to think about something other than yourself.

Dad wasn't waiting on the porch as he usually was, prompting Camille to curse.

"Damn it, Jim Maddox!" she said, gesturing that she was in a rush for me to open the door. She scrambled out onto the grass, ran all the way to the porch, jumped the stairs, and yanked open the rickety screen door.

Olive parked and tossed me the keys, waving. "Going next door to tell Mom I'm having dinner with Papa!"

I nodded, feeling a small lump in my throat. All the grandkids called Dad Papa, and I loved that Olive did, too, even though she didn't know how right she was.

I followed Camille into the house, wondering what we would find. The paint on the porch was peeling, and I made a mental note to bring over my sander. The screen door was barely hanging on, so I added that to the list, too. Mom and Dad bought the house when they first married, and it was nearly impossible to get him to let us make changes or updates. The furniture and carpet were the same, even the paint. Mom had decorated, and he wasn't about to let anyone go against her wishes, even if she'd been gone for almost thirty years. Like Dad, the house was getting so old that it was becoming unhealthy and, in some cases, dangerous, so in the last few months, Camille and I had decided to start fixing things without asking.

Just as the hallway opened up into the kitchen, I saw Camille running toward Dad, her hands held out in front of her.

He was bent over, just putting the aluminum-covered potatoes into the oven.

"Dad!" Camille shrieked. "Let me do that!"

He slipped them in and closed the door, standing and turning to face us with a smile.

Camille pulled a pair of oven mitts out of the drawer, shoving them at him. "Why don't you use the mitts that I bought you?" She walked over, inspecting his bandaged hands.

He kissed her knuckles. "I'm fine, kiddo."

"You burned them so badly last time," she said, wiggling out of his grip to further inspect the wounds under his bandages. "Please use the mitts."

"Okay," he said, patting her hand. "Okay, sis. I'll use the mitts."

Camille began opening cabinet doors to find the oil, seeing that the drumsticks had already been dipped in Dad's special flour mixture and were sitting on paper towels next to the pan on the stove.

She waved us away. "Go on. I've got this. Yes, Dad, I'm sure," she said, just as Dad opened his mouth to ask.

He chuckled. "All right, then. Dominoes, it is."

"Aren't you sick of losing? We played dominoes for two hours this afternoon."

"Did we?" he asked. He shook his head. "I can't remember to wipe my own ass most days."

I blinked, surprised he didn't remember, but he didn't seem concerned.

"Cards, then?" he asked.

"No, we can play dominoes. I owe you a rematch, anyway."

Thunder rolled in the distance as we sat down at the table. The front door opened and closed, and then Olive appeared at the end of the hall, holding her hands out to each side, dripping wet. "Oh. My. God."

I burst into laughter. "Ever heard of an umbrella, Ew?"

She rolled her eyes, stomping over to sit on the dining chair next to me. "Will you ever stop calling me that? No one gets it."

"You get it," I said. "How hard can it be? Your initials are O.O. Together, they make the sound *ew*. Like moo. And too." My gaze drifted up to the ceiling. "Shoo. Boo. Coo. Goo. Poo. I could go on."

"Please don't," she said, grabbing a domino and turning it over in her thin fingers. It was getting harder and harder to impress her. She used to think I was god.

"Oh! Damn!" Camille yelped from the kitchen.

I pushed out my chair, standing halfway. "You okay, baby?"

"Yeah!" she called back, appearing with her jacket and her keys in hand. "Out of oil."

"But I just bought him some last Friday," I said, looking at Dad.

"Oh. That's right. I knocked it over Sunday."

I frowned. "We had sandwiches for lunch and pizza for dinner Sunday. You didn't make chicken."

He mirrored my expression. "Well, damn it, one of those days."

"I'm going to run to the store. You need anything else?" Camille asked.

"Cami, it's pouring," I said, unhappy.

"I'm aware," she said, kissing at me before heading out the door.

Dad brought down the dominoes from the shelf, and we made small talk. He asked me a few of the same questions he'd asked me earlier, and I began to wonder if he'd been forgetful all along and I was just noticing it, or if his memory was getting worse. He had a doctor's appointment that Friday. I'd bring it up then.

My cell phone buzzed. I pressed the receiver against my ear. "Hey, cunt puddle!"

"They just keep getting better," Thomas said on the other end of the line, unimpressed.

"Christ on a bicycle, Trenton," Dad fumed, nodding toward Olive.

I winked at him. Shocking him with my insults had become a sport.

"How are Mom and baby?" I asked.

"We're headed home," Thomas replied. "I think … I think we're going to head that way earlier than expected."

"Everything okay?" I asked, noting that Dad's interest was piqued. I waved him away, assuring him nothing was wrong.

"Yeah … yeah. Have you heard from Trav?" Thomas asked.

"No. Why?"

Thomas had been an enigma since I could remember, and the questions only multiplied when he became an adult.

Dad was staring at me, both patiently and impatiently waiting for an explanation. I held up my finger.

"Just curious."

"You're going to put a newborn on a plane? I knew you were brave, big brother, but hell."

"We thought Dad might like to meet her."

"He would. Dad would love to meet …" My mind drew a blank.

"Stella," Olive whispered.

"Stella!" I repeated. "Dad would love to meet Stella." Dad popped me on the back of my head. "Ow! What'd I say?"

"So we'll be in tomorrow," Thomas said, ignoring the circus on the other end of the line.

"Tomorrow?" I said, looking at Dad. "That quick, huh?"

"Yeah. Tell Dad not to worry. We'll get the room ready when we get there."

"Cami has been keeping the guest room ready. She knew you'd be over some time with the baby. She even got a pack 'n whatever."

"She purchased a Pack 'n Play for Stella? Really?" Thomas asked. "That was nice of her. How is sh … that was nice of her."

"Yeah," I said, suddenly feeling awkward. "We'll see you tomorrow, I guess."

"Tell Dad I love him," Thomas said.

"Will do, shit pouch."

Thomas hung up, and I shot Dad a wide grin. The two lines between his eyes deepened.

"I should have spanked you more," Dad said.

"Yes, you should have." I looked down at the dominoes. "Well? They're not going to shuffle themselves."

I settled on a dining chair, the golden brown leather making fart noises under my jeans. Even though I'd moved out, Camille and I visited Dad at least once a day, usually more. Travis visited when he wasn't traveling for work. I glanced up at the shelf that ran just below the ceiling, filled with dusty poker memorabilia and signed pictures of our favorite players. A few cobwebs had formed. *I need to get up there and dust. Don't want the old man falling and breaking a hip.*

"Cami didn't say anything about the test today," Dad said, moving the dominoes around in a circle on the table.

"Yeah," I said, staring at the white rectangular tiles as they slowly circulated around, under Dad's hands, moving in and out of the pack. "It's a monthly thing now. I think she's tired of talking about it."

"Understandable," Dad said. He gave a side-glance to Olive, and I knew he was choosing his next words carefully. "Have you been to the doc?"

"Gross," Olive said, disgusted despite his efforts. She wasn't a little girl anymore.

"Not yet. I think she's afraid to hear it's something permanent. Honestly, so am I. At least now, we have hope."

"There's still hope. Even the worst circumstances have a silver lining. Life isn't linear, son. Each choice we make or every influence branches off the line we're currently on, and at the end of that branch is another branch. It's just a series of blank slates, even after a disaster."

I peeked up at him. "Is that how you felt after Mom died?"

Olive let out a tiny gasp.

Dad tensed, waiting a moment before speaking. "A while after Mom died. I think we all know I didn't do much of anything right after."

I touched his arm, and the tiles stopped spinning. "You did exactly what you could. If I lost Cami ..." I trailed off, the thought making me feel sick to my stomach. "I'm not sure how you survived it, Dad, much less got yourself together to raise five boys. And you did, you know. You got yourself together. You are a great dad."

Dad cleared his throat, and the tiles began turning again. He paused just long enough to wipe a tear from beneath his glasses. "Well, I'm glad. You deserve it. You're a great son."

I patted his shoulder, and then we picked our bones from the boneyard and set them on their sides, facing away from each other. I had a shit hand.

"Really, Dad? Really?"

"Oh, quit your whining and play," he said. He tried to sound stern, but his small grin betrayed him. "Wanna play, Olive?"

Olive shook her head. "No thank you, Papa," she said, returning her attention to her phone.

"She's probably playing dominoes on that thing," Dad teased.

"Poker," Olive snapped back.

Dad smiled.

I turned to look up at our last family portrait, taken just before Mom found out she was sick. Travis was barely three. "Do you still miss her? I mean … like before?"

"Every day," he said without hesitation.

"Remember when she used to do the tickle monster?" I asked.

The corners of Dad's mouth turned up, and then his body began to shake with uncontrollable chuckles. "It was ridiculous. She wasn't sure if she was an alien or a gorilla."

"She was both," I said.

"Chasing all five of you around the house, hunched over like a primate and making her hands into alien suction cups."

"Then she'd catch us and eat our armpits."

"Now, that's love. You boys smelled like rotting carcasses on a good day."

I laughed out loud. "It was the one time we could jump on the furniture and not get our asses beat."

Dad scoffed. "She didn't have to spank you. The look was enough."

"Oh," I said, remembering. "The look." I shivered.

"Yeah. She made it look easy, but she had to put a healthy amount of fear into you first. She knew you were all going to be bigger than her one day."

"Am I?" I asked. "Bigger than she was?"

"She was a bitty thing. Abby's size. Maybe not even that tall."

"Where did Travis's gigantism come from, then? You and Uncle Jack are bloated chipmunks."

Dad howled. His belly bobbled, making the table jiggle. My dominoes fell over, and I spat out a laugh, too, unable to hold it in. Olive covered her mouth, her shoulders shaking. Just as I began setting the dominoes back onto their edges, a car pulled into the drive. The gravel in the driveway crunched under a set of tires, and the engine shut off. A minute later, someone knocked on the door.

"I'll get it," Olive said, pushing her chair back.

"Oops," I said, standing. "Cami's back. Better help her with the groceries."

"Atta boy," Dad said with a nod and a wink.

I walked into the hall and froze. Olive was holding open the door, staring at me with a pale, worried expression. Behind her on the porch were two men in suits and soggy trench coats.

"Dad?" I called to the dining room.

"Actually," one of the men said. "Are you Trenton Maddox?"

I swallowed. "Yeah?" Before either of them could speak, all the blood rushed from my face. I stumbled back. "Dad?" I called, this time frantic.

Dad put his hand on my shoulder. "What's this?"

"Mr. Maddox," one of the men said, nodding. "I'm Agent Blevins."

"Agent?" I asked.

He continued. "We came with some unfortunate news."

I lost my balance, falling with my back flat against the paneled wall. I slid down slowly. Olive went down with me, grabbing both my hands and bracing us for an alternate, painful reality. She held tight, anchoring me to the present, the moment in time just before everything would fall apart. I'd known in the pit of my stomach not to let Camille drive in the rain. I'd been feeling off for several days, knowing something bad was looming. "Don't fucking say it," I groaned.

Dad slowly kneeled at my side, placing his hand on my knee. "Now, hold on. Let's hear what they have to say." He looked up. "Is she okay?"

The agents didn't answer, so I looked up, too. They had the same expression as Olive. My head fell forward. An explosion boiled inside me.

A sack fell and glass broke. "Oh, my God!"

"Cami!" Olive cried, releasing my hands.

I stared at her in disbelief, scrambling to my knees just before throwing my arms around her waist. Dad breathed out a sigh of relief.

"Is he okay?" Camille asked. She pulled away from me to look me over. "What happened?"

Olive stood and held on to Dad.

"I thought you … they …" I trailed off, still unable to complete a coherent sentence.

"You thought I what?" Camille asked, grabbing each side of my face. She looked at Dad and Olive.

"He thought they were here to inform us you'd …" Dad peered at the agents. "What in the Sam Hill are you here for, then? What's the unfortunate news?"

The agents glanced at each other, finally understanding my reaction. "We're so sorry, sir. We've come to inform you about your brother. Agent Lindy requested the news be brought straight to you."

"Agent Lindy?" I asked. "You mean Liis? What about my brother?"

Dad's eyebrows pulled in. "Trenton … call the twins home. Do it now."

# CHAPTER FIVE

## TRAVIS

ABBY WAS STANDING AT A WINDOW near the front door of our French Provincial home, peeking out from behind the gray sheer curtains she'd picked five years before to replace the old ones she'd picked three years before that. So much more than just the curtains had changed in the last eleven years. Weddings, births, deaths, milestones, and truths.

We'd rejoiced in the birth of our twins and mourned Toto's death. He was the twins' personal bodyguard, following them everywhere and sleeping on the rug between first, their cribs and then, their toddler beds. The hair around his eyes began to gray, and then it was becoming harder for him to keep up. His was the second funeral I'd ever attended. We buried him in our backyard, the Bradford pear his headstone.

Just a few months before, on our eleventh anniversary, Abby had confessed to knowing I worked for the FBI. Swollen with our third child, she'd handed me a manila envelope full of dates, times, and other pertinent information between her father, Mick, and Benny, the mafia boss I'd just shot in the face for threatening my family.

Abby's SUV usually sat parked in front of my silver Dodge truck, but it was notably missing, and my wife wasn't happy about it. We'd traded in the Camry years ago for the black Toyota 4Runner Abby drove to her teaching job. She'd always been good at numbers, and she'd begun teaching the math lab for sixth grade almost right after graduation.

College seemed like a week ago. Instead of dorms and apartments, we had a mortgage against a two-story, four-bedroom home and two car payments. The Harley had been sold to a good home before the twins arrived. Life had happened when I wasn't looking, and suddenly, we were adults making decisions instead of living with someone else's.

Abby put a hand on her round middle, rocking back and forth to relieve some of the aching in her pelvis. "It's going to rain."

"Looks like it."

"You just washed the truck."

"I'll take yours." I smirked.

She glared at me. "Mine is totaled."

I pressed my lips together, trying to suppress a smile. My shoulder burned from where a bullet had grazed me and drove through my seat, and my head was pounding from slamming into a tree on the side of the highway. I'd just begun to heal from the beating I'd taken beneath the streets of Vegas by Benny's men, and now, I had a fresh black eye and a one-inch vertical cut through my left eyebrow. I just happened to be driving Abby's SUV to pick up some ice cream, being a model husband while also using that time to get an update on Thomas from Val. The Carlisis thought I was in California, so they went there first, but Val said it was only a matter of time before they arrived in Eakins. That was when the first bullets shattered the passenger side window.

Abby was pissed, but she chose to be angry about the truck because she couldn't be mad about the situation. Anger was easier than fear. Even after I'd already eliminated the threat, I wanted to empty my clip into every single one of them when I saw the photos in the vehicle that had run me off the road. They had pictures of my wife, my kids, my nieces and nephews, my brothers and their wives. Even Shepley, America, their sons, and my aunt and uncle. They were planning to wipe out the Maddox family.

They chose the wrong family.

"They'll replace it," I said, trying to mask my growing anger.

"They can't replace you," she said, turning with her arms crossed and resting on her belly. "Are you going?"

"To meet Liis when she lands?"

"You should. She'll need to see your black eye and the cut on your eyebrow, to see the danger is real and has extended to the rest of the family," Abby said.

"I can't leave you here alone, Pidge." I sighed. "I didn't realize how much we'd used Lena until she left."

Abby shot me a knowing grin. "You miss her, don't you? She's the little sister you never had."

I smiled but didn't answer. Abby already knew that I did. Lena was a tiny thing, shorter than Abby. She was an exotic beauty, as deadly as she was stunning, handpicked by the Bureau to protect our children before they were born. Because my undercover position was atypical in that Benny knew who I was, where I lived, and that I had a family, the Bureau took extra precautions. Lena quickly fit in and was a huge help to a new mother with twin infants, especially when I was gone. She was like a little sister to Abby and me, and she loved to gang up on me with Abby. Like an aunt to the kids, she accompanied them to parks, nature walks, playing cars and Barbies, and teaching them Portuguese and Italian. She even taught them how to defend themselves, which we learned wasn't the best idea for Jessica. I should've known no daughter of mine would be afraid to use her new knowledge if someone picked on her brother at school.

Eighteen months ago, Agent John Wren replaced Lena. Suddenly reassigned, we didn't know where she was going, just that she was nervous as she packed her things and was devastated that she didn't have time to say goodbye to the children.

"I'm not alone," Abby said, snapping me to the present. She gestured over her shoulder to the window.

I didn't need visual confirmation to know that Agent Wren was outside in a black car, along with two more agents in undisclosed locations. Now that we knew our entire family was a target, we had to be vigilant. The Carlisis weren't known for their patience; they typically attacked at the smallest sign of weakness.

Lena's sudden departure deeply affected the children. James began experiencing nightmares, and Jessica was depressed for months. Abby insisted we not put James and Jessica through that kind of anguish again, so the Bureau sent an agent we thought the kids wouldn't become attached to. The twins were old enough that it was unnecessary for our new security to be handpicked because of his rapport with children; rather, he was chosen for the fact he was classified as *hyper lethal.* To date, Wren was the only agent I'd met with that classification.

"I still feel bad that he has to sit outside in this heat," Abby said.

"His car is air conditioned, and you were right. The kids were getting attached … and so was he."

As aloof as Wren was, the kids had grown on him. We were just as surprised as he was the first time Jessica nearly knocked him over with a hug. They beamed every day when they saw him sitting outside their school, and as each day passed, their acceptance of and love for him broke down his walls. As it turned out, that only made Wren more determined to keep them alive, a positive side-effect none of us saw coming. Abby wasn't happy about their growing attachment, though, so the rules changed. He had to keep his distance, and for a second time, the kids were heartbroken.

Abby nodded and turned away from the window, walking over to join me. She looked down at her stomach. "What do you think about Sutton?"

"You're talking names now? Sutton for a boy?" I asked, trying to keep my expression neutral. Pregnancy made my wife even more unpredictable than usual, but I just rolled with it. Pointing it out just made her cranky.

Abby's gray eyes brightened, relishing in the truth I couldn't hide. "You don't like it? I know it doesn't start with a J like the twins, and that's kind of the Maddox thing, but …"

My nose wrinkled. "It's not a Maddox thing."

"Taylor's are Hollis and Hadley," she said. "Shepley's: Ezra, Eli, Emerson. The T's? Diane and Deana? James and Jack? You're really going to deny it?"

"It's a regional thing."

"Your mom and aunt grew up in Oklahoma."

"See?" I said. "Regional."

Abby pressed her fingers into her back, waddling to the couch. She negotiated the space and her body, keeping the right balance as she lowered herself to the cushions. "Get this thing out of me," she groaned.

"Definitely not naming him *this thing*," I teased.

"Well," she began, breathing heavily. "We're going to have to name him something."

I thought for a moment. We'd been through four baby books twice. "Why not Carter?"

"Your middle name? I was actually trying to think of first names to go with Carter. If we made it his first name, what will his middle name be?"

I shrugged. "Travis."

"Carter Travis Maddox," she said, pausing to get comfortable. Even moving made her breathe hard. "You don't think that would be confusing to have a Travis Carter and a Carter Travis in the house?"

"No. Well, possibly, but I still like it."

"Me too."

"Yeah?" I beamed.

"Kind of goes along with our theme of naming the kids after us … sort of. James after your dad. Jessica after me … ish."

Jessica James was the name on Abby's fake ID. It was how she got into bars when we were freshman, but more importantly, how she gambled in Vegas. I remembered watching her in awe as she went head to head with gambling legends, hustling them for thousands, all to save her dad from being killed over an unpaid debt to Benny Carlisi. That trip to Vegas, fighting for the balance of what Abby didn't make, and the fire at Keaton Hall was the cosmic trifecta that landed us in our present situation. I was investigated for my involvement in a fire that had broken out on campus, resulting in the deaths of dozens of my classmates, and my brother just happened to be investigating Benny. When he learned my girlfriend was the daughter of a washed-up Vegas gambler who had ties to the Carlisi family, I was brought into the federal fold in exchange for immunity from prosecution for the fire.

I was relieved that when Abby had figured out I'd been drafted into the FBI for most of our marriage and had lied to her about it, she'd helped me bring the Carlisi case closer to a conclusion instead of leaving me. I was able to hand over years of bank account statements, emails, letters, and text messages Abby had gathered by hacking into her father's email account and phone, all tying Carlisi members to various felonious crimes.

Abby thought that would mean I'd be home more. Instead, the Bureau was going a hundred miles per hour trying to close the case. Now that Benny was dead and they were hell-bent on vengeance, we were all racing against the clock.

Abby smiled, resting her head against the couch cushions. Her hair was shorter than it was in college. Her caramel locks now just grazed her shoulders. She combed back what she called side-swept bangs with her fingers, but they fell right back into her eye. Abby would turn thirty in September. As wise as she was at nineteen, she was nearly clairvoyant now. I was sure that only made her more dangerous, but she was on my side—thank Christ. Her gentle curves filled her maternity jeans, her cleavage bursting from her bright tank top, and I chuckled thinking about how many times I'd begged her to have another baby—shamelessly enjoying the changes her body went through to carry our sons and daughter.

"What?" she said, catching me staring at her tits … again. Would I ever grow up? If it meant I had to stop appreciating how sexy my wife was, I hoped not.

I cleared my throat. "I'd like to meet Liis at the airport, but"—I looked at my watch—"you'll be leaving soon to pick up the kids."

"You should go." She sighed, struggling to lift her chest to get a full breath.

"No," I said, shaking my head.

"I can get the kids from school," she said. "Wren is here. He can drive us if you're nervous."

I frowned. "This needs to be over."

"And it will be," Abby said, standing. She walked over to me, sliding her hands under my biceps and locking them at the small of my back. She had to bend over slightly to nuzzle her head under my chin, pressing her cheek against my chest, but even her sweet touch couldn't cheer me up. We both knew the end of one case only meant the start of another. Abby was responsible for the break in her father's case. Mick Abernathy was a washed-up gambler who had an in with the Vegas mob. She had found out I was working for the Bureau and only wanted to help end a case that kept me away too much. Since handing over information that would put her father and the underboss away, she was asked to be an occasional consultant for the FBI. They were still waiting for her answer, and so was I.

Her tip had allowed me to climb the ranks quickly. No legal employment in Eakins would pay what I was making with the Bureau. If Abby took the consultant job, she would be able to stay at home with the kids. Either way, we'd made a good life here.

"Dad is excited," Abby said, "to see Stella."

"It never gets old, I guess. No matter how many kids his sons keep spitting out, there's nothing like holdin' a grandbaby for the first time."

Abby wasn't amused. "I believe it's the daughter-in-laws who do the spitting."

I kissed her on the forehead. "Touché."

"You should go to the airport, Travis. I'll pick up the kids from school with Wren and meet you at Dad's. Thomas would have wanted you to."

My brows pulled together. Hearing Thomas's name in past tense was unsettling. "Make sure Wren stays out of sight. Dad already knows something's up."

"He knows, Trav. He's known. I'm pretty sure since the beginning. He knows about the twins, too."

"What about the twins?" I asked.

Abby simply giggled, shaking her head. "You Maddox boys are terrible liars."

My face twisted in disgust. "No one's lying."

"Omission is lying," she insisted. "Making up cover stories is lying."

When I was recruited into the FBI at just twenty, I was also obligated to keep it from my wife. Unfortunately for the Bureau, Abby was too smart and stubborn to remain oblivious. Unfortunately for me, Dad was equally as sharp, and it was a full-time job to keep it from him. I wasn't sure how Thomas had been able to do it for over a decade. According to Abby, he hadn't. She was sure my father had known the entire time, too.

I kissed Abby's soft cheek, still smelling faintly of chocolate from the cocoa butter she slathered all over her skin the moment she'd started to show. That prompted me to kiss her again before heading out to my truck.

I used the small radio clipped to the lapel of my sports jacket to call Agent Wren. "Heading to the regional airport for pickup."

"I'm sure Agent Lindy will be happy to see a familiar face, sir."

I sighed. "Maybe. Maybe not." I slipped behind the wheel, taking in a deep breath before twisting the key in the ignition. Liis had traveled halfway across the country with a newborn. A funeral was the only reason she would risk it, especially knowing the mafia were committed to punishing her by targeting the only weakness Liis Lindy had: the people she loved. It wasn't enough anymore that she was surrounded by the Bureau. She needed the Maddox family now. She knew we would keep Stella safe.

I kept a tight grip on the steering wheel until the gates of the regional airport were in sight. No one had followed me. The security guard at the gate seemed alert but relaxed. I showed my ID, and he allowed me to continue. It was unlikely anyone in Vegas could have found out Liis was heading home to Illinois in enough time to beat her here.

As I pulled up to the terminal, I could see the Bureau's jet already parked near a county hangar. It was swarming with suits: men and women clearly armed and dangerous. The moment my truck rounded the corner, they were focused, ordering me to slow down, park my vehicle, and show my hands.

I did as they commanded, holding up my badge. Most of them knew who I was the moment I stepped onto the tarmac.

"Travis!" Liis called from behind a wall of men.

I jogged over to her, pushing agents to the side to get to my sister-in-law. Her red-rimmed eyes were puffy and tired. "Oh my God, your face," she said, gently touching my purple, swollen skin. Liis wasn't the most affectionate person, but she immediately melted into my arms. "You came," she said softly.

I placed my hand on the back of her long, dark hair and kissed the top of her head. "Damn right, I did."

"Abby?" she asked, looking up at me. "Everyone's all right? Nothing suspicious?"

"Everything is good. They're all waiting to help you with the baby."

"I haven't slept in three days," Liis said, her almond-shaped eyes staring up at me.

"I know," I said, holding her to my side as we walked toward the truck. "I know."

# CHAPTER SIX

## SHEPLEY

I HELD OUT MY HANDS in front of me. "Stop! No! Don't do it!"

My sons stared back at me with their mom's no-bullshit, round, sapphire eyes, ice cream cones in hand. Ezra, Eli, and Emerson were all standing on our porch, their faces as filthy as their shirts. Their mom would freak if they went inside like that, and they knew it. I'd taken them out in the first place to give her some quiet time to clean the house the way she wanted without one of our little monsters messing it up behind her. If I let them in covered in milky, sticky goo, America would kill us all.

"Guys," I said, still holding up my hands, "I'm getting the hose. Don't. Move. Mom is in there. Do you know what she'll do if you step foot inside the house?"

Eli looked at Emerson with his trademark evil grin.

"I mean it," I said, pointing at them. They giggled as I took the three steps from the porch to the sidewalk and then veered off into the grass toward the side yard to find the spigot.

America and I were both only children, and we knew we wanted more than one, and close together. By the time we'd had Emerson, we'd decided we were in way over our heads. Ezra was just a month older than Travis and Abby's twins. Eli came two years later. Emerson two more after that. Unlike Travis and Taylor's sons, mine were all quick to throw a punch, taller than every kid in their perspective grades, and unmistakably Maddox mean. Good thing I'd had some experience with that.

I grabbed the nozzle and pulled it from the retractable hose reel, unraveling it as I walked toward the porch. As soon as I rounded the corner, I dropped the hose and ran. The door was wide open, and the boys were gone.

"Damn it!" I growled, running toward the sound of America's shrieking.

She was in the kitchen, already moving at warp speed. Emerson was sitting on the counter with his bare feet in the sink under running water while she was temporarily blinding Eli by yanking a shirt over his head. She was already threatening Ezra.

"If you move, so help me God!" she warned.

"Yes, ma'am," Ezra said, standing uncharacteristically still next to the refrigerator.

The boys weren't great at listening to me, but none of them dared to test their momma when she'd had enough. She wasn't afraid to let us know when we were close to crossing that line, either.

"I'm sorry, honey," I said, grabbing several rags from a drawer.

America was in the zone, far away from me. There was no time for meaningless apologies—or her acceptance of them. She was concentrating on the next thing that had to be done. By the time we'd wiped the last of the melted white mess from their mouths and hands, the boys were already running at turbo speed to their rooms, and America was sitting on the floor looking spent.

"God bless Diane for keeping your cousins alive for as long as she did," America said.

I sat beside her, resting my forearms on my bent knees. "House looks good."

"For the moment," she said, leaning over to kiss me. "Still questioning our decision to remodel before they leave for college."

I chuckled, but that faded as I pushed up to stand, bringing my wife with me. We both groaned, our aging bones just beginning to show signs of three decades of wear and tear. We'd spent a lot of time on that kitchen floor, making meals, making babies, and then on our hands and knees replacing the linoleum with updated tile. The popcorn ceilings scraped, granite countertops and new carpeting or tile installed throughout, every room but the boys' painted Tony Taupe, lighting updated, and hardware replaced. The only things untouched were the oak wood cabinets and trim. Our house was nearly as old as we were, but America liked character and turning old into new rather than living in a space that didn't need us.

Emerson ran in and hugged America. "Love you, Mom." He darted off just as fast as he'd appeared, and she held out her shirt, revealing a white smear.

"We missed a spot," she said, exasperated. "I wonder how many more spots we missed. We should do a second sweep."

"He loves you, Mom. They all do."

America's eyes softened as she looked to me. "That's why I let them live."

From the moment two lines appeared on the pregnancy test, America was in love: more than she loved her parents, more than she loved Abby—more than she loved me. She made no apologies for putting the boys first, even before herself. When America took it upon herself to help me wrangle my roommate and cousin, Travis, neither one of us knew she was practicing to be a Maddox boys' mother herself. The way she commanded their respect and retained her soft maternal side reminded me of my Aunt Diane almost daily.

"Summer camp?" I asked. I was a football scout for the Chicago Bears and traveled for a good chunk of the year. America was a saint. She never complained and never resented me for being on the road, or continuing in a job I loved, even if it meant a lot of lonely nights and solo parenting. Even if she had, I'd still think she was a saint. Sometimes, I wished that she would.

"Oh, yes. Fishing, camping, and starting fires. They can't wait. We still have insurance, right?"

"Right."

America sighed, intertwining her fingers in mine. Covered in cleaner, fingers pruney, and with a dust bunny hanging from her blond ponytail, she was stunningly beautiful. I felt a pang in the pit of my stomach. "I love you," she said, and I fell in love all over again.

I opened my mouth to respond, but my phone rang. I rolled my eyes and then used my index finger and thumb like tweezers to pull it from the front pocket of my khaki pants. "Hello?"

"Hey, Shep. It's, uh … it's Trent. Are you home?"

"We're home. What's up?"

"You should come over."

I paused, not expecting his answer. "N-now?"

"Now," Trenton said without hesitation.

I shifted my weight from one foot to the other, already uneasy. "Is it Jim?" As expected, my question caught America's attention. "Is he okay?"

"He's okay. We just need you to come over."

"Sure," I said, trying to keep the worry from my voice. I knew Jim had been off lately, and I imagined that he might have gotten bad news from the doctor. "We'll be there in twenty."

"Thanks, Shep," Trenton said before hanging up the phone.

"Jim?" America asked.

I put my phone away and shrugged. "I don't know. They want us to come over."

"Sounds urgent," she said, watching my face for clues.

"I honestly don't know, honey. Let's just herd the boys toward the car. Twenty minutes is optimistic by anyone's standards."

"I can do it," she said, walking toward the hall. "Boys! Car! Now!"

I watched her disappear into Eli and Emerson's room and then searched for my keys and phone for a full minute before realizing they were both in my pockets. I cursed under my breath all the way to Ezra's room, and then encouraged him to put on his Chuck Taylors so we could go. I knew for a fact America had started cleaning their rooms before even thinking about the rest of the house, and Ezra's floor was already covered with clothes, toys, and …

"Rocks? Really?" I asked.

"Got them from James. He won them in a poker game."

I subdued a smile, knowing exactly where James got his hustling skills from. "Tie your laces. C'mon, buddy, we gotta go."

"Where?" Ezra asked in his mini-man voice. He reminded me of Thomas, always needing to know the details.

"To Papa Jim's," I said.

Travis and Abby's twins had come a little early, making James and Jessica just a month younger than Ezra. Even without the influence of Travis's kids referring to him as Papa, my kids would've still considered Jim their other grandpa.

"Yessss!" Ezra hissed, slipping on his Chucks without tying them and running for the door.

"Tie your shoes, Ezra! Ezra!" I called after him.

America was already standing next to the car just inside the open back door, reaching over Eli to buckle Emerson into his car seat. Ezra slid in on the other side, his laces dangling. America simply nodded to his feet, and his knee was bent, following orders.

"How?" I said, walking to my side.

"They know exactly what they can get away with," she said, pulling open the passenger side door. She clicked her seat belt and then leaned back, taking the precious few minutes we had in the car with the kids strapped down to relax. I barely heard her next words over the engine igniting. "Every kid has a currency, love. They also know I will annihilate theirs."

I chuckled, knowing full well she was serious. I'd seen many a toy plane and racecar bagged up and taken to charity or stored until the boys earned it back. America was militant at times, but she was right. One day, they would be bigger than she was, and it was important for her to establish respect before that happened. As I drove to Jim's, I thought about what it would be like if Diane had been around to raise my cousins. Everything America did as a mother was exactly the way I pictured my aunt. I wasn't sure how an only daughter kept a handle on a brood of rowdy Maddox boys, but from the moment she pushed Ezra into the world, she somehow always knew when to be soft and when to be tough.

I pushed down the blinker, waiting for oncoming traffic before turning left into Jim's drive. The two gravel slits on each side of a runway of freshly mowed grass sat on the left side of Jim's house and ran deep, past the backside of the house. So many cars were already parked, the ass of my minivan hung out into the street more than two feet. Good thing the parked car in front of Jim's house would keep the flow of traffic away from the van.

"What the hell?" America said.

"Mom," Ezra scolded. "Don't say hell."

"*You* don't say hell," America said back.

"You first."

She turned slowly, shooting him a death glare. He sank back into his seat, already afraid for his life.

No one was waiting for us on the porch. Something was wrong. I unfastened Eli and Emerson and kept pace with America as she led Ezra by the hand to the front door. I knocked twice and then opened the screen door, making a mental note to come by and fix it before it fell off its hinges. Trenton and Camille had been busy trying to get pregnant, and Travis had just come home from working out of town. I pitched in to help when and where I could.

America took my hand, just as wary about what we were walking into as I was. Except for quiet murmuring in the kitchen, the house was quiet—strange with that many people in the house.

"Hey," I said when Trenton came into view. He looked like shit, and I could see that both he and Camille had been crying. Travis and Abby were leaning against the counters next to the fridge, watching Trenton tell me whatever news I'd come to learn. "Where's Jim?" I asked.

He hugged me quickly. "Thanks for coming so fast."

"Trenton," I said. "Tell me what's going on."

"It's Tommy," he said, his voice ragged.

"Oh, God. The baby?" America asked.

My stomach sank. Stella was only a couple of days old.

"No"—Trenton shook his head—"no, she's fine. Super healthy." He looked down at the boys. "James and Jess are upstairs. Why don't you guys go find 'em?"

All three boys took off, and America grabbed my arm with both hands, bracing us both for what Trenton might say.

"Tommy was shot outside his house earlier. Just after they brought Stella home."

"Shot?" I said, feeling dizzy. All the air had been sucked out of the room while I tried to process his words. "But he's okay?"

Trenton's face fell. "It's bad, Shep."

I was getting angry, and I wasn't sure why. "Like a drive-by or . . .?"

"We're not exactly sure. The agents have been instructed to wait for Liis before giving any more info," Trenton said.

America's nose wrinkled. "Agents?"

Trenton gestured over his shoulder to the men in suits sitting at the dining table. "FBI."

I leaned over to get a better look and then stood back upright. "What are FBI agents doing here?"

"We're not sure about that, either. I think it has something to do with who shot Tommy. Maybe they're on the Ten Most Wanted or something."

"But why wouldn't they give you more information? Have they asked you any questions?" America asked.

"No," Trenton said.

America approached Abby, whose entire body looked swollen, even her nose. "You don't find this situation odd? Where's Travis?"

Abby touched America's arm, giving her an unspoken signal to be patient.

"It's going to be okay, Mare," Abby said. "He went to pick up Liis from the airport."

"Liis is here? Why isn't she with Thomas?" I asked.

Before Abby could answer, Jim hobbled in from the living room.

"Uncle Jim," I said, hugging him.

He patted my back. "Just waiting to hear something." When he pulled away, he looked weary and heartbroken, as if he already knew what was coming.

"Can I get you something, Dad?" Abby asked.

"Just getting some coffee," Jim said.

"I'll get it," Camille said. "You should both be resting." She meant Abby and Jim, but I felt like sitting down myself.

"She's right. Put your feet up," America said.

As America walked past me, leading Abby to the living room by the hand, I noticed the absence of the same fear and devastation that was weighing down the faces of everyone else in the room—everyone but Abby. Normally, she would be interrogating those agents until she got answers.

America nodded, a glimmer of understanding in her eyes. I wondered what she knew that I didn't. The boys screamed, and America rushed to the bottom of the stairs, looking up as she yelled, "Any blood?"

"No ma'am!" all three called back in unison.

Camille smiled and filled a glass with ice and water, handing it to Dad before escorting him back to his chair.

"This doesn't look like coffee," Dad said with a smirk.

"I know," Camille said.

America and I joined everyone but Trenton in the living room. He was in the hall on the phone, trying to reach the twins in Colorado. America sat on the couch, and I settled in on the floor between her legs, trying not to groan when she began rubbing her thumbs in circles over my shoulders.

Trenton walked in, holding his phone in the air. "Twins got a flight for the morning. I'll pick them up."

"I'll follow you in the van," I said.

America's fingers pressed into my sore muscles even further. "When do we find out more about Thomas?" she asked.

"Soon," Abby said.

America shot her a look. Something was up, and my wife never appreciated being kept out of the loop. I thought that when Travis and Abby eloped, America would strangle them both. Apparently, they hadn't learned their lesson.

The front door opened and closed, and Travis walked around the corner, loosening his tie. He'd gotten a job with Thomas's advertising firm. It was based in California, and the story was that he was taking over for Thomas since he'd moved out to manage their East Coast office, but Travis somehow managed to stay in Eakins. None of it made much sense, but I hadn't thought to question them until now. America and I had been busy with our own family. It'd been far too easy to overlook things.

I stood, hugging Travis. "You okay? Is that a fresh black eye?"

Travis grimaced. "I totaled the SUV."

"Where's Liis?" I asked.

"Her friend Val took her to get diapers and such," he said, looking tired.

"Can someone answer the fucking question?" America blurted out. "Why is Liis here without her husband?"

"Mare," Abby warned.

Camille brought Dad a steaming mug, and his eyes lit up for a few seconds.

"Decaf," Camille said.

"Why are we here, Abby?" America demanded.

"To keep you safe," she blurted out. "To keep us all safe."

"From what?" I asked.

Travis shifted. "From whoever shot Thomas."

I looked up at my wife. Her mouth hung open a bit, and she'd stopped rubbing my shoulders.

"What the fuck does that mean?" Trenton asked, reaching for Camille's hand. She took it, looking just as stunned and worried as America did.

"It means …" Jim began, taking a deep breath. "The FBI are here, and they seem to think whatever happened to Thomas wasn't an accident. Now … everyone, just calm down. You're safe here.

The kids are safe. When Taylor and Tyler get here, they'll be safe too."

"So that's the plan?" Camille asked. "To hole up here like a safe house?"

"Do they really think someone is targeting our family?" Trenton asked. "Why?"

Travis seemed irritated with each question. "It's possible."

"The whole family?" Trenton asked.

"Possibly," Travis responded.

"Olive," Trenton said, running down the hall and out the door.

# CHAPTER SEVEN

## LIIS

## 24 HOURS EARLIER …

I SAT IN A SEEDY HOTEL ROOM, judging the peeling white paint and outdated furniture. I'd stayed in a lot of shithole places during my time with the FBI but never with a newborn. I'd been holding her since we'd arrived, too nervous to set her down before scouring the room with a black light.

After a short knock, Agent Hyde cracked open the door. "It's me."

"Come in," I said, half relieved, half annoyed. She'd come empty-handed when I'd specifically asked for clean sheets, pillows, blankets—not from the motel—rags, and Lysol—and a lot of it.

"I know what you're thinking," Hyde said. Her dishwater blond hair was pulled back and secured at the nape of her neck. She was Quantico's top female agent after me. I was glad she was there, but she wasn't exactly the warm and fuzzy type. I wanted to be tough, buttoned-down, and unfazed, too, but it was hard to keep up that persona with my nursing bra unsnapped and smelling of baby vomit.

"You don't have a clue what I'm thinking," I said.

"It's all on its way."

*Maybe she does.* "It'd better be. He knows I hate D.C., and this motel is atrocious."

"Talking about taking one for the team." When Hyde saw my expression, she swallowed. "Sorry, Agent Lindy. Bad joke. But after what happened to Salvatore Cattone in the nineties, the mob isn't going to come anywhere near D.C. This is the safest place for you."

"A bacteria breeding semen storage facility?" I asked. Hyde wasn't fazed, and she didn't respond. I looked up and sighed. "How is he?"

She only offered one word. "Sore."

I looked down, angry that my hormone levels were changing too dramatically to control. Tears streamed down the bridge of my nose, dripping from the tip onto Stella's pink and brown polka-dotted footie pajamas. Just a few days before, the crying had been foreign to me. Now, it was all I could seem to do.

The Bureau had just fifteen minutes' warning that the Carlisis had split up and were closing in. They had traveled with the intention of assassinating Thomas and Travis. One small group had been traced to Quantico, the other to California. Travis's hitmen had bad intel, something that had been planted and circulated back in his undercover days when he was just an ad exec to the rest of the world, but it was only a matter of time until they tracked him to Illinois.

Fifteen minutes to form the plan that Thomas would risk being assassinated in our front lawn. Snipers were in place when the car came screeching down the road. As they sprayed the front of our house with bullets, one sniper blew the back of the rented Nissan Altima's tire, and another targeted Thomas's vest. My husband went down, and he stayed there until the ambulance arrived. The Nissan sped away, caught after a twenty-minute car chase. The agents in pursuit finally tackled them after they'd fled on foot. Vito Carlisi pulled a gun, and he was shot and killed. The others were arrested. Thomas couldn't have executed a more perfect plan.

I could still feel his lips on mine from just before he walked out the front door. I'd kissed him goodbye, not knowing if it was real or not, or for how long. Possibly forever. But Benny was dead, and we'd finally cornered one of his men to testify against the remaining Carlisis: a washed-up Vegas gambler who was now shaking down small-time strip clubs for Benny, who happened to be Abby Maddox's estranged father. Mick Abernathy was now in custody. Abby had handed over a six-inch stack of intel on her own father, giving him no choice but to testify against the remaining Carlisis. We knew they wouldn't stop without blood. It was our hope that Benny's men would believe Thomas's death would serve as a warning and keep Travis or me from testifying.

I could have planned a lifetime and still never prepared myself to see the father of my child gunned down in our front lawn. That moment was when the tears began to fall, and they hadn't stopped.

After a specific knock on the door, Hyde did a quick check, sidearm ready, and then let in another agent in plain clothes, holding large plastic bags. "Afternoon, Agent Hawkins."

He nodded to Hyde and then me. "Agent Maddox."

"Lindy," Hyde corrected him. "She's still Lindy."

"I'm so sorry," he said, stuttering over his words. "I thought …"

I could only shake my head, feeling tears pool in my eyes again. It made me angrier each time. Where was that phenomenon people always talked about? Being *cried out*?

Thomas had proposed to me several times, but that wasn't in the plans, and I always stuck to the plan. The day Stella came into the world, plans changed, and I decided it might not be so bad after all. The next time I saw Thomas again, he'd promised to propose. No airplanes writing in the sky, no flowers, no Eiffel Tower or any other theatrics, but we had a new plan. I just had to make sure I would see him again.

Agent Hawkins laid out a thin blanket and began unpacking the plastic bags. "The queen size sheets and comforter you requested. The crib sheets, pillow, rags, and Lysol. The sheets have all been laundered. The crib sheets with the detergent you requested."

"Thank you," I said, watching as he excused himself.

Hyde was already wiping down the crib as I turned to place Stella on the thin blanket. I unfolded her crib sheet and smelled it to confirm it had been laundered in mild baby soap. I breathed in deep, remembering how much Thomas loved this smell as we readied the nursery. A nursery we weren't using.

I made Stella's bed and then picked her off the thin blanket to place her tiny body in the center of the crib. She flailed and cried while I changed her diaper and then settled down as I dabbed her shrinking umbilical cord with alcohol and buttoned her PJs back up from ankle to chest. I placed a pacifier in her mouth, and she suckled on it until she stilled and fell asleep. She looked so small in that filthy motel-issued crib. She had a brand-new, breathtaking nursery at home, and she'd barely seen it. She didn't deserve this germ-infested room.

My throat tightened, and the tears flowed again.

Hyde held out a tissue, her expression emotionless.

"You must think I'm nuts," I said, wiping my eyes.

"No. My sister's had kids. It doesn't last forever."

"I didn't know you were an aunt. Nieces or nephews?"

"Both," Hyde said. She was trying to hide a smile. "Hunter is five. Liz is three. Noah is eight months."

"Wow," I said, breathing out a laugh.

Agent Hyde's expression softened. "You've been through a lot, Lindy. Cut yourself some slack."

I thought about her words, and she was right. I would never be so harsh to anyone else in my situation. I nodded, wiping the tip of my nose. "Thank you. I will." I cleared my throat, trying my best to think and feel like the agent I once was. "Any new information on Maddox?"

"He's alive," she said.

I swallowed down an urge to cry. "And the Carlisis?"

"In custody. One dead."

"Which one?" I asked.

"Vito," Hyde reported.

I rubbed the tension from my neck. The stress and the baby were taking a toll, and I could barely keep my eyes open. "Benny's favorite. That's going to hit them all hard."

"Don't discount Giada. She's unstable."

Hyde was right. The Carlisi's matriarch could be considered even more dangerous than Benny was. She stayed in the background, but she had ordered many of the hits, via whisperings in her husband's ear. "It will either break her or resolve her to finish this." I nodded, reaching for my phone.

"Agent Lindy," Hyde said, taking a step forward. When I froze, she continued. "I can contact the director if you'd like to notify him of Giada."

"Oh, right," I said, setting down my phone. The Carlisis thought I was a grieving widow. If there was a trace or mole or any other intel being given to the Carlisis—which we could only assume since they'd known Thomas's exact location, and later found out Travis's—I had to be careful. Only a small handful of people knew that Thomas was alive. It made sense to have protection and to be moved from our home to a safe location, but if I was making calls to the director about anything other than my anger over what had happened to Thomas, it could tip them off.

"We need to find who or what they're using for the info," I said.

"We're on it."

"Do we have a lead?"

"Agent Lindy, the baby is sleeping. My sister always naps when the baby is sleeping. It's about the only time she—"

"Okay," I said. "You're right."

Hyde seemed surprised at my response but quickly recovered, stripping the bed and remaking it with the clean sheets, pillow, and blanket in the time it took me to take a shower. I plodded to the bed in house shoes, unwilling for my bare feet to touch the crusty carpet.

I lay down, smelling the slightest hint of lavender. Hyde noticed me looking around and sniffing.

Hyde shifted her weight, and her face flushed. She was noticeably uncomfortable with my unasked question. "I asked Hawkins to track down a couple of air freshener plug-ins. Your home smells a little like lavender, so I thought it'd make you feel more at ease. Just a couple. If it's too much for the baby …"

"No," I said with an appreciative smile. "No, that was very thoughtful of you."

"It was Agent Taber who suggested them."

"Val," I said with a smile, but then my eyes began leaking again.

"She'll be on the first flight. She insisted on accompanying you to Illinois."

"Thank you," I said, already feeling desperate to see my closest friend.

Hyde didn't smile or show much of a response, but even that made me feel comforted because I was used to that with my mother. She showed her love in what she did for me. My father was the affectionate and animated one. Maybe that was why the director had chosen Hyde as my personal security. Besides being one of the Bureau's best drivers and best with a pistol, she was also somehow maternal.

I rested my head against the pillow. It also smelled a bit like lavender, and I had to wonder if Hyde had spritzed it to further help me relax. I wouldn't ask. I didn't want to embarrass her again.

I watched Stella breathe, the buttons on her footie pajamas rising and falling. She looked so peaceful. I wondered if she missed Thomas's voice, or if she knew this wasn't where we belonged. I didn't realize I was crying again until the pillowcase felt wet, and I closed my eyes, begging myself to relax enough to get some rest. Stella would be awake soon, and I couldn't take care of her if I didn't take care of myself. We were leaving for a different location in the morning, and Eakins the morning after that. I would need all of my strength to break over a dozen hearts.

"Hyde? Will you be there tomorrow? In Eakins?"

"Where you go, I go, Agent Lindy."

"Can you tell whoever you need to tell to call Thomas? Tell him I love him?"

"I will."

I felt my muscles melt into the mattress, but as hard as I tried, I couldn't sleep.

# CHAPTER EIGHT

## FALYN

THE PACKING TAPE made a high-pitched noise when it pulled from the roll, and I froze. Our only television was on in the living room down the hall, and I listened through the muted conversation between SpongeBob and Patrick Star for footsteps padding toward the closed door of my bedroom. I'd wanted to get a head start on packing but wanted Taylor there when we broke the good news to the kids. I smiled because they would be so happy. But my smile soon faded. Any misery they'd felt the past few months was my fault.

The wall was paneled except for one section, revealing the sheetrock behind it. The bed was a king but not nearly as comfortable as the queen I left behind. Our quilt didn't quite reach across the mattress, but it had gotten me through a particularly snowy Colorado winter. A picture of Taylor with the kids sat on the night table. Even though Taylor didn't share my bed, I still slept on the same side I'd chosen after we'd moved in together. Hadley would sometimes crawl into Taylor's side in the middle of the night, but other than that, it stayed empty.

Hollis and Hadley were so close in age that they were able to start pre-school together, and now, they had just finished the second grade. Looking at Hollis's dark hair, bronze skin, and blue eyes was like looking at Alyssa, the woman Taylor had met in California during the week we'd broken up. As angry as I was when I learned he'd gotten another woman pregnant, the night Taylor and Alyssa spent together made Hollis possible, and I wouldn't trade my son for anything. Hadley was the spitting image of me except for her warm chocolate irises. She kept her wavy blond hair long, and she had the same splash of freckles across her nose and cheeks.

Neither of them had looked at me much since we moved from Estes Park to Colorado Springs. Hadley was a bit more forgiving than Hollis. Sometimes, she would even forget how angry she was with me, and I'd get a hug or even an evening of snuggling on the couch while we watched a movie, but Hollis took every opportunity to remind me how I was ruining his life. It was becoming more difficult to argue with him. He'd had trouble making friends, but everyone in Estes Park loved him. He was picked first for teams, charmed the girls, and sang like the star of a boy band. In the Springs, he was the new kid who was a threat to the established class hierarchy.

Second grade was a lot different than I remembered.

My phone buzzed, and I picked it up, expecting an update from Taylor. Instead, it was Peter. I still wasn't sure how he'd gotten my number, but he was incessant. I still wasn't sure if it was my fault the night we met; if I had looked in his direction too long or absently smiled at him. Men like him thought every woman who laughed at a single joke was begging to be fucked. So, no. It wasn't my fault. He was raised with privilege and without accountability. He'd graduated from a rich pansy-ass snot rag to the rapey egomaniac otherwise known as Mayor Lacy's son. Peter had his eye on me from the moment we stepped into the bar to celebrate Jubal's promotion to lieutenant. Taylor and I didn't get out much, and I wanted to make the most of the babysitter we'd procured on late notice.

For weeks after I'd left, I wished we'd just stayed home. But the longer I was gone, the angrier that made me feel. Taylor was long overdue for some self-control. He'd put his job at risk—his brother's job at risk. I frowned. What used to be cute and maybe even flattering was now detrimental. I didn't want to teach our children that they could punch their way out of every situation without consequences, or do it anyway, consequences be damned.

I tossed my phone to the mattress and covered it with a stack of folded towels. They were frayed at the edges and none of them matched, but they smelled like home, so I kept them in a bag in the back of my closet and opened it when I missed Taylor the most. *Only slightly psychotic.*

The doorbell announced someone's arrival with its flat and offbeat chime that begged to be put out of its misery.

"Daddy!" Hadley said.

Taylor greeted the kids, his hellos cut off by tackle hugs. A few moments later, my bedroom door burst open, and Hollis stood there with Taylor, who was carrying Hadley on his back. Hollis wore a wide grin on his face, his left dimple sunk in, the eyes I loved looking up at me not remotely resembling Taylor's or mine.

"Dad's here!" Hollis said. He was so excited he didn't notice the box on the bed, but Taylor did.

"I see that," I said with a grin.

"Uh … why don't you kids pack an overnight bag? I'm going to chat with Mom."

"Overnight? Really?" Hadley said, sliding off Taylor's back. She looked at me. "Really, Mom?"

"Really," I said. "Go on."

They raced each other to their bedrooms, making as much noise as possible. A day before, I would have been worried about the neighbors complaining, but we were finally leaving this dump behind.

"How's it going?" Taylor asked, noting the box and my cluttered bed.

"Just getting started. It was tough packing in secret and making dinner and …" I trailed off, noticing a smear of soot on his face. "I checked the news on my phone. The fire's still going."

Taylor nodded. "It's a beast."

"You're sure Tyler was okay with you leaving them to it?"

"Yep," he said, looking around. He found a broken down box and opened it, taping the bottom closed. He seemed conflicted about something, and when his brow furrowed, I braced myself for what he might say. "Uh … Falyn …?"

"Dad!" Hollis said, bag in hand. He glanced at the empty box in front of Taylor and then at the one in front of me. "What's going on?"

I turned toward the kids, both of them confused. "Let's talk at the table. Come on."

Hollis and Hadley followed me to the dining room, which was really just a corner of the living room with a table and chairs. We sat down, and they both rested their elbows on the table, crossing their arms just like Taylor.

"We need to tell you something, but before we do, I need to explain. Dad and I are not back together, and we will not be getting back together—at least, not for a while. We have a lot of things to work out."

The kids' eyes fell to their hands and so did Taylor's.

"The good news is," I said, looking at Taylor. "You want to . . . ?"

Taylor instantly masked his sadness with a cheerful smile. "The good news is you're moving back to Estes Park."

"What? With you?" Hollis said, jumping up from his seat. He threw his arms around Taylor's neck, and I tried not to let it hurt too much that he was so eager to live with his Dad.

"With Mom, too," Taylor said. Both kids' gazes bounced between Taylor and me. "That's the confusing part."

"Mom's moving back, too?" Hadley echoed. Cautious hope flashed in her eyes.

"Your dad and I think it's a better idea if we move back into the house in Estes, where you can have your old rooms back and go back to school with your old friends."

"But you're not together?" Hollis said. I could see the confusion on his face.

Taylor swallowed, already hating what he was about to say. "I'm going to get an apartment until your Mom and I figure things out."

"An apartment?" Hollis groaned. His eyes glossed over, and he collapsed on his chair. "That's fucking stupid."

"Hollis Henry Maddox!" Taylor growled.

He wasn't used to the cursing, the mood swings, or the anger like I was. As far as the kids were concerned, I had ruined their lives, and Dad was their savior.

Taylor regained his composure, and he pulled Hollis in for a hug, forcing him onto his lap. "You're not happy here, and your mom sees that. It took a lot for her to call me and figure out how to get you back home. I don't mind finding an apartment for a while."

"For how long?" Hollis said, trying not to cry. His cheeks flushed red, making his already faint freckles less noticeable.

"Hollis," I began. "We've talked about this. Sometimes moms and dads need some time to—"

"This is bull crap!" Hollis said. "If we're going to live in Estes, we should all live together."

"But we can't," I said, firm. "Not yet."

Hollis stared at me for a moment, hatred in his eyes. At these moments, I waited in fear for him to scream that I wasn't really his mom, but he hadn't yet. Teeth clenched, he pushed up from his chair, the legs whining against the tile, and he stomped to his room.

Taylor sighed. "That didn't go as well as I thought it would."

"You should go talk to him," I said.

Taylor kissed Hadley's forehead and then nodded, following Hollis to his room.

"Mom?" Hadley said. "He can have my room." I looked at her for a moment, confused. Her platinum hair reminded me so much of Olive, down to the splash of freckles across her nose. "Dad. If you don't want him sleeping with you, he can have my room."

I reached for her hand, and to my surprise, she took it. "I wish I could explain this to you so you could understand."

"I understand," she said. "He got arrested, and you got mad at him. But you've been mad at him for a long time. Can't you be done being mad now?"

I looked down. "It's just not that simple, love. I wish it were."

She nodded, her gaze falling to our hands in the center of the table.

Taylor walked in, his hands in his jeans pockets. "He's okay. He's packing. You should get to packing too, baby girl."

Hadley hopped up from the table and hurried toward her room, stopping long enough to throw her arms around Taylor's waist. He pulled her in tight and then let her go, watching me rest my chin on the heel of my hand.

"They've hated me since we left. It's been tense," I said.

"They could never hate you."

"You don't know that," I said.

"Yes, I do." He stared at me for a moment, neither one of us saying a word. I swallowed, knowing that we still loved each other, but also sure that I wasn't ready to move forward together. It was a fine line—being cautious, so I didn't make a bad decision based on emotion and holding out just to further punish him. "C'mon," Taylor said. "We'll start in your room." He held his hand out to me, and I hesitated. He pulled back, returning it to the pocket it was in. "I get it, you know. The kids don't, but I do. They don't know what happened. They don't know I deserve this."

"That doesn't make me feel any better."

"They don't deserve this, though. We're better than this, Falyn."

"Taylor, don't." I stood, walking past him. He gently caught my arm, and it took all of my strength not to fall into him. I'd missed his touch, being so close to him, hearing his voice in the same room, watching him watch me.

"I still love you," he said, anger on the edge of his words. I couldn't blame him. Our family was broken, and our children were hurting.

"I know," I said. My resentment wouldn't let me say anything else, and I pulled away from him to walk to the end of the hall.

Taylor gathered a few boxes, taped them together for the kids, and then returned, helping me to load my things into the cardboard. We gathered socks from the drawers and shoes and Halloween buckets from the top of the closet. I'd missed how tall Taylor was, too. He could reach everything I couldn't. He could lift and open everything I couldn't and sometimes, even if I could, just so I could watch him do it.

"I still love you, too," I said. Taylor turned around, an indistinguishable expression on his face. "And I miss you. Maybe the kids are smarter than I am on this one. Maybe we should try to fix this from the inside out instead of hurting the kids while I pretend to wait for an epiphany."

"Is that what you're doing? Hoping for a sign that I've changed?" He took a step toward me, dropping everything in his hands. "Because baby, I've changed. I don't want to lose you. I don't want to lose the kids. I—"

My phone buzzed, cutting him off. I looked around, touching my jeans pockets. It buzzed again, and Taylor pointed at the stack of towels.

"It's coming from there," he said, stepping toward the bed. "It's late. Think it's Ellie?"

"Oh, yeah. I—" *Oh. Fuck.*

Before I could stop him, Taylor lifted the towels and picked up my phone, his face instantly twisting into disgust. "Why the fuck is Peter Lacy calling you? How does he have your number, Falyn?"

"I don't know," I said, reaching for my phone. "It doesn't matter. I never respond."

Recognition lit Taylor's eyes, and he became angrier. "How many times has he contacted you? What the fuck, Falyn? Is this why you want to move back?"

My mouth fell open. "No! And he hasn't contacted me at all because I don't answer!"

"How did he get your fucking number?" Taylor screamed. His veins were bulging from his neck, his eyes practically glowing and wild. His chest was heaving, and I could see the restraint. He wanted to punch something or someone. If Peter had been there, he might have killed him. I remembered now. The man standing in front of me now was the Taylor I left.

My eyes fell to the floor. The hope I'd had just moments before gone. When I looked up again, and Taylor's eyes met mine, I could see the anger melt away and shame take over. Even then, he couldn't let go. He picked up the stack of towels and shoved them into the box on top of some trinkets, ripping at the tape and slamming it across the top. He grabbed a thick black marker and wrote *master* across the top and then hurled the box into the corner of the room behind the door, its contents scattering.

Two dark silhouettes were standing in the hall, and when I realized the kids were present once again for the shitshow that was our marriage, I covered my mouth, unable to stop the tears from falling.

"No, baby, don't cry…" Taylor glanced down at the hall. "I'm sorry," he said to the kids. He sat on the bed, hunched over. "I'm sorry," he choked out.

"Can we still go?" Hadley asked, stepping from out of the shadow of the hall.

"I'm still going," Hollis said.

I wiped my cheeks and walked to the doorway, holding Hollis and Hadley as if they might shatter like the ceramics in the box. "Yes. Yes, we're still going. Dad wants us to, and I want us to. We're happier in Estes, right?"

"Right," they both said, looking up at me and nodding.

Soon, Hollis would be taller than I was. Maybe taller than Taylor. I couldn't let him think it was okay to use violence and intimidation to solve anything. I couldn't let Hadley think Taylor's was acceptable behavior, and that it was okay to stay without real change. And I couldn't let them—or my own guilt—talk me into taking Taylor back before we were ready.

Taylor's phone rang, and he fished it from his back pocket. He sniffed once before answering. "Hey, Trent." The longer he listened, the more his shoulders sagged. "What? What do you mean shot? Like with a gun? How? Is he okay?"

Taylor let the phone fall to the floor, and I scrambled to pick it up, holding it to my ear. All the blood had drained from Taylor's face, and he was staring at the floor, a single tear streaming down his cheek.

"Trent?" I said. "It's Falyn. What happened?"

Trenton sighed. "Hey, Falyn. It's, uh … it's Tommy. He, uh … there's been an accident."

"An accident? Is he okay?" I asked.

"No. Taylor and Tyler need to come home. Can you get them here?"

"*No?*" I asked. I had heard him, but the words didn't make sense. Thomas Maddox was the strongest of all five boys; the smartest. He had the best head on his shoulders, and Liis had just given birth to their first baby. He was a new father. *How can he* not *be okay?*

"It's bad," he said, his voice low. "Just get them home, Falyn. Call Tyler. I don't … I don't think I can."

"I'll take care of it. How's Liis?"

"She's with Stella. You'll get 'em on a plane?"

"Yes. We'll all be there tomorrow."

"Thanks, Falyn. See you soon."

"Mom?" Hollis said, watching Taylor with worried eyes. "Is Uncle Tommy okay?"

I held out my hand to the kids, letting them know to wait before inundating us with questions, and to let me care for their dad first. I kneeled in front of Taylor, searching for words to say. There were none. He was still trying to process what Trenton had said.

"Honey?" I said, gently tugging at his chin. "I'm going to call Tyler, and then I'm going to call the airline."

"He's at the fire," Taylor said, his voice monotone. "He won't answer."

I dialed Tyler's number with my husband's phone, listening as it rang several times before his voice mail picked up. I tucked the phone into my back pocket and pointed at the children. "Pack for five days. Five jeans, five shirts, five socks, and five pairs of underpants. Toothbrush and toothpaste. Go now."

The kids nodded and ran to their rooms. I emptied a small roller bag Taylor had already filled with my unmentionables and packed for five days as well. "Where's your bag?" I asked Taylor.

"Huh?"

"Your bag. You packed a bag to come here, right? Do you have at least two days' worth?"

"Three days. It's in my truck."

"Okay," I said, pulling up the handle on my bag. "Let's go. I'm driving. I'll reserve tickets on the way."

"To where?"

"Estes Park. We're going to tell Tyler, and then we're driving to Denver to catch a plane."

"Falyn …" Taylor began, but he knew he couldn't be the strong one this time. We were broken, but we weren't alone.

I held out my hand to him. "Come with me."

He looked up at me, seeming lost. Taylor reached for me, intertwining his fingers with mine and bringing my hand to his lips. He closed his eyes tight, breathing hard through his nose.

With my free hand, I cupped the back of his head and hugged him to my middle. "I'm here."

He let go of my hand and wrapped his arms around me, burying his face in my shirt.

# CHAPTER NINE

## ELLIE

THE TELEVISION WAS THE ONLY LIGHT in our dark living room, dim and then bright and back again, depending on what scene and camera angle was presented at the time. I'd told myself not to watch this movie, knowing it was about an alcoholic, foul-mouthed reporter. Even after a decade on the wagon, my throat tightened every time she took a drink; my heart pinged when she was out, laughing hysterically, sloppy drunk with her friends, taking dick from anyone who had one. I'd made it to the last scene, and she had fallen in love with a decent dude. *Fuck*. I was too old to say dude. At least, that was what Gavin had told me because he was five and knew everything.

I ran my fingers over the prickles of Gavin's dark, buzzed hair. He'd fallen asleep using my lap as a pillow like he always did when his dad was on shift. Tyler and I had fallen in love sometime between a one-night stand (mostly my fault) and a stint in rehab (totally my fault). Somehow, we lived in a three-bedroom house with a dog, two cats, and a son who wasn't into throwing temper tantrums and never held on to anything—not a bottle, a pacifier; he even potty-trained early. Addiction didn't seem to be in his future. I just hoped his penchant to let things go didn't spill over into his love life.

I glanced at my watch and sighed. It was nearly three a.m., and Tyler was still fighting the fire at the warehouse. Years of sleepless nights kept me from trying to go to bed before he was back at the station, so I waited for the call that he was safe at his second home.

Just as the credits began to roll, a light knock sounded on the front door. I carefully moved Gavin's head off my lap and slipped out from under him. I approached the door with caution. We lived in a nice neighborhood in a smallish tourist community, but whoever was at my door in the wee hours of the morning wasn't selling LipSense.

"Who is it?" I said, trying to be both loud enough to be heard and quiet so I wouldn't wake Gavin.

"It's Taylor," a deep voice said.

"And Falyn."

I twisted the bolt lock and yanked open the door, staring at my in-laws as if they were a hallucination. Taylor had both of their sleeping children hanging over his shoulders, his face pale and his eyes glossed over.

"What are you doing here?" I asked, and then covered my mouth. I hadn't heard from Tyler in nearly an hour. A lot could happen in an hour. "Oh, God."

"No," Falyn said, reaching for me. "This isn't about Tyler."

I pulled her in for a hug, squeezing her tight. She was surprised, and I couldn't blame her. I wasn't typically the snuggly type with anyone but Tyler and Gavin.

"Have you heard from him?" Taylor asked, walking past me.

"You can put them in the guest room," I said but wasn't sure why. Taylor knew exactly where it was and was already headed that way. Taylor and Falyn had spent a lot of their time in our home and vice-versa until Falyn had left. She hadn't been gone that long, but it somehow still felt strange being under the same roof with both of them again.

Taylor returned. His hands were free, and he didn't quite know what to do with them, so he crossed his arms across his middle.

"Are you okay?" I asked.

"I've been trying to get a hold of Tyler."

I shook my head and then glanced back to check on Gavin. "He should be wrapping up at the warehouse. I haven't heard from him in the last hour."

Taylor sniffed. "Guess I'm going to have to go to the warehouse."

"They should be finished soon," I said. "Everything okay?"

"He's grown so much," Falyn whispered, walking over to my son sprawled out on the sofa. She kneeled beside him, smiling as she took a closer look. "Gavin looks identical to Taylor and Tyler when they were his age."

"He misses you," I said. "He asks about you a lot."

Her expression fell. "I miss him, too. And you." She stood. "Taylor got a call from Trent."

"We're going home," Taylor said.

"To Eakins? When?"

"Tomorrow," Falyn said. "You and Tyler, too."

"We are?" I asked, touching my chest. "What's going on? Is it Jim?" I knew Dad's health wasn't the greatest. He was overweight, ate bacon every morning for breakfast, and smoked cigars. By the look on Taylor's face, I knew something terrible had happened.

Taylor opened his mouth to explain but couldn't.

Falyn continued for him. "It's Thomas."

"*Thomas?*" He'd just become a father. "Oh, God. The baby?"

"No," Falyn said. "Thomas was shot."

"*Shot?*" I said, my voice going up an octave. The room began to spin.

"We don't know many details."

"Oh, Liis," I said, covering my mouth with my hand. My heart instantly broke for her. My gaze drifted to Taylor. I felt bad, knowing he would have to hear the story again when we broke the news to Tyler. I closed my eyes, feeling hot tears streaming down my cheeks. My heart broke for my husband.

"You should sit down," Falyn said, trying to keep her composure.

I lumbered to Tyler's recliner and collapsed. "Fuck. *Fuck.* This doesn't make sense. Did they catch the shooter?"

"We're not sure," Taylor said. He clenched his teeth, his jaw muscles dancing under his skin.

"Liis is flying into Eakins in the morning," Falyn said.

I lifted my head. "She's not staying with Thomas?"

Falyn shook her head. "It … it sounds like it's pretty bad. Her flying to Eakins …" she trailed off.

Bile rose in my throat. He wasn't going to make it. Liis was flying home to be with his family.

"I already booked the tickets," Falyn said.

"For us, too?" I asked. She nodded, and I stood, looking around, my mind already filling with packing lists and who would care for the animals while we were gone. I paused and then walked the few steps to where Taylor stood, hugging him to me. He felt a little limp in my arms.

"I fucking knew it," he said. "I had a bad feeling when I left the fire earlier, but I thought it was Tyler. I should have called home."

Taylor knew as well as I did that calling home wouldn't have helped anything, but he was doing what Tyler was going to do when he heard the news: blame himself. I let him go and walked back to the sofa, picking up my phone from the end table and disconnecting the charger.

I texted Tyler to call me, and then we all waited. Within three minutes, my phone rang. I answered immediately.

"Hi baby," he said, sounding tired and out of breath, but happy. "Just getting in the truck."

"I … need you to come home," I said. It just occurred to me that he would want to know why, and I didn't want to tell him over the phone.

"What happened?" he asked, already suspicious.

"Taylor and Falyn are here. Just come home, okay? As soon as you can get here."

"On my way," he said. I heard the sirens in the background, and then the line went silent.

I breathed out a long breath, knowing within a few minutes, those sirens would be blaring in the distance, getting closer until they turned off when Tyler entered the neighborhood. I tried not to think about him speeding home to hear what he already knew was bad news. He just didn't know how bad—or who.

# CHAPTER TEN

## CAMILLE

AS EVERYONE ELSE WAS SETTLING IN for the night, I was leaving for work. I started at Skin Deep Tattoo as the receptionist, but now, I was the business manager. I hired and fired, kept books, and worked the business side that Calvin, turns out, wasn't doing. The shop nearly closed down, but I navigated an agreement with the IRS, and we were finally making enough profit to hire a couple of new artists. Tonight, though, I was heading to The Red Door. I filled in when they needed me to cover the east bar. Very few could handle it, and Raegan and Blia had left years ago when they graduated college. Hank and Jorie had been so good to me; I couldn't tell them no.

The federal agents asked that I not leave, but I'd promised Hank I'd cover a shift for one of his newer bartenders. The house was overfilling, anyway. Olive was sleeping on the sofa in Jim's living room, and Shepley's parents were even spending the night. Travis felt it was safer if everyone was under the same roof until Liis arrived in the morning—apparently with more agents.

Agent Perkins was on watch, staring out the window when I left with Trenton. He dropped me off at the side of the building, as close to the door as he could get. He was unhappy about me going to work, too.

I leaned over to kiss him. "I'll be fine. Drew is in there. He's a beast."

"I'll be here waiting at two."

"It'll be two-thirty," I said.

"I'll be here at two."

He looked worried, so I didn't argue.

A few years past thirty, my clothes covered more, but I found that fast service made just as many tips as tits and ass. I waved to Drew as I made my way to the door. He jogged to meet me, twisting the knob and pulling before I could. He held the door open with a smile.

"Thanks, Drew," I said, patting his bicep. I would have had to reach up to pat his shoulder. Drew was a sophomore at Eastern State, six-foot-seven, with arms as big around as my head. His father was a champion weightlifter, and Drew was on his way. The moment he stepped into Hank's office to apply for the bouncer job, he was hired. The only problem—if you could call it that—was Drew being so polite that he sometimes wasn't as aggressive as Hank wanted. He was an awe-shuck, rock-kicking cowboy, but he could hold two men apart while they were swinging and yelling, asking them to please get along. Admittedly, it was always entertaining, but Hank wanted a bouncer, not a peacekeeper. Lucky for Drew, his presence was usually enough.

"Yes, ma'am. Do you have my number? I'd be happy to meet you in the parking lot when you pick up a shift. It's not safe for ladies to be walking alone at night."

I gave him a side-glance. "Have you met me, Drew?"

He chuckled. "Once or twice." He paused while he decided if he was going to say the next part. "I'd still feel better about it. If you don't mind."

"Okay. I'll call ahead."

He smiled, relieved. "Thank you, Mrs. Maddox."

"Cami," I reminded him.

Drew turned right, toward the entrance, and I went left to the east bar. Shayla was already stocking beer in the coolers. She was high-strung but worked fast enough to keep up with the east bar's traffic.

She sighed. "Did Natasha call in sick again?"

"She did."

"Hank's going to fire her."

"I doubt it."

"He misses team Cami and Raegan. He tells us all the time."

"That's non-productive," I said, pouring a bucket of ice into the last cooler.

"I don't blame him. I like working with you, too."

I smiled. It was nice to feel needed, even if I was spread a little thin the past few years with Jim. I'd made sure he was in bed before I left, propping his cane against the wall next to his bed and setting a cup of ice water on his nightstand. Night-lights lit the way from his room to the bathroom, but I still worried. Jim was like a father to me; he was the only one I had. My alcoholic, abusive father had died years before from cirrhosis of the liver. I didn't miss him, but Mom moved to Ohio with my oldest brother and his family, and the rest of my brothers were scattered all over the country.

I was lucky to have a family like the Maddoxes, but I was desperate to keep Jim as long as possible. His health had declined in the past few years and had me worried. I wanted to give him a grandchild and for him or her to know Jim; to remember him. It seemed no matter how many vitamins I gave him every morning, how many walks we went on, or how healthy I cooked for him, we couldn't fight time. The hardest part was that he was embracing it. He looked forward to seeing his wife again, and it felt self-serving to beg him to try harder.

The DJ started up the sound system and checked the mics, making me snap out of my stare off with the beer cooler.

"You okay?" Shayla said. She was staring at me like I was nuts. She was barely twenty-one and had no way to relate to what I was feeling, so I kept it to myself.

Jorie sauntered by, her eyes lighting up when she saw me. She wouldn't stay long. She was seven months pregnant and was concerned about the loud music affecting the baby. "Cami!" She rounded the bar and threw her arms around me.

"You look great," I said, feeling both happy for her and guilty for my envy. Liis, Abby, and Jorie were all pregnant at the same time, and every month when I looked down at my negative pregnancy test, I thought of them. I didn't want to be envious. I didn't want to be angry that it was so easy for them and so far had been impossible for me. I didn't want to hate them a little bit, but I did. Desperation created its own emotions.

"Thanks," she said, looking down and running her hand over her baby bump. Her gaze returned to mine. "You look tired. Everything okay?"

I rolled my eyes, shoving two more beer bottles in the bucket of ice. "Tired is code for you look like shit."

"No. Your eyes are bloodshot. You have circles under your eyes. Your shoulders are sagging. So … I take it back. You do look like shit."

I chuckled at her bluntness. One of the many reasons I loved her. "We got some bad news today."

She gasped. "Jim?"

"No. Thomas …" I trailed off, unsure what to say. My brother-in-law being shot was so unbelievable. There were FBI agents at Jim's asking us to keep it quiet. "… was in an accident."

"Oh, fuck!" she said, touching her belly. "He's going to be all right, though, right?"

"We're waiting. We don't have a lot of information yet, but they say it's bad."

"Who's *they*?"

I paused. "Liis."

Jorie covered her mouth, her eyes glossing over. "Oh, Liis." She hugged me as if she were hugging Thomas's girlfriend. It felt strange because, at one time, I was. Her reaction brought long buried feelings to the surface. I'd been worried for Trenton and Jim but hadn't taken a moment to really understand my own emotions. Thomas was my first love, and at one time, we considered me moving out to California to take it to the next level. And then … Trenton came along. Thinking back, Trenton and I made much more sense, and Thomas was perfect with Liis. But it took several years for all of us to work it out in our hearts and minds. In that moment, hugging Jorie, I was right back where I started … loving them both.

I released her; even though Jorie's soft curves were comforting. She might have been curvier than she used to be, but she still had long, platinum blond hair. Instead of black peek-a-boo streaks, her style now featured teal tips. She would be the kind of mother I wanted to be: maternal, wild, fierce, and fun. I just had to get pregnant.

She wiped her eyes and then waved goodbye, retreating to Hank's office to get another hug before going home.

"Wow," Shayla said, her eyes wide. "What did you say to her?"

"My brother-in-law was in an accident." *Fuck*. Now, it felt weird to say brother-in-law. Even having confusing feelings felt like a betrayal to Trenton. I cared about Thomas and loved him once. Now, my love for him was in the realm of how I felt about any of

Trenton's brothers. But losing him was a very real possibility—at least, according to the federal agents at Jim's. I remembered the times we'd laughed and talked about our deepest thoughts and feelings. We'd created a bond before I'd ever fallen in love with Trenton, and that was a strange place to be in. I wanted to pull out my phone and text Trenton to work out the thoughts spinning in my head, but there was too much to do before the doors opened.

"Oh, damn. I'm sorry. Did Jorie know him?"

"Yeah," I said, being vague on purpose. I didn't want to explain how Jorie knew him when we were dating. I understood how on the outside looking in, the whole situation was very incriminating. It was hard to explain the way I felt about Thomas without sounding like those feelings betrayed Trenton. In truth, I loved my husband more than I'd loved anyone, including Thomas. Trenton got me in a way no one else did, and he loved me more than anyone else had. Even if the tables were turned, and Trenton had the accident and Liis had never come along, I still wouldn't turn to Thomas. Now that Trenton had shown me what love was, I knew that wasn't what Thomas and I had. My feelings ran deep, and something about him was hard to shake, but Trenton Maddox was the love of my life. No one else.

Within ten minutes, Hank was making his way to me, sympathy in his eyes. "Jorie just left. She told me about Thomas. I'm sorry, sweets."

I shrugged to stave off the tears. I'd been obsessing about how I felt since Jorie had walked away, and Hank talking to me nearly sent me over the edge. For some reason, when men showed me sympathy, it made me feel things more intensely. I wasn't sure if it was because my father showed a little compassion, or it was just a universal thing that women felt when men allowed themselves to be vulnerable for half a second. Men holding and cooing to babies, men crying, men admitting they were afraid or just showing sensitivity, in general, had always made me overly emotional. It just seemed like such a beautiful moment of vulnerability and bravery to me.

Hank took me into his arms, and the tears flowed. He held me tighter. "You should go home. You can't work like this."

I pulled away, and I could see that in his eyes he didn't mean it. He knew better. I needed to stay busy to cope. "No, thank you."

"Let me know if you change your mind."

I was glad when the doors opened, and I could put on my game face. It was coin beer night, and the east bar was surrounded six lines deep. I took an order, made the drink, jabbed the buttons of the register, took the money, watched the tip go into the jar, and started all over. After just half an hour, I pulled the horn for more beer. After three hours, I pulled the horn for more of everything. The dance floor was full, the patrons were happy, and Drew didn't have to break up one fight. It was a good night, and after everyone had cleared out and housekeeping was sweeping up the mess left behind, I grabbed my middle to hug myself, and I bawled.

So many memories stood behind the bar with me. Feeling giddy when Thomas walked in and proceeded to flirt with me, and then feeling empowered when he came back and asked me out. Seeing Travis and Abby sit on the stools in front of me for the first time. Watching the Maddox brothers fight at the drop of a hat. The time Trenton leaned over the bar and kissed me on New Year's Eve. Working with my best friend and roommate, Raegan, and watching her fall in love with Kody. Crying when they moved away, and celebrating when Jorie and Hank learned they were finally pregnant. The Red Door was a part of me and being there was an escape right up until the doors closed. I didn't want it to be over. Not even just for the night.

After I'd dried the last glass and put it away, Drew smiled. "Ready?" he asked. He walked all the females to their cars at the end of every night. Drew was a good kid.

"Ready. Trenton should be right outside."

Drew's eyebrows pulled together. He looked confused. "No, ma'am. At least, he wasn't when I checked a few minutes ago."

"Maybe he's late," I said, grabbing my purse and slinging it over my shoulder. But as I said the words, a bad feeling came over me.

Drew opened the side door, and after I had noticed Trenton wasn't where he said he'd be parked and waiting for me, I scanned the dark lot.

"It's not like him to be late, is it?" Drew asked.

"No, it's not." I typed out a text to him and waited. After a few minutes and no reply, my body began to shake. Adrenaline was surging through my veins as my mind went over the worst scenarios.

A black car slowed to a spot where Trenton was supposed to be, and instinctively, I stretched my arm across Drew, moving him backward. "Go inside," I hissed.

"Who is that?" Drew asked, moving to stand in front of me.

The window rolled down, revealing one of the agents from Jim's. "We're here to pick you up, Mrs. Maddox."

I relaxed but hesitated. "Where's Trenton? Why hasn't he texted me back?"

"I'll explain when you get in," he said.

Drew held me back just as I stepped forward. "Do you know this guy?" he asked.

"Yes. It's a long story." I reached for the door handle, but Drew stopped me.

"She's not going anywhere with you until she's heard from her husband."

"That will be difficult," the agent said.

My stomach sank. "Why?"

"You need to get in the car, Mrs. Maddox. I can't explain further in the presence of your current company."

I grabbed Drew's arm, and he looked down at me, pleading me with his eyes not to go. "He's okay," I said simply. "He's a friend of Jim's."

"Trenton's dad?" Drew asked, suspicious. When I nodded, Drew didn't seem convinced. "I have a bad feeling, Cami. I think you should stay here until Trenton calls you."

My gaze fell back to the agent. "I don't think he's going to."

# CHAPTER ELEVEN

## ABBY

TRAVIS SQUEEZED MY HAND, and I squeezed back, letting him know I understood how hard this was for him. Everyone was upset and exhausted, speculating what had happened to Thomas while also expressing anger at the agents for withholding information—which forced them to speculate. Now, he lay flat on his back in the center of the sunken-in, full-size mattress he'd had since the eighth grade, a hand-me-down from Thomas. Our twins were on pallets on the floor, both snoring softly.

We'd talked Shepley and America into coming over and even Jack and Deana. Even though it only raised more questions, it was safer to have everyone under one roof until Travis and the agents had more backup. For all we knew, the entire Carlisi crime family could be in Eakins at any moment.

Travis turned over on his side, burying his face in my neck. He'd just come to bed after doing a second sweep of the house for bugs. We couldn't be too careful. "This fucking sucks. This makes me wish I still smoked."

"Your emergency pack is at home, and you're not leaving us, so forget it," I said.

"I know, but this feels like an emergency."

I turned over to meet his gaze and hooked my leg over his hip. It was the closest we could get with my belly between us. "The Maddox family is capable of almost anything. Actors they are not."

"Maybe they could. We don't know that."

"They're not trained like you are, Trav. Someone will make a mistake. You wouldn't have agreed to this unless you knew for a fact this was the only way to keep everyone safe."

He nodded, touching his forehead to mine. "You're my favorite wife."

"Just try to put it out of your head until Liis gets here tomorrow. Most of the burden is going to be hers."

He sighed, looking up at the ceiling. He crossed his arms over his middle. "She just had a baby, Pidge. She's alone. How can I make her do that?"

"She's not alone. We can support her. We can help."

He was quiet for a moment. "There has to be another way. Dad is going to have a heart attack. This is going to kill him."

"He's stronger than you think."

"We can't do this," he said. The panic that had been just beneath the surface all evening was now evident in his voice.

I grabbed his face, forcing him to look me in the eyes. "We don't have a choice. Think about what they did, Travis. They thought they were shooting at me. They thought they were running me off the road. Jessica and James could have been in the car. We could have been killed. Everyone could have been coming home for our funeral. If we don't do this, it still could be our funeral—or Shep's, or even Olive's. As of yesterday, we know we all have targets on our backs. Even the kids. When Liis makes the phone call to the Bureau that she's not testifying, and my dad goes missing," I said, making quotation marks in the air with my fingers. they'll back off. Then you can hunt every single one of them down until they're not a threat anymore, and anyone else will think twice about threatening your family again."

Travis blinked. "You're right. I know you're right."

I leaned in to kiss his lips, just as soft and warm as the first time I'd felt them on mine. He pulled my bare leg closer to him, kissing me harder, deeper. Travis always thought I was beautiful, but up until the moment I told him we were pregnant again, I'd forgotten just how the idea of carrying his child made Travis insatiable.

"If you want me to stop ..." he trailed off. "Any contractions today?" I smiled and shook my head. I'd been having strong Braxton Hicks for nearly three weeks. We'd even gone to the hospital once but were sent home. He slipped my silk nightgown over my head and kissed my belly. He knew I had no intention of saying no.

We were at the part of my pregnancy that made my curves more difficult to work around, but Travis easily navigated every high and low, running his tongue over my stretched skin more eagerly than our first time in his apartment.

He sat on his knees at the end of the bed, holding my right foot in his hand, kneading my aching arch with his thumbs. He lifted my toe to his mouth and kissed the tip and then continued with my massage, moving up to my calf. Each time he finished a section, he would say goodbye with a kiss. My insides tensed when he found his way to my thighs. His head disappeared behind my pregnant belly, and I rested my head back.

"Where did you go?" I whispered.

His tongue made a wet line from my thigh to the inner folds of my most sensitive parts, and I let out a quiet sigh. "Oh. There you are."

Travis gripped my hips and pulled me toward him, just as eager for him to be between my legs as I was. I could hear his legs brushing against the sheets, getting more excited with each flick of his tongue.

Just as I felt my insides building to release, he crawled to lay beside me, pressing his lips against my skin. Running his tongue up my belly, he followed the dark line that had formed beneath my belly button, spanning to my pelvic bone sometime during my second trimester. The baby stirred, and Travis jerked his head up, smiling and running his palm over the place our son had moved. It was such a strange combination—sex and parenting. It didn't seem to be a struggle for Travis, to go from foreplay to attending to a wet bed or nightmare, and then returning to feeling sexy and desirable. Transitioning from mom to lover was more difficult for me.

Travis pulled me on top of him, running his hand over the small of my back to my ass. His fingers pressed into my skin as his eyes scanned my naked body from my hair to where our skin met. Everything around us melted away, and I was nineteen again, feeling his hands on me for the first time. Sex with Travis Maddox had always been amazing, but something about the way he worshiped my body when I was pregnant made it even better. I had never felt more beautiful or wanted than at that moment, and I would feel even more beautiful and wanted the next time he made love to me.

Travis gripped my thighs, steadying me as I slowly lowered myself onto him. The black leather braided bracelets on his wrist tumbled up his tensed forearm, drawing my attention to his tattoos dancing on the surface of his skin. I let my head fall back, biting my lip to keep myself from moaning. A quiet sigh left my lips instead. Travis rocked his hips just to reposition, and I tensed, already feeling close to climax. My body reacted so differently during pregnancy, to everything. Best of all … sex. Not everything was such a bonus, but bigger breasts, my husband catering to my every craving, and the ability to come faster than my husband were certainly the highlights. All Travis had to do was slip his fingers beneath my panties, and I was a flustered mess.

I slowed my movements, and Travis complied, letting me set the pace. His russet irises pored over me, relishing the moment. His eyes rolled back, and he groaned. As soon as the noise escaped his lips, we froze, waiting to hear a pause in the light snoring on the floor below.

I covered my mouth, trying not to giggle.

Travis smiled for a moment, and then his gaze fell to the place where our bodies met. He rolled his hips again, arching his back to bury himself deeper inside me. I had to concentrate to hold back, both hoping he would hurry and dreading the end.

"My God," he whispered. "It blows my mind every fucking time how good you feel."

I anchored my knees on each side of him, lifting up so I could feel him against me as I slid down around him again.

Travis paused, his eyes moving around the room. I started to speak, to ask him what was wrong, but he held his finger to his mouth.

We heard raised voices downstairs, and Travis closed his eyes, disappointed and regretting his next request. He patted me gently on the thigh, and I climbed off him, watching as he hopped out of bed and pulled on a pair of red basketball shorts. He put on a navy blue baseball hat and swung it around backward, hiding the mess I'd made of his hair while he was between my thighs.

"I'll be back," he said, leaning down to kiss me. His lips still tasted like me.

The muscles of his chest rippled as he moved, rushing to get downstairs to find out what was going on. He closed the door behind him, and I fell back against my pillow, frustrated. As Travis made his way downstairs, the snoring of the twins picked up, echoing one another. Travis's voice joined the symphony of deep tones, and then I heard him yell.

I jumped up, glancing out the window to check for any signs of danger before wrapping myself in my robe and rushing downstairs. Travis was standing in the center of the living room, toe-to-toe with Trenton. Shepley was standing between them, his hands flat against their chests.

"What the hell?" I hissed, trying to keep my voice down.

Travis immediately relaxed and took a step back, letting Shepley stand between him and his brother.

Trenton watched me for a moment and then frowned, looking up at his bigger little brother. "I'll be right back."

Travis pointed at the floor. "I said no one leaves the house. That means no one, Trenton, Goddamn it! You shouldn't have let her leave in the first place."

"Who the fuck put you in charge?" Trenton snapped.

Travis tried to stay calm. "You have no idea what you've done."

"What have I done?" Trenton said, taking a step toward Travis. "You seem to know more than the rest of us. Why don't you enlighten me?"

Travis sighed, frustrated. He wasn't allowed to say anything until Liis called the next day. "You stay here. One of the agents will pick her up from work."

"I'm not sending a stranger to pick up my wife," Trenton spat. "You wouldn't, either."

"Trent, you can't go out there."

"*Why*?"

"Because you can't," Travis said.

America padded down the stairs, flinching from the dim lighting offered from the lamps in the living room. She hooked her arm around mine, waiting to hear more in hopes of understanding what was going on. The brothers hadn't argued in years, certainly not like this. It was unsettling, and I could see they were both upset about being on opposite sides of a disagreement.

"I'm going," Trenton said.

Travis went to grab his arm, but Shepley stopped him. He communicated with his eyes what we all knew. If Travis attempted to physically stop Trenton from leaving to pick up Camille, there would be a brawl in the living room.

"Trent," Shepley said, following him down the hall. America followed him.

Travis was breathing hard through his nose and shifting his weight from one foot to the other, trying to release the negative energy. It reminded me of the way he behaved just before a fight.

"You're okay," I whispered, touching his shoulder. "He doesn't understand you're just trying to keep him safe."

Travis was glaring at the hallway, listening to Shepley try to persuade him to stay. "If he'd just trust me for once. Stubborn motherfucker."

"He trusts you," I said. "He's thinking about Camille."

Travis's shoulders relaxed, and he reached back to touch my belly. "We have to think about everyone."

"Let Shepley and Mare talk to him."

Travis rubbed the back of his neck and began to pace, waiting for his cousin and my best friend to talk sense into his brother. I had planned for broken hearts and tears. I even assumed there would be anger once we came clean about the lies; even when we explained it was the only way to buy time while keeping everyone safe. I wasn't prepared for the brothers to turn on each other.

# CHAPTER TWELVE

## AMERICA

SHEPLEY FLATTENED HIS HAND against the door, begging Trenton with his eyes not to take it further. Jim, Jack and Deana, and the kids were still asleep, although I wasn't sure how with all the loud whispering. The lamp in the living room was the only light on in the house, and the air conditioner had just kicked on, drowning out the crickets whose chirping was just announcing the arrival of summer.

At three a.m., there was no traffic outside and no headlights sliding across the wall, just the old bulb in the corner of the living room surrounded by a dirty white drum held up by a five-foot tall Lucite column with a brass base. The entire home looked frozen in 1980, except that it hadn't frozen. Everything was worn, stained, tattered, or marred, mostly by the five boys who grew up here.

The light from the lamp didn't quite reach the hallway, so we stood with Trenton in the dark.

"Shep, I love you, but get the fuck outta my way," Trenton said. His dark form moved toward the door, but Shepley moved in front of him.

"C'mon, cousin. You're going to punch me in front of my wife?"

Trenton frowned and then turned to me. "Turn around for a second, Mare."

"No," I said, crossing my arms.

Trenton sighed. "I have to pick up my wife from work. I have to leave now. I don't want her to have to wait on me."

"Agent Perkins can do it," I said. "He can leave right now. He's ready to go, standing in the kitchen, keys in hand."

As Trenton became more agitated, I threw my arms around him and squeezed. "Our kids are here; your nephews and nieces. Your dad is here. Travis and Shepley can't save everyone. We need you here, Trenton."

"What if something happens to Camille?" he asked, conflicted.

"Do you think whoever the agents are protecting us from are going to hit The Red Door before the house? She doesn't even work there anymore. Not technically," Shepley said.

Trenton glared at my husband. "Would you leave it to a stranger to pick up your wife when we all know people are out there hunting us down?"

Shepley sighed, and his shoulders sank. "No."

Trenton put his hand on the knob. "Then don't ask something of me you couldn't do yourself."

Just as he opened the door, an agent standing on the porch turned to stand in the way. He wore a suit like the other two agents, but he was much bigger. "I'm going to have to ask you remain inside the home, sir."

Trenton looked up at the agent, and then back at us and over my shoulder. I turned to see Travis standing at the end of the hall.

"What the fuck is this?" Trenton asked.

"That's Agent Blevins," Travis said, smug.

"Why are you asking him?" Shepley asked. "Travis is just as clueless as the rest of us."

Trenton's brow furrowed, and he lifted one hand to point four fingers at Travis. "He knows all of their names. Do you happen to know all the names of everyone who works at the FBI, Shep, because I sure as shit don't."

"What are you trying to say?" Shepley asked.

Trenton's face screwed into disgust, but at least he stepped away from the door. "I don't know. I don't know what the hell is going on, but I know *he* is part of it." He pointed at Travis.

Shepley and I traded glances. This was going downhill fast.

"I'll go with you," Shepley said.

"Shep!" I said. "You will not!" I turned to Trenton. "You were told not to leave the house, but you took her anyway."

"She works to blow off steam, Mare. You know that," Trenton explained. "She's had a rough day. I was just trying to ..."

"We need to do this their way, Trent," I said. "They're just trying to keep us safe. Why would you do anything to make their job harder?"

Trenton shifted. "You sound like Mom."

"I know you want to pick her up so she feels safe, but we need to worry about what we can all do to actually be safe. No more crazy talk. No more Maddox machismo. Agent Perkins is going to bring Cami back, and you're going to follow orders until we get this figured out."

Agent Perkins jingled the keys in his hand, and Agent Blevins stepped to the side to allow him to pass. The door closed, and Trenton stomped past us up the stairs. Shepley followed him.

I returned to the living room where Travis and Abby were standing. When I was within earshot, they stopped whispering.

"Well done," Abby said, patting my shoulder. I pulled away from her. My reaction startled her. "Oh, I'm sorry. I didn't mean to—"

"What aren't you telling me?" I asked.

Abby's gaze drifted to Travis.

"Don't look at him," I snapped. "I'm asking you. My best friend. My sort of sister-in-law."

"Mare," she began.

I arched an eyebrow. "Choose your words carefully, Abby. My kids are in the house hiding from some unknown assailant, and if you know why, you'd better tell me."

"I," Abby began but winced. She touched her belly.

"Oh, stop," I said. "Don't even try it."

She blew out a breath and then reached for Travis. He held her to his side.

"Really?" I asked. "You're going to fake a contraction to get out of telling me the truth?"

"She's been having them for weeks," Travis said.

I crossed my arms. "Something else you're not telling me."

She stood upright and nodded to her husband, signaling that it was over.

"Well?" I said.

"Mare, not now. Abby needs to go upstairs and rest. Stress isn't good for her."

I rolled my eyes. "Oh, please. I birthed three gigantic Maddox boys. No less than forty-seven hours of labor, and they were all over nine pounds. I only went to the hospital to have Emerson after I picked up Ezra from a two-hour T-ball practice. She's not the first woman to have a contraction."

"America!" Shepley said from behind her.

I crossed my arms, unwavering. "The truth. Now."

Trenton returned, wearing an apologetic expression on his face. "I'm sorry, guys. I—"

What sounded like a gush of water sloshed onto the carpet just beneath Abby's robe.

"Oh. My. Lanta," Abby said, looking down.

We were all confused at first. Travis was the second to react. "Was that you?" He lifted up her robe a bit and then looked up at her, his eyes wide. "Your water just broke?"

She nodded.

"Oh, shit," Travis said.

"I guess we can leave now," Trenton deadpanned.

I smacked the back of his head.

"Ow!" Trenton said, rubbing the point of impact. "What'd I say?"

"We're down to two agents," Travis said to Abby.

She breathed, focusing on another, more intense contraction. From experience, I knew the ones that came after my water breaking were always ten times worse.

"We should have someone come here," I said.

"No," Abby moaned. "I need drugs. I want drugs. Lots and lots of drugs."

"Then what should we do?" I asked.

"Get a towel and put me on the couch until you figure it out," Abby said through her teeth.

I ran for a towel while Travis picked her up and carried her to the sofa.

"Shit. *Shit!*" Abby cried. The demonic sounds she made after that sounded like a feral cat preparing to fight for territory.

I folded the towel and placed it on the couch, and watched as Travis carefully lowered her to the cushions. He kneeled in front of her.

"If I take you, they'll just have Agent Blevins until backup arrives, and that could be a while."

"We have the other two," Abby said. Her face turned red, and she focused, breathing in through her nose, and out through her mouth. Her eyes filled with tears. "It's too early, Trav."

"What do I do, baby?" he asked.

"We have to go," she said, the contraction finally over.

He nodded and pointed at me. "America, get the kids. Trenton, get Dad. Shepley, get the cars. We'll need enough seats for everyone. Tell Blevins to prepare to follow and to stay alert."

"On it," Shepley said, rushing to the key ring holder to fish out the right sets.

I rushed upstairs, going first to Travis and Abby's room. "Hey," I said with a soft voice, rubbing the twins' backs. They stirred but were pretty out of it. "James. Jess. It's Aunt Mare. I need you to wake up. We're going to the hospital. Mom's having the baby."

"What?" Jessica said, sitting up. She rubbed her eyes and then poked James. He sat up, too.

"C'mon, kids. I need you to get your shoes on and go downstairs."

"Right now?" James asked. "What time is it?"

"It's the middle of the night. But Mom's having her baby, so we need to go."

"Really?" Jessica said, scrambling up from her pallet on the floor. She was pulling on her shoes when I headed for the next room.

"Really. Downstairs in two minutes, please!" I said, rushing down the hall to where Olive was sleeping. "Olive?" I said, switching on the light. I sat down on the twin bed next to her. "Olive, sweetie, I need you to wake up."

"Is everything okay?" she asked, rubbing her mascara-smeared eyes.

"We're going to the hospital. Abby is having her baby."

"But it's not time yet, is it?"

"No," I said. "It's early, which is why she has to go soon. We all have to go together, so please get moving."

She stood up, stumbling around the room to dress, and I rushed into the next room. "Boys?" I said softly. Emerson sat up, rubbed his eyes, and then jumped on his brothers. They began to fight. "Stop. Stop it. Knock it off. Right now!" I snapped.

They froze.

"Aunt Abby is having her baby. We're going to the hospital. Get shoes on and let's go."

"In our pjs?" Ezra asked.

"Yes," I said. I searched for Emerson's sandals, finding one beneath his pillow. I wondered why for half a second before resuming the task of getting all the children dressed and downstairs.

At the same time Jim was stumbling from his bedroom with Trenton and Deana was helping Jack with the zipper on his jacket, all six kids were in the hallway ready to go.

"You're amazing," Abby said.

"I'm sorry I gave you a hard time earlier," I said.

She waved me away, letting me know that no apology was necessary. We were working on two decades of friendship, and nothing was going to interfere with that.

Travis helped Abby to the truck, and Olive climbed into the back with him. Trenton drove, and Jim sat in the passenger seat. Jack and Deana climbed in with Agent Blevins. I made sure everyone was buckled in the van before hopping in next to Shepley. Agent Blevins' headlights flashed on, and then another two sets flashed on further down the block.

"Shepley," I warned.

"I think that's the other agents they were talking about." He clicked his seat belt into place, and we surged forward behind Travis's truck.

With every bump, every red light, I thought about Abby.

"Why does it seem like the hospital is a hundred miles away when you're trying to get a laboring woman there?" Shepley grumbled.

I remembered the first time Shepley drove me to the hospital, terrified the whole way that I'd give birth in the car and wishing I'd had a home birth. But I wasn't in premature labor, either. Abby was particularly calm for what she was facing, but she was famous for her poker face. I imagined she was trying to keep it together for Travis and the kids.

I wrinkled my nose and turned around, irritated that I couldn't reminisce or have a moment of internal dialog without the sounds of fighting children in the background.

"Jessica Abigail! No hitting! Ezra! Don't try to put toys up your brother's nose! Emerson! Stop screaming! James! Stop farting!"

It was quiet for a full minute before they all began chatting again as if nothing had happened. I rolled my eyes and glared at Shepley.

"Why do you always do that?"

"Do what?" I said, my eyes narrowing.

"Give me a dirty look when the kids are driving you nuts? Like I magically impregnated you when you weren't looking?"

"That is your DNA back there. It's your fault."

Shepley frowned, turning on his blinker and surging forward so he could continue to follow Travis's truck instead of being stuck at a red light. He stretched his neck to peer into the rearview mirror, checking that Agent Blevins was still behind us.

"He probably just ran the red light," I said. "He's a federal agent on duty. I'm sure he's not worried about a ticket."

"He did," Shepley said. "Damn. This is something."

"You mean scary?" I asked.

The kids got quiet.

"Is Mom going to be okay?" Jessica asked.

I closed my eyes. It was so easy to forget when they were all chattering away that they were still paying attention. Kids could ignore us all day, but the moment we utter something we don't want them to hear, they develop superhero powers. A few times, I was sure Ezra could hear me whisper the F word under my breath through two walls. Shepley glanced over at me and interlaced his fingers in mine. He'd told me hundreds of times how proud it made him to watch me mother our boys, and I took pride in it, too. They were messy and rough and sometimes deaf, but I handled it. Shepley didn't think I'd never made a mistake, and I loved him even more for that. I could lose my shit, threaten, yell, and cry, but my boys didn't want perfect. They wanted present.

Shepley pulled into the parking lot near the ambulance bay, and we unbuckled the kids while Travis carried Abby into the Emergency Room. Someone must have called ahead because a nurse was already at the door waiting with a wheelchair.

Trenton fell behind, holding Jim's cane in one hand and hooking his dad's arm with the other. After Abby had settled into the seat, she waved to her in-laws and then to us, blowing a kiss to the kids as the nurse wheeled her inside. We had just stepped through the sliding door of the ER waiting room when they disappeared behind double doors. Travis was walking next to

Abby's wheelchair, holding her hand. He was encouraging Abby to breathe, telling her how good she was doing, and how amazing and strong she was. We followed them until they slipped behind the doors. That was when Jessica looked up at Agent Blevins, enormous and towering over us all, and began to cry.

Trenton kneeled beside her. "Mama's okay, baby girl. She's done this before. You just don't remember."

"Are the babies going to be okay?" James asked.

"There's just one this time, buddy," Shepley said, mussing his nephew's hair with his fingers.

"They haven't even named it yet," Jessica cried.

Trenton picked up Jessica and carried her away from the double doors, her gangly legs hanging loosely while he walked. She laid her head on his shoulder, and he flattened her tangled hair against the back of her head, kissing her temple and swaying from side to side.

"You okay, Jim?" I asked, touching his shoulder. He still looked half-asleep and a bit confused.

"I guess they'll tell us where to wait?" Jim asked.

I nodded. "I'll ask someone. You can sit if you want."

He looked around for the closest chair and chose one next to Trenton, who was still standing with Jessica in his arms.

"I'll go," Shepley said, kissing my cheek.

He approached the admissions desk, waiting for the clerk to finish up with an elderly couple. Once they walked away, he began speaking with her. She seemed pleasant, pointing and nodding and smiling. Shepley patted the desk a couple of times before saying thank you and then returned to us.

"They're taking her to the maternity wing on the third floor. They said we should go to the waiting room up there."

"Then that's where we'll go," I said.

Agent Blevins was in my peripheral, using his tiny radio, I assumed to update the person on the other end of our whereabouts. I knew he couldn't tell us any more information, so I tried not to dwell on it. An entire department of people in the FBI knew more about what danger our family was facing than we did. The very principle, even beyond a sound reason, infuriated me, but I had to focus on Abby.

We found an elevator and crowded inside—all eleven of us—including Agent Blevins. The elevator dipped a bit when he stepped on, but he didn't seem worried. Olive pressed the button, and the doors swept shut. The kids were uncharacteristically quiet while the red digital number above the door climbed with each floor. Finally, the door opened, and Trenton stepped off, the rest of us filing out behind him.

Trenton immediately fished out his phone, looking at Agent Blevins. "Have you heard from Perkins yet?"

"He's arrived at the location. He's currently waiting for Mrs. Maddox to enter the vehicle. There is a security guard presenting a small problem."

Trenton smiled. "That's Drew. He's the bouncer. Good kid. I should call her. Tell her it's okay to leave with him."

Agent Blevins touched his ear. "She's in the car, sir. Agent Perkins will deliver her to the hospital shortly."

Trenton seemed satisfied and put his phone away before approaching the nurse's station. A woman with big green eyes and a platinum blond bob led us to the waiting room, even though most of us knew where it was already. Travis and Abby's third child would be the sixth Maddox grandbaby born in Eakins. We were very familiar with the maternity ward.

"In here," the nurse said. "Snacks and drink machines are out and around the corner." She gestured to the hall and to her right. "Someone will be in to update you as soon as they know something."

"The baby is early, but he'll be all right, right?" I asked.

The nurse smiled. "Our entire staff is waiting and ready to make sure he's given the best care possible."

I turned to my family. "I guess he heard Stella was coming and couldn't wait to meet her," I said with a contrived smile. No one responded except for Shepley, who simply patted my leg. For James and Jessica's sake, I tried not to show any worry. Abby's due date was still seven weeks away, and even though the delivery might go smoothly, we wouldn't know how the baby was doing until after he was born. It was enough of a hint that the adults were so quiet, very different from the giddy excitement the other times our family had spent time in that room.

The nurse returned with blankets and pillows. "These are if the kids want to rest for a bit. Abby's water broke. They've done an ultrasound, and the doctor has evaluated the baby. He feels that to avoid the risk of infection and complications for both mom and baby, he will let the labor proceed."

"Can I see her?" I asked, trying to keep my voice level.

The nurse thought about it for half a second and then nodded. "Of course."

I kissed Shepley quickly on the lips and waved to the kids. He switched off the light, and Trenton and Olive began making pallets on the couches. The kids whined before crawling in.

"Mommy!" Emerson cried.

"I'll be right down the hall," I said. "Daddy will tuck you in, and I'll sit with you when I get back."

"When will you be back?" Eli asked, pouting. He was trying not to cry.

"Soon. Before you fall asleep. Snuggle with your brother until then."

Eli turned his back to me, hooking his arm over Emerson. Shepley sat next to Ezra and winked at me before I left them to follow the nurse to Abby's room.

The hard soles of my shoes echoed in the hallway, the warm color of the wallpapered walls a contrast to the cold, white tile floors. Generic pictures of mother and babies, traditional families with infomercial smiles, lined the walls, selling their brand of normality. Most people would go home dealing with a colicky baby, or postpartum depression, or the struggles of a broken family. Abuse, drugs, insecurity, poverty, fear. First-time moms left this place every day, going home with the vision we see in every diaper commercial of a mother rocking her sleeping infant in an immaculate nursery. Within a month, those same moms would be begging their baby in the wee hours of the morning to sleep, answering the door with vomit on her shirt, and choosing whether to shower or eat, clean, or sleep. I wondered how many four-member families actually left the maternity ward financially stable and emotionally whole because our baby was coming into the world greeted by two great parents who were crazy in love and a large, loving extended family yet still needed the protection of federal agents. What was normal, anyway?

I paused in the middle of the hall, the circumstances finally coming together. Abby's father, Mick, was tangled with the Vegas mafia. She'd had more than one run-in with them to keep him alive. My intuition told me Mick was involved, but I couldn't figure out what Thomas had to do with it. *Why would they go after him?*

The nurse stopped in front of a door and flattened one hand on the wood, the other on the handle. "Everything all right?" she asked, pausing when she realized I wasn't right behind her.

"Yes," I said, joining her outside the door.

Just as she began to push the door open, another nurse yanked on it from the inside, nearly running into us.

"I was just bringing her sister in to—"

"I'm sorry," the nurse said. "No visitors at this time. NICU will be standing by. She's having the baby tonight." She shouldered past us, and I peeked in as the door slowly closed. Several more nurses were working feverishly around Abby, but I couldn't see her. I caught just a glimpse of Travis, looking over his shoulder at me with fear in his eyes.

# CHAPTER THIRTEEN

## TAYLOR

THE MOMENT THE WHEELS OF THE PLANE touched down at O'Hare in Chicago, I switched my phone off the airplane mode and watched as the messages filled my lock screen. Before we'd taken off, Dad said everyone was at the hospital with Travis and Abby. According to the messages, the baby still hadn't arrived, but Abby was close.

I scrolled down the partial messages before stopping at one and tapping the screen. It was a group message for Tyler, Falyn, Ellie, and me from Shepley.

> *A federal agent will be at baggage claim to bring you all to the hospital. He'll have a van, plate number 978 GOV. DO NOT get a ride with anyone else. Not even a cab. Will explain later.*

I frowned and looked back at my brother, holding up my phone. He was a few rows back but nodded, knowing what I meant. I tilted my phone to show Falyn, who was sitting across the aisle from Hollis and me with Hadley. She leaned over, squinting her eyes. She'd needed glasses for at least two years but refused.

"Can you see it?" I asked.

"Yes, I can see it," she snapped back, confusing my need for her be informed with a dig.

"Baby," I began, but she was already looking out the window, hugging Hadley to her side.

I sat back, resting my head against the headrest.

"She's just tired," Hollis said.

I patted his knee without making eye contact. We were all tired. It made me sad to hear Hollis trying to make excuses for why we didn't listen to each other anymore. Somewhere along the way, we started hearing insults instead of questions. I sighed. I didn't know how to fix it.

The seat belt sign turned off, and a ding sounded over the PA system. Hollis jumped up, opening the bin and handing Hadley her carry-on to her before getting Falyn's and mine. He made me prouder every day. Moving to Colorado Springs had made him into a little man, trying to take care of everyone.

I hugged him to me, kissed his head, and then gestured to his sister. "I just got a text from Uncle Shep. Aunt Abby is having her baby, so they sent a driver. Don't run off. Both of you stay where I can see you."

They nodded.

"I mean it," I continued. "It's important. You can't even go to the bathroom alone."

"What's going on, Dad?" Hollis asked. "Does it have to do with Uncle Tommy?"

"Yes, but we don't know what."

They nodded again, trading glances.

We moved in a slow line down the aisle and out of the fuselage, staying in one unit with Tyler's family up the Jetway and into the terminal. I could tell Tyler was on edge, looking around with his family's bags either on his back, over his shoulders, or being pulled by a handle. Ellie was holding their sleeping son, keeping his head steady on her shoulder.

"What do you think's going on?" Tyler asked me. He kept his voice low.

I shook my head. "I don't know. Sounds like Tommy wasn't the only target."

"Like they're after the family? Why?"

I shrugged. "Could be a million reasons."

Tyler frowned. "You have a better imagination than I do. I can't think of one."

"Dad was an investigator. Abby's dad is a gambler. Remember when Trex came to question us about Travis and the fire? Everyone has an enemy. Maybe Travis or Abby inadvertently made the wrong one. Wasn't she raised around mobsters in Vegas?"

Tyler didn't respond, but I could tell his thoughts were spinning.

"Abby was raised around mobsters?" Ellie asked.

"Sort of," Falyn said. "They don't really talk about it. She was born in Vegas. Her dad was a fairly famous poker player. Then he started losing, but he didn't stop gambling. He lost everything and got in pretty deep with some loan sharks. Abby had to go to Vegas just before she and Travis got married to bail him out. They were going to kill him."

"Whoa," Ellie said. "But she's really good at poker, right? She went there to win the money?"

Falyn nodded. "She won most of it."

"How did they get the rest of it?" Ellie asked.

Falyn made a face, drifting off into thought. "I'm not really sure. Do you know?" she asked me.

I shook my head. "They've never really said."

"You've never asked?" Ellie said.

Tyler shook his head. "I figured if they wanted me to know, they'd tell me."

We arrived at baggage claim, looking at the screens.

"Thirteen," Falyn said, dragging Hadley by the hand.

"Hold on," Tyler said, trying to get a handle on their roller bags.

"I can help," a woman said with a smile. She was wearing dark slacks, a button-down shirt and a dark blazer, her sunglasses hanging from where the top button of her blouse was undone. She flashed her credentials that were clipped inside of her blazer and then tucked them away.

My stomach felt sick, and I looked back at Falyn, who was watching Alyssa Davies's eyes turned soft when she looked down at Hollis.

"Cute kid," Alyssa said. "I'll be driving you to the Eakins hospital."

Taylor and Ellie were unfazed, but Falyn looked at me, confused and angry. Alyssa was the woman I'd taken home from the bar during the week Falyn and I had broken up. Falyn needed space, so I left for California to visit my brother Thomas in San Diego. He'd taken me to a local bar to cry in my beer, and I met Alyssa, Thomas's colleague. A few weeks later, Alyssa ended up pregnant and gave me the opportunity to take full custody before opting for an abortion. She carried Hollis to term, and Falyn and I stood outside the hallway of a San Diego hospital while she labored and gave birth. The nurses handed my son to me, and Alyssa returned to her life without looking back.

"Wait, wait, wait," I said, holding up my hands. "You're *FBI*?"

"I am," Alyssa said. "I realize this is somewhat awkward ..."

"*Somewhat* awkward?" Falyn repeated.

"But you're in advertising. With Thomas," I said, bewildered.

Alyssa sighed. "You're my assignment. I'm all you've got. If you ask me, I'm the best one for the job since I have slightly more invested in getting you from A to B in one piece than any other agent, and … I'm a badass."

Hollis smiled. Falyn pulled him against her front with her free hand, hanging on tightly to Hadley with the other. Alyssa—or Agent Davies—represented more of a threat to our family than our failing marriage did.

"Can we see those credentials again?" Falyn asked.

Alyssa pulled her ID until it unclipped from her pocket and handed it to Falyn. "Look it over, but please be quick. We don't want to stay in one place too long."

Falyn studied the ID, and then handed it to me, glaring at Alyssa. "Do you even work with Thomas?"

"Yes," she said simply.

"So you're in advertising too?" I asked, handing her ID to Tyler.

"No, Thomas is FBI," Ellie said, realizing the truth as she said the words. "And you…" she trailed off, looking at Falyn with sympathetic eyes.

Everything clicked, and all at once, every lie Thomas had ever told me boiled in my blood.

Tyler offered the ID to Ellie, but she declined. "We should go. This is awkward as fuck," he said.

We followed a diligent Alyssa to a black van with dark windows. Tyler climbed into the back with Ellie. There was already a car seat ready for Gavin. As Tyler and Ellie struggled to strap in their unconscious toddler, Alyssa buckled in and checked all of her mirrors, radioing in to someone that we were all accounted for and en route.

"Falyn," I said, reaching for her hand. She yanked it away, and I clenched my teeth. "How in Christ's name is this my fault?"

"Shut up," she hissed. From hairline to neckline, red splotches began to form. Her eyes watered like they always did when she was embarrassed.

Alyssa wasn't paying attention to our spat, but she did look in the rearview mirror at Hollis more than once. I was waiting for Falyn to catch her and say something, but when their eyes met, Falyn took the high road.

Hollis, to my surprise, rested his head against Falyn's shoulder. She put her arm around him, and both of them seemed to relax. Falyn ran her fingers through his hair, softly singing the same tune she'd sang to him the night we brought him home. Alyssa watched with curious eyes, without judgment or jealousy, like she was observing the passing cars.

Hollis had no clue he'd just made my life a lot easier and his mom more at ease. Falyn leaned down to kiss his forehead and then looked out the window, still humming.

I rested my arm at the top of the bench seat, turning around to face my brother. He and Ellie were both staring at me, and Gavin was still sleeping, his head propped against the side of the car seat with his mouth gaping open. Ellie offered an encouraging smile. We'd spent long nights talking after Falyn left. Ellie had been to therapy enough for all of us, and I'd benefitted from it. I'd told her more than once that her advice and friendship kept me going.

Ellie reached up and placed her hand on my elbow, and I nodded to her in appreciation. It was nice to know she understood what a tense situation Falyn and I were in, and that she was right there with me.

I tapped Falyn gently with my finger, and she instantly tensed. She didn't turn to me, so I accepted that she wasn't going to speak to me as long as Alyssa was in the car. "I love you," I said, running my thumb along the skin between her shoulder and neck. She didn't shrug me off, which was the first surprise, but then she turned to me and smiled. I figured I'd say it again, hoping to get an even better reaction. "No matter what. I love you."

A tear welled up in Falyn's eye and spilled over onto her freckled cheek. I used my thumb to wipe it away and then held my palm against her face. She leaned into it, and my heart burst in my chest.

*Thank you*, she mouthed.

So that was it. She just needed Alyssa to know where she stood. Actions, not words. It made sense now why she wanted nothing to do with a quiet attempt to hold her hand. She needed a show. Women were exhausting. Ellie had tried to explain to me the logic for leaving and staying gone. It had made more sense to me to work things out together, but Ellie had assured me that it was better to try to gain some insight on the whys rather than to let my frustration lead to anger. Falyn's reasons were always far deeper than I could understand, and sometimes deeper than she would admit. Things like needing control or leaving before she was left. Shame. Guilt. Or even worse—apathy. My brothers all seemed to get their wives better than I did, but Falyn kept me in the dark most of the time.

I was desperate to understand her and for her to understand me. Just when I was beginning to lose faith, we would have a moment, and I would feel a flicker of hope. By the look in her eyes, I could see she felt that way, too. It was so much more than her being a bitch and me being dumb. It was two people who had lugged all of their baggage into a relationship trying to sift through their own shit to see the love that brought them together in the first place.

I slipped my hand beneath her hair and began to rub her neck with my thumb and index finger. I used to do that when we'd sit on the couch and watch a movie after the kids fell asleep. It had been a long time since I'd been able to do that, and her tense muscles melted under my touch.

Alyssa touched her radio. "I have a possible on my four o'clock, six back." I couldn't hear a reply, but Alyssa didn't seem alarmed.

"Someone is following us?" Hollis asked.

Alyssa smiled. "Possibly, smarty pants."

"Is it the same guy who shot Uncle Tommy?"

"No," Alyssa responded.

"How do you know?"

"Because he's in jail."

"How do you know?" Hollis asked again.

"Hols," Falyn said, tapping him.

"Because I put him there myself," Alyssa answered.

"You did?" Hollis said, leaning against his seat belt. "How many people have you arrested?"

"A lot."

"How many people have you shot?"

I frowned. "C'mon, buddy."

Hollis waited for Alyssa to answer.

"Only the ones I had to," she said.

Hollis sat back, impressed. He hesitated before asking his next question. "Has my Uncle Tommy ever shot anyone?"

"Ask him yourself," Alyssa said. Hollis was satisfied, but Alyssa wasn't. "I like your name."

"Thanks," he said.

"What about mine?" Hadley asked.

"Yours, too," Alyssa said.

"We should let Alyssa concentrate on driving," Falyn said.

Alyssa didn't skip a beat. "I can do both."

The muscles in Falyn's neck began to tense, and I looked for a sign that would tell us how many miles to Eakins.

"If you think someone is following us, maybe you shouldn't," Falyn said.

The moment the words came out of her mouth, she regretted them. Hollis looked up at her, surprised at her rudeness. Falyn and I had many late-night talks about what we would do if Alyssa wanted to be in Hollis's life again or if he started asking questions. He knew Falyn wasn't his biological mother, but he didn't know more than that, and he certainly had no idea that the cool, gun-toting woman in the driver's seat was the enigma he'd no doubt wondered about his whole life. Falyn didn't really want to keep them from talking, but I knew it had to be hard for her.

"I mean," Falyn said, clearing her throat. "I'm sorry. I shouldn't tell you how to do your job. You know better than me what you're capable of."

"It's fine," Alyssa said, unaffected.

Falyn's apology won her big points with Hollis, and he snuggled up against her again.

Alyssa exited off the highway, and I sat up, trying to see where we were. It definitely wasn't Eakins. She drove three miles, turned down one road, and then another after another three miles, parking in a dirt driveway. She turned off the motor and tossed me the keys.

"Stay put," she said.

"What are we doing?" Tyler asked. "This isn't Eakins."

A red Corolla pulled up behind us, and Alyssa unholstered her side arm. "Hadley. Hollis. Close your eyes and cover your ears."

"What's going on?" Hadley whined.

"Just do it."

She stepped out and walked to the road.

"What the hell?" Ellie said. "I'm uncomfortable with this, I—"

A set of shots rang out, and I threw myself over my family. Tyler did the same. After another set of shots, the only sounds we could hear were the cicadas in the trees, and the crickets in the grass surrounding the van.

The driver's side door opened, and Alyssa climbed back in. She held her hand out to me, and I handed her the keys.

"A little warning would have been nice," I said.

"Did you … did you shoot the people who were following us?" Hollis asked.

"Well," Alyssa said, starting the van, "to be fair … they shot at me first." Hollis swallowed, and Alyssa backed out and drove toward the highway. She touched the small black apparatus in her ear. "Clean up on aisle five." She waited for confirmation. "I got tired of waiting on you. Yes. We're three less Carlisis. Three miles west and three miles north." She smiled. "Thank you."

I was worried that as we passed the Corolla, the kids would see a gruesome scene, so I covered their eyes, but each of the victims in the car had their shirts or a newspaper covering their heads. The moment we were out of range, I removed my hands from the kids' eyes, and I patted Hollis's shoulder and kissed the top of Hadley's head.

"Who the fuck are the Carlisis?" Tyler asked.

"You'll have answers when we get to our destination, I promise," Alyssa said.

"Did that just happen?" Falyn asked, breathing hard and holding onto the door. "What the hell is going on?"

I shook my head, unable to answer. I wasn't sure whether to be freaked out that our driver was the one-night stand who gave me full custody of my son, or that it made sense now why she'd done it, considering she was a trained killer, or that the woman I had once spent an entire night banging while she'd yelped like a dying poodle had just killed three people without blinking.

"Thank God Gavin sleeps like me and not you," Ellie said to her husband.

Alyssa navigated the van to the on ramp, and we returned to the highway, gaining speed toward Eakins. Alyssa drove faster than she had since we'd left the airport, and I looked down at the passengers in the cars we passed. They had no idea that we'd just been involved in an execution just a few miles off the highway or that our driver was the executioner. I felt more uneasy the closer we got to Eakins.

"What's your total now?" Hollis asked.

"Hollis!" Falyn shrieked.

"Don't answer that, Alyssa," I said. Falyn craned her neck toward me. That was the first time I'd uttered Alyssa's name in years, and it obviously didn't sit well with my wife. "Agent Davies," I corrected, and then swallowed.

Alyssa chuckled.

"What's funny?" I asked.

"You're just a lot different than I remember."

"Yes, he's sober … and clothed," Falyn snapped.

"Oh, my God," Tyler said. "Is she …" he thankfully trailed off, not wanting to drop that bomb on Hollis.

"Holy fuck," Ellie said under her breath.

I sunk back into my seat, reliving the moment I had come clean to Falyn all over again. It was even worse that she didn't blame me since she'd been the one who'd asked for the break. Where Falyn hadn't raked me over the coals, Ellie never missed an opportunity—not only to let me know how shitty it was that I slept with someone days after my girlfriend asked for some time to think but how ridiculous and flat-out gross it was that Falyn blamed herself.

Either way, no one could call it fault because the result was Hollis, and no one wanted to think about what life would be like without him.

I caught Alyssa stealing another glance at Hollis in the rearview mirror.

"Any updates on Tommy?" I asked.

"No," she said, but I could tell she was holding back.

"None?" Ellie asked, suspicious.

"None that I can relay."

"That's messed up," Tyler said.

"That's the way it is." Alyssa shrugged, unapologetic.

We sat in silence the rest of the way to Eakins, but a new energy filled the van when we pulled into the hospital parking lot. Tyler unfastened Gavin, who was finally awake, and Falyn scrambled to open the door. I met her and the kids at the back of the van, anxious to get our luggage and see our family.

Once everyone but Gavin had weighed themselves down with backpacks, bags, and roller luggage, we ran to the hospital entrance and straight for the elevator. I was the last to step in, but then Alyssa stepped in behind me.

Falyn wasn't happy.

"I have to accompany you upstairs," Alyssa explained. "Then you'll be rid of me."

Falyn blinked. "Thank you. For getting us here safe."

Alyssa seemed genuinely touched. She looked down at Hollis and mussed his hair. "My pleasure."

The elevator doors opened to reveal our family standing on the other side.

# CHAPTER FOURTEEN

## TYLER

"YOU MADE IT," Dad said, beckoning me in for a hug. He'd picked up his cane, and I was so happy to see him, I failed to let go of all three roller bags that I'd been lugging around all day as I swung my arms around him. Dad pulled Taylor in too, shaking because he was so happy to see us.

After Dad finally let us go, we took turns hugging Jack and Deana, Trenton, Shepley, and America, and they all hugged the kids.

"Where are the boys and the twins?" Falyn asked.

"All asleep," America said, "in the waiting room with Agent Blevins. We made them pallets on the couches and floor, and then turned out the lights. It's been a long day."

Dad gestured for us to follow him, a pattern of taking a small step, limping, and using his cane for support, and then picking it up and starting over. "This way. Fair warning. Agent Blevins is a giant."

"Bigger than Uncle Travis?" Hadley asked.

Dad hugged Hadley to his side. "Bigger than anyone I've ever seen."

Hadley's eyes widened, and Dad chuckled.

"How's Abby?" I asked.

"Getting close," America said. She smiled, but I caught a spark of worry behind her eyes.

"She's early, isn't she?" Ellie asked.

America nodded. "Seven weeks early. But they decided not to stop her labor."

I wasn't sure if that was a good thing or not, but Ellie and Falyn weren't happy about America's answer.

I knew which room was the waiting room because a dark-skinned giant was standing outside the door. His hands were clasped at his waist. He looked more like secret service than FBI. He spoke, his voice abnormally deep. "The nurse is on the way with more blankets and pillows."

"Th-thank you," Hadley said, stretching her neck to gaze straight up.

Agent Blevins winked at her as she passed by.

Ellie and Falyn ushered the kids into the dim waiting room, followed by a nurse with short blond hair and a Crest smile. She was holding a stack of blankets and pillows, thanking Agent Blevins as he held the door open for her.

"Where's Cami?" Taylor asked.

Trenton glanced at his watch then at Agent Blevins.

"Five minutes out," the giant said, acknowledging Agent Davies with a nod. I was glad he was assigned to the kids. The Maddoxes were almost all together, and even though we were a force to be reckoned with, Agent Blevins was his own army. "Heard you made a pit stop."

"I did," Agent Davies said.

I couldn't stop looking at her. Not because she was beautiful—although she was—but because Hollis looked so much like her. I was curious, wondering how she could carry him for so long and just walk away. Then I thought about how selfless it was of her to offer that to Taylor. Most guys didn't get a choice. She could have just had an abortion, and he would have never known. None of us could imagine a world without Hollis Maddox. He was smart as a whip and way too good-looking and charming for his own good. Knowing his biological mother was a lethal federal agent made perfect sense.

Falyn and Ellie snuck out of the waiting room, and my curious staring ended. I pulled Ellie to my side and kissed her temple. "Gavin went back to sleep?"

"I know," she said. "I can't believe it, either. He must be growing."

"If he grows any more, he'll be in the NFL soon," Dad said.

My chest puffed out. I couldn't help it. He was a good-sized kid. Reminded me of Travis when he was his age. If he didn't slow down, even Agent Blevins would be looking up at him soon. I hugged Ellie tighter. "And Ellie lugged him around all day. I'm surprised her arms didn't fall off."

"I'm used to it," she said.

She was right. Long before Gavin came, she was following around my crew of wildfire hotshots into the mountains to document the fire season for the local magazine, *The MountainEar*. Not long into her second season, she was lugging equipment miles into the wilderness and onto helicopters like the rest of us. She'd worked so hard to get her life back, and she made sure to appreciate the second chance she'd been given by the Alpine Hotshot Chief to tag along with her camera. She'd had a couple of setbacks, but we'd gotten engaged pretty quick after she got back from rehab and then married not long after. A wedding, living together, and working together were a lot for her to process in one year, but I was glad we didn't give up. It hadn't been perfect, but I wouldn't have traded one moment of my bad days with my wife for good days with anyone else.

It took a long time for her to believe she was ready or deserving to be a mom, but once Gavin arrived, she was a natural. She started staying home full-time when he was born, playing the part of both parents when I was gone on the job.

"Can't wait 'til morning," Dad said. "Travis and Abby's son will be here, Liis will be here with Stella, and all my grandkids will be in one place for the first time in a long time."

"You're sure it's a boy?" I asked.

"That's what Abby said," Dad said with a shrug. "I'm betting she's right."

"I know better than to bet against Abby," Trenton said, glancing at his watch again. He looked at Agent Blevins. "It's been five minutes, boss."

The elevator opened, and Camille stood there with who I assumed was another agent. Trenton jogged over to her, throwing his arms around her middle and lifting her feet off the ground. He planted kisses on her mouth for a full minute, and then they joined us in the hall.

"Here, Dad," Camille said, directing him to sit on one of the benches pushed up against the wall. No arms or back, they were just long seats covered in green, fake leather, sitting on silver legs.

Dad sat, his belly covering half his thighs. He was wearing a jacket over his pajama shirt, slacks, and suede moccasins. He looked tired but happy.

Just as we all found a seat, a doctor rounded the corner and paused at our sheer number. Even with the kids and Shepley's parents asleep in the waiting room, we were a good-sized group.

He was bald with a white goatee and in decent shape for his age. His round glasses made him look more hippie and less doctor, and I liked that about him. "Good morning. Baby's fine. Mom's fine. We'll be moving the baby to NICU here shortly to observe him, but he's strong. Dr. Finn, the pediatrician, doesn't believe he'll need anything more than some supplementary oxygen, but she's keeping an eye on him. The nurses will be wheeling him down the hall soon. You can catch a glimpse of him then."

"They're taking him from Abby?" America asked.

The doctor smiled, patient with the barrage of questions. "All babies under thirty-five weeks go to the NICU. Mom and Dad can visit as soon as we evaluate and get him hooked up to the good stuff."

"How big is he?" Falyn asked.

"I think they said five pounds, five ounces," the doctor said, smiling when everyone gasped. "A good size, considering."

"Thank you," Dad said.

The doctor nodded, in a hurry to get home and get some sleep before what was likely a full day of prenatal appointments. A group of nurses and a doctor wheeled past with an incubator, pausing when they saw us down the hall. America jumped up first, followed by Shepley, and then the rest of us. Camille and Trenton stayed behind, helping Jim to his feet and walking with him down the hall.

We oohed and ahhed over Travis's youngest son.

"He looks just like Travis!" America said, her eyes filling with tears.

"I don't know," Dad said. "I see that stubborn chin sticking out."

"You're right," America said. "That's definitely Abby's chin."

"Hang in there, little guy," Trenton said, holding tight to his wife.

I wondered what it was like for Trenton and Camille to see us one by one, as we all had our second and third child, and they were still trying. I knew they were happy for Travis and Abby—I could see it on their faces—but I could also see a longing; an ache that wouldn't go away until they had one of their own.

The nurses wheeled him down the hall, and everyone but America returned to our uncomfortable bench seats. I smiled when I saw Travis tap America on the shoulder, and she threw her arms around him and cried happy tears. They talked for a moment, and then he walked her down to where we sat.

I stood up, shaking his hand a couple of times before giving him a hug. "Congratulations. He's a good lookin' boy."

"That he is," Travis said. He looked both tired and energized, happy and worried.

"What'd you decide to name 'em?" Dad asked.

Travis clapped his hands together, already proud of the name. "Carter Travis Maddox."

Everyone gasped and then laughed with glee.

"That won't be confusing at all!" Trenton said. Dad smacked him on the back of the head. "Ow!" He rubbed the back of his head. "What'd I say?"

"James, Ezra, Hollis, Eli, Emerson, Gavin, and Carter Maddox," America said. "Poor Jess, Hadley, and Stella."

"Ten," Dad said, sitting up a bit taller. "I have ten grandkids so far."

"So far," Trenton said. "We're going to add to that soon."

Camille offered a contrived smile. I couldn't tell if she was tired or had lost hope.

"I'm going to head back," Travis said.

"Can I go with you?" America asked. Travis nodded; she hopped up, kissed her husband goodbye, and they were gone.

We settled back in our seats for the fourth or fifth round in the short time we'd been there. Everyone was quiet at first, settling in, exhausted and happy to be together. I could still see the shock in Ellie, Falyn, and Taylor's eyes that I felt. We were feet away from three deaths, and we still weren't sure how to process it. I wasn't even sure if we should bring it up.

Dad finally spoke up. "We should all try to get some sleep. Liis will be here in the morning."

# CHAPTER FIFTEEN

## TRENTON

"DID YOU KNOW, DAD? About Thomas?" Tyler asked.

"Which part?" he answered.

"That's he's FBI."

I laughed but seemed to be the only one in on the joke. I shook my head. "No way. Tommy's an FBI agent?" I glanced around, my gaze pausing on my wife. Her cheeks flushed. "You knew?" I asked, hurt.

"Baby," Camille said, reaching for me. I backed away. A few hours before, I was ready to punch someone if they didn't let me go get her from work. Now, I wasn't sure I could look at her. "Dad?" I said. "You knew, too?"

Dad was quiet for a long time and then nodded. "Yes. Since the beginning."

Tyler frowned. "How?"

Dad shrugged. "I picked up on little things. I do pay attention, you know."

"What else do you know?" Taylor asked.

Dad smiled and pressed his lips together. "I know everything, son. You're my boys. It's my job to know."

"What are you talking about?" I asked.

"We're, um," Taylor began. "We don't sell insurance."

Ellie had taken Tyler's hand before he spoke. "We're firefighters."

"No shit," I said, in shock. "Am I the only one who's not lying about their career?"

"Well," Ellie said. "If Thomas isn't in advertising, then Travis didn't take over for him."

Everyone looked around at one another for answers.

Ellie raised her brows. "Or maybe he did, just not as an ad exec."

"No way," I said. "Travis a fed?" I glanced at Camille, who looked sheepish. "Are you fucking kidding me?" I stood.

Dad's brows pulled together. "Trenton. Language."

"You've known all this time about my brothers? And kept it from me? What the fuck, Cami?"

She stood, too, holding out her hands. "It wasn't my secret to tell."

"Bullshit," I said, pointing to the floor. "I'm your husband. You don't keep secrets from me … about my own brothers. It's already happened once, and I forgave you, but Cami …" I walked away from her, my hands on my head.

"Trent," she said, surprise and hurt in her voice.

When I returned to where she stood, I noticed everyone else trying to look everywhere but at us. I'd seen my brothers argue with their wives, and it was always awkward as fuck, but we didn't have a choice but to stand there and hash it out. I couldn't yell at Thomas because he was fighting for his life halfway across the country. I couldn't yell at Travis because he was with his wife who'd just had a new baby. I turned to Camille but just shook my head. Her eyes filled with tears, so I looked away.

I pointed at the twins then set my hands on my hips. I was breathing hard as if I'd just ran a mile up a steep hill. "What if something had happened to you guys? That's how you're going to let me find out? Like I did with Tommy?"

"We were keeping it from Dad," Tyler said. His voice was low and calm as if he was talking someone off a ledge. That only made me angrier, as if they thought I was overreacting.

"Why?" I yelled.

"You don't remember, Trenton," Taylor said. "He promised Mom to keep us safe. She didn't want him in law enforcement. She didn't want any of us following his footsteps. I'm sure Thomas lied for the same reason we did. We loved our jobs, but we didn't want to hurt Dad."

"So we all just lie to each other? That's how this family works now?" I seethed.

"I knew," Dad said. "I knew, and I didn't tell you because the boys were keeping it from us for a reason. I didn't keep it from ya because I love them more, son. It simply wasn't my place."

I shook my head again, hands on hips, pacing. Camille tried reaching out to me, but I yanked my arm away. Everything I knew about my brothers was a lie. Their experiences in the field, their colleagues, their training—I'd missed out on it all. But my wife knew.

"Did you know about Taylor and Tyler, too?" I asked Camille. She shook her head, tears streaming down her face. "And now look at us. Tommy's hurt. We're being babysat by federal agents. People are trying to kill us!"

"Keep your voice down," Tyler said.

"Fuck you!" I snapped back, still pacing.

Tyler stood up, but Dad held up a hand. "Sit down, son."

I pointed at Camille. "You've already lied to me once. Now I find out you never stopped? What am I … what am I supposed to do with that, Camille?"

"Don't call me that," she said. It was what her father called her when he was angry, and what Thomas called her when he was chastising her for being upset at not being put first. I always put her first. I fucking worshiped her, and she'd been lying to me. My whole family had, one way or another.

"You're lucky that's all I'm calling you," I growled.

Camille's mouth fell open, and the wives gasped.

"That's enough," Ellie fumed.

Shepley stood. "Let's go get some coffee, Trent."

Travis rounded the corner with America, the smile on his face fading. "She's ready for more visitors," he said, looking around. "Everything all right?"

"You've been lying to me?" I asked.

Travis blanched. "I'm … not allowed to discuss details until tomorrow when Liis arrives."

I took a step toward him. "We're your family, Travis. You and Tommy aren't in some secret fucking club where you get to gamble with our lives. And you don't ask my wife to lie to me for you."

"That's not what I was doing, Trent. I didn't have a choice in the beginning, and it wasn't my decision to tell Cami or to ask her to lie."

I narrowed my eyes at him. "But you went along with it."

Travis took a step toward me. "I had to, or I was going to prison for being involved in that fire on campus."

I balled my hands into fists. I wasn't sure who or what I wanted to punch, but it was just seconds away.

Dad stood up and put a hand on my shoulder. He wobbled a bit, making my rage dwindle. I helped steady him, and then he brought me in for a hug, holding on tight when I tried to let go. He held me until the anger subsided. I helped him back to the bench and then I sat on a section of the bench in the corner. Camille took a step toward me, and I held up my hand. "Don't."

Ellie patted the empty space next to her, and Camille sat down, her bottom lip trembling.

"So," Taylor began. "You're a fed. Thomas is a fed, and this is all because of some case you're working on?"

Travis took a deep breath, looked at Agent Blevins and Agent Davies, and then emptied his lungs. "Fuck it." He sat down next to Dad, resting his elbows on his knees, and put his hands together like he was praying, touching his fingers to his lips. He sat up. "I was there that night … when the building at Eastern caught fire. I'd talked Trenton into staying with Abby while I went toe-to-toe with John Savage. It was a small basement. Too small for a final fight. We'd almost been busted once, so Adam wouldn't allow any lights. We just had a few lanterns hanging from the ceiling. There was …" he trailed off, remembering, "furniture covered in sheets lining the room and the main hallway. A lantern fell, and the whole place went up in flames in seconds. I was separated from Abby and Trent, and I had to go find them. I found Abby, but didn't find Trent until later. Scariest night of my life."

I sunk back, realizing I'd been lying for years, too. I'd lied to the FBI about being in the building when it caught fire, and only Travis and Abby knew that I'd left Abby because I was scared. I waited for him to out me.

Travis continued, "A lot of kids died that night. Adam was arrested. I knew I was next, even though Abby had concocted a plan for us to go to Vegas and get married to try to make it seem like we weren't."

America looked up at Travis. "You knew about that?"

I looked down. I knew about that, too, and kept it from him. *Fuck, now I'm a hypocrite.* I thought we were a tight family. Turns out we were just spiders caught in our web of lies. I felt my face flush. The anger was returning.

"How could I not? She suddenly wanted to run off to Vegas an hour after we'd escaped a fire. After our classmates had died? Either she was crazy, callous, or concocting a plan. Whichever it was, I was desperate to be her husband. I ignored it. Probably not the most honest thing to do. Thankfully," he said, gesturing toward Abby's room, "it worked out."

"But that agent," I said. "He came to the house. He was asking about you. They didn't just buy the Vegas wedding story, did they?"

"I was given a choice," Travis said.

"But why you?" Tyler asked. "Why not Adam … why—"

"Mick Abernathy," Dad said.

"I'm not sure if you're lucky or not," Taylor said.

"So how does Tommy fit into all of this?" I asked. "He was a fed before that. Long before that, I'd guess." I looked at Camille, who was still staying maddeningly quiet. "Even now?" I asked her. "It's all coming out, and you're just going to sit there … loyal to him?"

"She couldn't tell you, Trent," Travis said. "It was a safety issue."

I stood, looking around, holding out my hands. "Because we're all safe now? Awake at three a.m. with two … sorry, three feds babysitting us to make sure whoever you pissed off doesn't gun down our kids?"

"I know it sounds bad, and I understand you're angry. And it's not over yet. I'm sorry, Trent, I really am. I never meant for any of this to happen."

Travis being so patient and calm only made me angrier. I took a step toward him, but Camille stood between us.

"Trenton!" she yelled, holding up her hands.

"Travis, go back to your wife," Dad said. "Trenton, sit your ass down. Now. We're not going to understand tonight, and we don't have to. What's important is keeping our family safe."

I grudgingly sat down, obeying my father. He was feeble. Not nearly the intimidating man I remembered from my childhood, but he was my dad, and he deserved my respect.

Camille took a few steps toward me, asking permission without using words. I scooted over and held out my arm, and she rushed to sit next to me, burying her face in my neck and wrapping her arms around my middle. Deep down, I knew her keeping Thomas's secret wasn't a matter of her choosing to be loyal to him or honest with me, but it was hard to push that completely from my mind. I hugged her to my side, but only because I refused to let a seven-minute-old feeling of betrayal overshadow the love I'd felt for Camille for most of my life.

"Is Abby sleeping?" Ellie asked.

"She can't," America answered. "She wants to see Carter. They're supposed to tell us soon when she can."

"I'd like to see her if I can," Ellie said.

"Me too," Falyn said.

Travis gestured for them to follow, and they trailed behind him. Falyn turned to me with an unmistakable warning glare not to upset Camille while she was gone. I sighed and kissed my wife's hair. She was quietly sniffing, her body jerking against me. Still, I couldn't bring myself to say it was going to be okay. I didn't know if it would be or not. I wondered what new heartbreak the next day would bring and how much more our family could take.

# CHAPTER SIXTEEN

## TRAVIS

I WALKED INTO ABBY'S BIRTHING SUITE with Falyn and Ellie, instantly regretting bringing anyone but Carter. My wife's face lit up for a fraction of a second, and then she tried to hide her disappointment with her sweet smile.

"We can go see him in a few minutes," I assured her.

Abby's hair was barely sprouting out of a low ponytail. Pieces had fallen out to frame her face. Her eyes were still red from delivery and then the tears after. I'd never seen her as devastated as the moment they took our son away.

"He's beautiful," Ellie said with a smile.

"You saw him?" Abby asked. She sat up on the bed and tucked the loose strands of her hair behind her ear.

"In the hall. He's just at the end of this wing," Falyn said.

"That's comforting." Abby's eyes began to gloss over, and she looked up at the ceiling, trying to hold back the tears.

"It's okay to cry," Ellie said, taking the chair closest to the bed. "You've had a long day. You're exhausted. Your hormones are going nuts."

Abby wiped her cheeks. "I don't want to cry."

I sat down on the bed next to her, holding her hand. Several pieces of tape secured her IV that was now delivering antibiotics to stave off the infection that had caused her premature labor. She'd tried everything to get her contractions to slow down naturally, but the harder she tried, the more intense and closer together they were. When the doctor told her we were going to have a baby, she broke down. She had such a normal delivery with the twins, we were surprised that a single birth was anything but a breeze.

I knew more than just the infection was to blame. She also had the added stress surrounding my fucking job. Not only was I going to devastate my family to protect them, but it had put my wife and newborn son in danger. I was going to find a way to walk away from the FBI after this. Thomas and I would be lucky if our family was still intact.

"Stop," Abby said, seeing the expression on my face. "There was nothing we could do. It's just one of those things."

"And he's okay," Ellie said. "He was wailing like a banshee all the way down the hall. Strong lungs with the temper of a Maddox. He's golden."

"Do you think we'll be able to take him home?" she asked, suddenly hopeful.

I patted her hand. "Probably not. Not right away, anyway. But let's wait for an update from the NICU before we get too upset."

"You mean before I get too upset," she said.

I raised her hand to my lips and closed my eyes. The guilt was almost too much to bear. I was glad Dad had stepped in when he did with Trenton because I was desperate to go back to the days when I could punch my way out of things. Nineteen seemed like a lifetime ago, and quite frankly, adulting blowed. It was so much easier to lose my shit and start swinging rather than to listen to Trenton being an insecure dick stick and having to be the bigger person when all I was trying to do was save his life.

"Baby," Abby said, watching as my inner turmoil began to seep out.

"Trenton found out about the FBI," Ellie said. "And that Cami already knew. He's taking it pretty hard."

Abby looked at me. "He's taking it out on you."

"Who else is he going to take it out on?" I grumbled.

Abby's fingers intertwined in mine. "Just a little longer."

I nodded, knowing we couldn't say any more in front of Ellie and Falyn.

Abby recounted the moments of her labor and delivery, and they all cried again when she detailed watching the nurses wheel Carter out of the room. The sisters hugged, and then Ellie and Falyn returned to the hall outside the waiting room to check on their families.

Abby sighed, resting her head back against her pillow.

"Want me to lay the bed flat?" I asked.

She shook her head, wincing and pressing gently on her abdomen. "You should try to sleep. You've got a long day tomorrow."

"You mean today?"

Abby looked up at the clock on the wall. "Liis will land in a few hours. The nurse said the recliner lays nearly flat."

I stood up and nodded, walking around the hospital bed to the mauve recliner nearby. The nurse had already set a couple of folded blankets and a pillow in a stack on the seat. The recliner made a scraping sound against the floor as I pushed it closer to her bed. I sat down and shook out a blanket, pulled the lever, and leaned back.

Abby used the remote to turn out the lights, and for a few precious moments, it was quiet. Just as I felt myself drift off, the door opened, and I could hear the nurse swishing around the room. She turned on the dim overhead lamp just above Abby's bed.

"Hi there, Mrs. Maddox. I thought you might want to try pumping." She lifted a small machine with tubes and what looked like a mini air horn.

Abby looked horrified. "Why?"

"Carter isn't going to be strong enough to suckle just yet, so we'll have to feed him through a tube. We have a special preemie formula, but if you prefer, your milk is best. Is that something you'd like to try?"

"I …" she trailed off, looking at the pump. It was completely foreign to her. She'd breast-fed our twins, but she stayed at home, so she'd never used a pump. "I'm not even sure if I have anything to pump."

"You'd be surprised," the nurse said. "His stomach is smaller than a marble, so he won't need much."

"And it's okay with the antibiotics?" she asked, holding up her hand. I was so proud of her. Even exhausted, Abby thought to ask questions that wouldn't even cross my mind.

"Completely safe," the nurse said.

"Oookay," Abby said. She listened as the nurse gave her instructions. When we were alone again, she looked at the tubes and container with contempt.

I sat up. "Want me to help?"

"Absolutely not," she said.

"I can just—"

"No, Travis. If I'm going to have to sit here with this thing on me like a milk cow, you're not going to help. You're not going to watch."

"Baby, it's not a bad thing. You're doing it for our son."

"It just feels very … personal."

"Okay," I said, leaving the pile of blankets behind in the recliner. "You're sure?"

"I'm sure."

"I'll come back in fifteen. Need anything before I leave?"

"Nope."

"Good luck, Pidge."

Abby used the mini air horn as a thumbs-up, and I chuckled, willing to do anything to have a light moment in all of this. I closed the curtain and then the door behind me, and returned to the hall in front of the waiting room where my family was. Camille was sitting alone on a bench.

"Where is everyone?" I asked.

"The nurse brought cots. They're all sleeping in the waiting room except for Dad."

"Where's he?"

Camille nodded her head toward a birthing suite, and immediately, I heard the familiar Jim Maddox snore. He would breathe in through his nose, and then his cheeks would fill with air before it finally pushed through his lips.

"He talked them into giving him a room?"

"He was afraid his snoring would wake the kids. He insisted on having his cot out here, but the nurses caught wind of it, and you know ... Everyone loves Jim."

"Aren't you tired?" I asked.

She shrugged. "I don't think Trent wants my company."

I sat down next to her. "Cami … you know he loves you. It's a lot to process all at once."

"I know," she said, wringing her hands. "The thing with Thomas and me … It's been festering just beneath the surface all these years. I knew it would come out eventually, and I knew he'd be angry. I just didn't expect to feel this much guilt."

"Because you don't want to see him hurting."

"No, I don't."

I looked down at the ground. "No one's going to escape it this time."

"Have you heard from Liis? Any updates?"

"No," I said. It was the truth. I didn't need any updates. I knew exactly what was going to happen.

"They said she was flying in. Isn't that weird she would do that? While Thomas is recovering?"

"She has a new baby, and …" I trailed off. I didn't want to lie anymore, and the worst was still ahead.

Camille grew quiet. "He didn't make it, did he? She wants to tell us in person." When I didn't answer, Camille stared at me until I faced her. "Tell me, Travis. Is he dead?"

"You want to keep more secrets from Trenton? What if he finds out you knew something about Tommy before him? Again?"

"Just tell me," she said. "I deserve to know."

"More than anyone else?"

"Trav. I've been protecting his secret for him for years."

"And look where it got you."

Camille thought about my words and sat back. She closed her eyes, appearing pained. "You're right."

I stood up, leaving Camille alone with her quiet tears. As I walked away, I was surprised to feel even heavier than before. That would have been one less person I would've had to destroy. I froze in the hallway, in front of Abby's door, realizing we would have to tell the kids. *My* kids. I would have to look them straight in the eye and tell them their uncle was dead.

I closed my eyes, wondering how I could ever explain why they couldn't lie later in life. How could they ever trust me after that? I pushed open the door just as Abby was screwing the lid on the milk container.

"How did it go?" I asked.

She paused. "What's wrong?"

"The kids," I said.

She jerked up. "What about the kids?"

I sighed. "Fuck. No, I'm sorry. They're fine." I sat next to her, gathering the pump and tubing in one hand, the container in the other. I kissed her forehead. "They're fine. It just hit me that we're going to have to tell the kids about Thomas."

She looked up at me, her eyes wide. "They'll be heartbroken."

"And then … later …"

Abby covered her eyes, and I hugged her. "I know. I'm sorry."

"They'll never trust us again."

"Maybe they'll understand."

Her eyes filled with tears for the dozenth time that morning. "Not for a long time."

The nurse knocked on the door, her short blond hair bouncing. "Good morning," she whispered.

"I couldn't get much," Abby said as I handed the nurse the equipment and container.

The nurse held it up and narrowed her eyes then smiled. "It'll do. He'll be a happy boy."

"Can we see him?" Abby asked.

"Yes," the nurse said, pointing at her. "Right after you get some rest."

"We've been trying," I said.

"Not a problem. I'll make a note. Do not disturb."

"Unless," Abby began.

"Unless something comes up. Yes, ma'am." The nurse closed the door behind her, and I settled back into the recliner.

Abby turned off the light above her, and except for the sunrise peeking through the edges of the blinds, it was dark. The birds were chirping, and I wondered if I would ever sleep again.

"I love you," Abby whispered from her bed.

I wanted to crawl into her bed with her, but the IV made that precarious. "I love you more, Pigeon."

She sighed, the bed crinkling as she settled in.

I closed my eyes, listening to Abby's breathing, the IV pump, and the obnoxious bird happily singing outside. Somehow, I slipped beneath the waves of consciousness, dreaming that I was lying next to Abby for the first time in my college apartment, wondering how in the hell I was going to keep her.

# CHAPTER SEVENTEEN

## SHEPLEY

AMERICA HELD MY HAND, pulling me through Abby's hospital room doorway. It smelled like bleach and flowers, exactly why I was glad America had our last two boys at home. Hospitals gave me the heebie-jeebies, pretty much just holding bad memories for me. Mercy Hospital was the setting for the times I remembered going with my parents to see Diane, when I broke my arm, when Trenton got into that bad car accident with Mackenzie and again with Camille. The only good memories I have of Mercy Hospital were when Ezra and then Travis and Abby's twins were born.

"Hi," Abby said with a smile, embracing America when she bent over for a hug.

"You look so good!" America said, repeating the phrase every postpartum mom wants to hear.

Abby beamed. "They're taking me to see him soon."

"Good," America said, sitting next to her. She held her friend's hand. "That's good."

There was an elephant in the room. The four of us had been close since the first night Abby came to my apartment with Travis. It wasn't like them to keep things from us. At least, that's what I'd thought. America and I had several conversations about how the FBI seemed to have forgotten about Travis's involvement with the fire, how the questions and the suspicion stopped. And then the weird moment the morning after Travis and Abby's wedding in St. Thomas when he was so upset he couldn't speak. That was it. That was when it happened. Thomas had given him an ultimatum.

America fell quiet. The America I fell in love with would have raked Abby over the coals for being dishonest, but my wife and mother of three tyrants was wiser and slower to anger. She listened more and reacted less. Their friendship had lasted on the basis of full disclosure. How else could they love each other no matter what? But now we were in a time of our lives when we had to put our spouses first. Marriage made friendship—even old ones—complicated.

"Mare," Abby began. "I wanted to tell you."

"Tell me what?" America said. Now that the conversation had started, she wasn't going to let her off too easy.

"About Travis. I just found out myself a few years ago."

"When did you stop trusting me?" America asked, trying not to sound hurt.

"It's not about that. He wasn't cheating or fighting a drug addiction, Mare. He was undercover for the FBI. He was running with the mob, fighting at first, and then shaking down Vegas strip clubs and making threats. I couldn't call you about it or text. We couldn't whisper about it like gossip next to the pool while watching the kids play. Travis was being watched. Why would I tell you?"

"So you didn't have to carry it alone."

"I wasn't alone," Abby said. She looked at Travis with a small smile.

"That morning in St. Thomas?" I asked. "That was when you were recruited?"

"I didn't have a choice," Travis said.

I rubbed the back of my head, my thoughts spinning. How had Travis kept this secret all these years? When he was traveling for the gym, and then when he took over Thomas's job, it was always the FBI. That explained how they bought a house based on his personal trainer wages, but I still couldn't believe they'd kept it from us.

"So why Thomas?" I asked. "Why did Thomas keep it a secret?"

Travis shrugged. "Mom. She made Dad promise to quit his job as a detective, and that we wouldn't follow in his footsteps. But Thomas was born to do this job." He spoke of Thomas with reverence, and I believed him, even though I still didn't understand the lies.

"Jim would have understood, Trav. Surely, there's another reason."

Travis shrugged. "That's the only reason he's ever given me. He didn't want to disappoint Dad. He didn't want Dad to tell him not to pursue a career he was passionate about."

America watched Travis speak, her eyes narrowing. She picked up on something I didn't. "So Thomas knew that you were about to be arrested and talked someone in the Bureau into offering you a job because of your connections with Mick and Benny? Why not Abby?"

Abby chuckled. "Travis was capable of doing things for Benny I wasn't. And Travis would have never agreed to that." America nodded, but she still wasn't satisfied. Something wasn't adding up. They were still hiding something. "So now Thomas …" America trailed off. She did that with the boys a lot, hoping they would fill in the blanks.

Travis cleared his throat. "Was targeted, yes."

"And that cut on your head?" I asked.

He traded glances with his wife. "I was, too. That's why the agents came to Dad's. That's why they're here. That's why we have to stay together."

"You automatically assumed they'd be after the rest of the family because they went after you and Thomas?" America asked.

"They weren't after Travis," Abby said. "He was in my car. They were after the kids and me."

America covered her mouth.

Travis's gaze fell to the floor. "The men who ran me off the road … They were Benny Carlisi's men. They had pictures of us in the vehicle. All of us, our families, the kids ..."

"Why?" I asked. "Because your cover was blown?"

"I fucked up," Travis said. "I killed Benny. They're out for blood."

"You *killed* him?" America asked, stunned. "My friend Travis, my husband's cousin, my best friend's husband, killed a *mob boss*? Did we somehow fall into an episode of *The Sopranos*? How the hell is this happening?"

"He didn't have a choice," Abby said. "It was him or Benny."

"And Mick?" America asked.

"He was in protective custody. He's disappeared."

"*Disappeared?*" America screeched, looking at Abby.

"Keep your voice down," Travis said.

America stood and began to pace. "So now what? We'll be prisoners in our own home until they're all caught?"

"It won't be long," Travis said. "I promise, Mare. They gunned down one of our agents—my brother. We won't stop until they're locked up or wiped out." Travis crossed his arms across his chest. As big as he was in college, he was a beast now. His arms were thicker than my legs, his chest almost twice the width it used to be. He was solid muscle. I couldn't imagine anyone looking at him and thinking it was a good idea to go after his family, and it was hard to believe Thomas had dragged him into this mess.

Travis noticed that I was deep in thought. "What is it, Shep?"

I shook my head.

"Say it," Travis said.

"You said it was to keep you out of prison. Couldn't Thomas have done that without asking you to go undercover? Every time you were on an assignment, you were in danger. Why would Thomas do that?"

"It wasn't an easy decision for him," Abby said.

"That implies he had a choice," I said. "Did he?"

Travis shifted his weight from one foot to the other, uncomfortable with the direction of the conversation.

"What if you weren't you?" America asked. "What if Abby had been involved with her first boyfriend Jesse, or Parker, or someone not as … capable as you?"

Travis shrugged. "Then if he would have been stupid enough to be involved in The Circle fights and found himself guilty of gathering a hundred students in a small basement with questionable exits, he would have gone to prison."

"Or bartered with Abby for her cooperation and manipulation of Mick. I just …" I trailed off, hesitant to say anything more to hurt our family. "He could have found another way, if he wanted to. He could have, Trav. I realize it's probably not the best time to voice that opinion, but I didn't know back then. So I'm saying it now."

Travis looked down and nodded, pulling in a breath through his nose. He looked up at me as if I had invited in a truth that had been living in silence on the edge of his conscience. "He knows that. I see it on his face every time he sees me on the job."

"It seems a little too perfect," America said. "Thomas is in the FBI, and his brother just happens to be dating the daughter of a man involved with a crime family they're investigating?"

"Thomas got lucky," Travis said.

"*Lucky*?" America snarled. "Did he get a promotion?"

Travis and Abby tensed.

"Did he?" America demanded.

"Yeah," Travis said. "He did."

"Un-fucking-believable," America said, letting her hands fall to her thighs with a slap. "And you were okay with this?"

"No!" Travis said. His patience was running out. "No, I wasn't okay with it. I did what I had to do."

"Thomas sold you out," America said, pointing at Travis.

"So Liis is coming here? Without Thomas?" I asked. "I'm assuming he's in some secret federal hospital with a ton of security?"

"I can't talk about that," Travis said. "Not yet."

"We're your friends," America said. "At least, we thought we were."

Travis sighed, rubbing the back of his neck. "It's not about how much we trust you. It's about who's listening."

"The truth is dangerous," Abby said. "The more you don't know, the better."

"Abby," America said, disgusted. "We're in protective custody. We're already in danger."

Travis and Abby traded glances. "There's not much more you don't know," Travis said.

"Then fill us in," America said, standing. "I guess I'm missing where we aren't important enough, or smart enough, or have high enough security clearance to know why someone wants to kill us or our children."

"Did they … have pictures of our boys?" I asked.

Travis hesitated then nodded.

America retreated to my side, forming a united front. I knew what was coming, and by the look on Abby's face, so did she.

"You involved us in this without our permission," America said. "We've been behind you since the beginning. We've been there for you through everything. Then we find out you've been lying to us for years. Okay. I understand the circumstances, but it's time to be straight with us, *now*. Now, it's our business. It's our problem. Is there anything else we should know?"

She was right. Our boys were sleeping in a waiting room of a hospital, and before that, they were crowded on a makeshift pallet on the floor so we could be under the watchful eyes of the FBI. We weren't sure how long the Carlisis had been in town, or how long they'd been watching us. We couldn't protect ourselves or our sons without knowing exactly what we were up against.

"What are you going to do about it, Mare?" Travis asked.

"Trav," I warned.

"No, I'd like to know. You think Thomas or I wanted any of this? It's the last thing we wanted. That's why I've been undercover for—"

"Undercover?" America seethed. "Lying to mobsters about your loyalties doesn't make you undercover, Travis! They knew who you were, who you're married to, and where you live! We were in Vegas with you. They had photographs of my boys!" she said, her eyes filling with angry tears. "The second you agreed to this, we were in danger. Don't act like you're the savior in all this. You and Thomas are the *cause*!"

"America, enough," Abby said. "You don't know everything."

"Exactly," she snapped. She grabbed my hand, and we walked together toward the door.

"Shep," Travis pleaded.

I turned to him. I'd always been on his side, but for the first time, I wasn't sure if he had my back. I wasn't sure if I could believe anything he was saying. He hadn't chosen to lie to us, but he wasn't in control. "You haven't even apologized, Travis. I know you didn't want this, but you brought it on us. And for what?"

"To keep him out of prison," Abby snapped. "You would have done whatever you could to keep that from happening, too, and you know it."

"I wouldn't have painted a target on the backs of my sons," I said. "You did that." I glared at Travis and then pulled my wife out the door.

# CHAPTER EIGHTEEN

## LIIS

VAL LOADED STELLA'S AND MY THINGS into the passenger seat and floorboard of Travis's truck, except for the pink and gray baby bag Travis had slung over his large shoulder. I smiled for the first time since Thomas had left. Seeing a man as large and intimidating as Travis Maddox carrying anything girly struck me as amusing. Just as quickly as it came, the feeling vanished, replaced by bone-deep pain. I couldn't believe I was in Eakins, Illinois, with Stella but without her father. The past few days had left me in a daze.

Travis set the baby bag in the back on one side of an already-present rear-facing car seat. He seemed to have a lot on his mind besides the upcoming task of breaking the hearts of everyone in his family.

"I'll have to tighten the straps," he said, reaching for Stella. His voice went up an octave when he addressed her. "You're so tiny, but Carter makes you look like a giant. Yes, he does."

I walked around to the other side, settling in next to the car seat behind Val. She was already in the passenger side tapping away on her cell phone.

"Carter?" I asked.

Before Travis could answer, Val spoke up. "Why do men act so stupid around babies?"

"Glad to see you, Agent Taber," Travis said, his voice thick with sarcasm. He knew what to expect next.

"Fu …" Val began her trademark response, but she decided to mind Stella.

"Why does it bother you so much?" Travis asked. "Why go into the FBI if you detest being referred as an agent?"

"I don't. It's just an excuse to tell people to fu … you know."

"Any word, Val?" I asked.

"Significant improvement overnight," she said, resuming the tapping on her phone. "Also heard from Lena. Operation Coco is a go. She's in."

Travis sighed, relieved by both. He secured Stella while making sure she was snuggly tucked in. He kissed her head before manning the driver's seat, and I froze, remembering that Thomas had done the same thing just a few days before.

Travis closed his door and pulled his seat belt across his chest, fastening it with a click. "All set?" he asked Val. She ignored him, busy communicating with the director. Travis gripped the steering wheel and stared straight ahead without turning the ignition. "Liis?"

I closed my eyes. "I'm okay."

"I doubt that."

I looked out the window. "Let's just get it over with."

"You should know. I told them." Travis spat the words as if they'd been burning his mouth.

"What?" I said.

"What?" Val repeated.

"Most of it came out last night. They know Thomas, and I are Feds. They know my career started with the fire. Dad already knew, Liis."

"He doesn't know all of it."

"I know. But I had to lay some of it out before you got here. Otherwise, it'd be too much for him."

"And the others?"

"They know, too. Most of it. Except about you and … the plan."

"I understand," I said. It was all I could say. How could anyone prepare to tell their entire family they'd been lying to them? That I wasn't who they thought I was, and neither was Thomas? That he was gone and watch as they processed the worst pain they could possibly imagine?

"I'll be right there with you," Travis said.

It took a long time for me to speak. We were already passing through the airport gate by the time I could take hold of my emotions long enough to get the words out. "They won't forgive me," I said. Just those few words created a tightness in my throat.

"Yes, they will. They'll forgive us both." I'd known Travis long enough to hear when the calm in his voice was contrived. Abby was the better actress, but Travis had honed his poker face over the years. His wife was a good teacher.

"I don't know if I can do this. My emotions have been all over the place," I said.

Travis turned to face me. "You just had a baby, Liis. You went from a new family to a single mother in a day. Cut yourself some slack."

I glared at him, resenting his bluntness. As much as I wanted to hate what he said, it was true. "I'm still the same person. I'm not weak."

"Fuck no, you're not. Mothers are damn strong, anyway. And you, Liis? I've never seen anything like you."

I shifted in my seat. His response surprised me. "Besides Abby."

"It's not a competition," he said, offering a small smile.

My shoulders relaxed. Travis had a way of always making me feel safe, just like Thomas. As frightening as traveling with a newborn was, knowing I was going to be with the Maddoxes soon had been a significant comfort. "How are you doing?"

He cleared his throat, putting on the truck's blinker. "It's been rough. I'm not looking forward to this any more than you are."

"Where's Abby?"

"At the hospital with everyone else."

"The hospital? Why?" I asked, alarmed.

"The baby came last night."

Val and I both gasped. Abby was nowhere near her due date. I immediately felt ashamed. Years ago, I'd filled Abby in on the details of Travis's agreement with the FBI. She already had an idea, and I chose to spare Travis the burden of being the one to breach his agreement. I wouldn't go to prison if I told her, but Travis could have. In the end, it saved their marriage. She understood why he was so secretive and leaving so often, but the truth was a burden. From the moment you become aware of a secret, the inevitable question arises: what price will you pay to keep it?

"Are they okay?" I asked.

"Abby's doing great. Carter will be fine."

*Carter.* That's who he said made Stella look like a giant. She wasn't yet seven pounds. Carter must have been tiny.

"That's good to hear," Val said, sincere. It was her way of apologizing for giving him a hard time earlier.

"Is Abby alone at the hospital?" I asked, startled.

"The whole family is there with a half dozen agents, including Agent Davies."

"Sorry about that," I said. "She is the best …"

"I know. You won't have luck explaining that to Falyn, though."

"So … they know?"

"They'd figured most of it out. They put two and two together when Agent Davies picked them up from the airport."

I settled back into my seat, looking at Stella's peaceful, sleeping face. She was the perfect combination of Thomas and me. She was already on a schedule, sleeping and eating at the same times. She changed every day, and Thomas was missing it.

My eyes felt wet, and I had just reached into Stella's bag for a tissue when Travis reached back with one.

"It's going to be okay, Liis. I promise."

I dabbed beneath my eyes and sniffed. "It damn well better be, or the director will answer to me for a change."

"Yes, he will. And he knows it, too."

We drove from the outer edges of Eakins into town. It hadn't changed much. Only businesses like oil and industrial, gas stations, boutiques, tanning salons, and fast-food chains were thriving. Anything else was pretty much abandoned.

"Is that it?" Val asked as the taller buildings of the college came into view, reaching above the tree line.

"Yeah," Travis said, unhappy about the reminder. "Yeah, that's it."

The burned bricks of Keaton Hall had long since faded and the damage repaired. In the few minutes it took us to pass, Travis didn't look in the direction of the tiny college once. I assumed it was too much of a reminder of the strange direction his life had taken because of one night—the last time he'd participate in The Circle, Eastern State's underground fight ring. He looked away from the memories of the fire, of the night he'd nearly lost Abby.

"You know," I said, thinking aloud. "Whether or not Thomas had offered you as sacrifice to the FBI—"

"In return for immunity," he added.

"Yes, but between Abby's father and Benny Carlisi, you would have been involved in this mess. In a way, the fire kept you on the right side of it."

"I guess so," Travis said, lost in thought. "They didn't think I'd actually be worth a damn and turn from asset to agent, did they?"

"Actually, I think they did," I mused. "The FBI would take all five of you if Trenton and the twins would go for it."

"Trent?" Travis scoffed, placing an earpiece in his ear.

"He's got heart," I said. "Don't forget after his accident with Camille he carried her a mile with a broken arm."

"In two places," Travis specified.

"Exactly."

I caught Travis glance at the far corner of Eastern just before turning toward Mercy Hospital. We passed the street that led to the apartments where Travis and Abby fell in love and first lived, Trenton and Camille's apartment building, the street where Shepley and America's house sat, and then after six more blocks, he slowed.

Mercy Hospital loomed ahead, its aged, blond brick bright in the morning sun.

"Travis?" I said, angry at the sound of my voice.

"You're okay," Val said. "Just breathe."

Travis found an open parking space and pulled in, twisting back the key. We sat in silence for several minutes. Not even Val dared to speak.

"I can't!" I blurted out.

Travis pulled on the lever of his door and pushed, stepping out onto the gravel drive. "You can." He stepped back to open the back door and reached in, swung the baby bag over his shoulder, and then reached for Stella.

"Sh-should we leave the luggage here or …?" Val began.

I looked down, feeling hot tears drip down the bridge of my nose and fall away. "I hate all of you for making me do this."

"I'm not happy about the plan, either. But it's still the plan. You have to do it, and you know why." He tipped the carrier just enough that I could see the sweet face of my daughter. "If there was another way, do you think you'd be here alone?"

I shook my head and wiped my nose.

"Keep the tears," Travis said, laying Stella's blanket over the top of the handle to shelter her from the bright sunlight. "Tears are good."

"Fuck you," I said through my teeth.

A car door shut, and Val swung around, her hand on her sidearm. She relaxed, seeing Agent Hyde. "I didn't realize you'd be joining us," Val said.

"I'm on Agent Lindy's protection detail," Hyde said.

Val looked to me for confirmation, and I nodded. "She's out of Quantico. She's better than good. Assigned by the director."

Val scanned Hyde from hair to shoes, sizing her up. "Is that so?"

"It's so," Hyde said, lifting her chin with confidence.

"It's just Liis for now, Agent Hyde," Travis said. "My family doesn't know Liis' involvement with the Bureau just yet."

"Yes, sir," Hyde said.

Travis closed the door and walked around to my side, helping me out and walking me to the hospital entrance. Val trailed behind. Besides Travis and I, we would have Agents Hyde, Wren, Blevins, Davies, Perkins, and Taber—all agents who'd been on this case from the beginning. All agents we trusted with the lives of our family, and the only agents besides the director who knew the truth about Thomas.

Travis touched his earpiece. "We're on our way up," he said simply.

The elevator door opened to an eerily quiet hallway. Hyde stepped out first, and then Travis with Stella. Val followed me, the last to leave. She seemed uneasy the moment we landed in Eakins. A nurse rushed by, startling her.

Travis smiled. "A little jumpy?"

Val snarled. "Fu..." She clenched her jaw, frustrated.

Travis led me into the waiting room, stepping to the side so I could walk in. Everyone stood, tired but smiling. The kids' hair was all smashed or sticking up, frizzy and ratted from a long night on uncomfortable sofas and pallets on the floor. The adults were in worse shape, all staring at me, waiting for news. The look on my face must have confirmed their fears, because Falyn covered her mouth, and Ellie hugged Tyler.

"Hey there, sis," Jim said, trying and failing a few times to rock himself up off the sofa to stand. Camille finally helped him to his feet. He was trying his best to smile, to stay positive despite the fact that I'd arrived without Thomas. He hugged me tight.

"I came as soon as I could. I wanted to tell you in person," I said. Already the lie was scratching at my throat, making it feel raw. "Thomas ..." I looked around the room. They knew, but they were still waiting, still holding out hope.

Travis held me to his side.

"Thomas has passed away."

Jim's bottom lip trembled, and then he took a step back. Camille helped him to his seat and threw her arms around him. Trenton did the same.

"How?" Trenton said. "Why?"

Jim fished a handkerchief from his shirt pocket. He wiped both eyes and then mashed the embroidered white cloth back where it belonged. "Sit down, sis," he said, scooting away from Camille to make room.

Stella began to wail, and Travis set the carrier on the floor, unbuckled her, and quickly put her in my arms. It was obvious that he was a veteran dad, already searching her bag for something to help me calm Stella down.

I rocked her for a moment, turning toward Jim so he could get a look. He leaned in, smiling with unbridled pain behind his wet eyes. He looked up at me. "She looks like you and a little like Tommy, doesn't she?"

I nodded, feeling my bottom lip tremble. "A lot. She looks *a lot* like him."

"She's beautiful," Jim said, using his index finger to pet Stella's fist. "She favors my Diane."

I nodded and then watched as Jim's expression crumpled. Trenton curled his arm around his dad's shoulders and pulled him against his side. Camille reached over to squeeze Jim's knee. It was hell. I was supposed to be celebrating the birth of my daughter, and instead, I was mourning the loss of her father.

Taylor's bottom lip trembled. "Can we see him?"

"They're shipping him home tomorrow," I said, wiping away an escaped tear. "He wanted to be buried here."

I inwardly cursed the Bureau and this fucking plan. The director had called me himself the day before to apologize, but success would be the only thing that would convince me the risks we'd taken were worth it. Success meant keeping anyone else in our family from being targeted. Their safety relied on Benny's men believing they'd retaliated, but just as important, they had to believe that if they continued, they'd suffer more casualties of their own. Travis had already taken care of the second part. He'd been consulted and had agreed. The intel told us faking Thomas's death had worked. The Carlisis had returned to Vegas, and for now, at least, no hit had been put on Stella or me. The moment they realized it wasn't real, it would start all over again. We had to make Thomas's death look real. It was a huge risk. We were lucky they didn't aim for the head. Thomas's vest took the hit, but the mafia was watching us all.

"I'm so sorry," I said to Jim, and I meant it.

"I just can't believe he got shot. I mean … what the fuck?" Trenton said, his bottom lip trembling.

Everyone looked in my direction for the answer.

I looked around and took a breath before spewing the poison that would slowly kill Thomas's family. Travis handed me Stella's pacifier, and I sat back, rocking her back and forth until her cries were reduced to whimpers.

"We, um … we'd just gotten home from the hospital. It happened in the front lawn as he was walking out to get the rest of Stella's things. Travis told me you know that Thomas is an agent with the FBI. What you don't know … is that I'm an agent, too."

Falyn and Ellie gasped, and Trenton's mouth gaped open.

"That's how we met." I accidentally met Camille's eyes then looked away. "When Thomas learned of the fire and the charges Travis was likely facing—"

"He wasn't at the fire," Jim said.

"Yeah, I was, Dad," Travis said, ashamed. "I was. I was there."

Jim's brows pulled together as the truth set in.

"… he went to the director and asked for a deal. Thomas knew by then that Travis had crossed paths with Benny Carlisi, the head of an organized crime family in Vegas."

"When?" Jim asked Travis.

Travis swallowed. "Abby's father got into some trouble. Owed Benny money. He came to Abby for help. We went to Vegas, and she won most of the money. I won the rest."

"How?" Tyler asked. "Not poker."

"Fighting," Travis said simply.

I continued. "Thomas knew that Travis had an unbelievable in with Benny that he could use in exchange for immunity. Thomas had a limited amount of time to get Travis to agree, and he wanted to do it in person, so we told him the day after the vow renewal."

"In St. Thomas?" Falyn asked.

I nodded, feeling my eyes tear up at the memory. It wasn't a good one. I had never been able to forget the shame in Thomas's eyes. "So we brought Travis into the fold, and he's been working undercover, giving us information."

"I don't understand. Why keep it from us?" Trenton asked.

"It was the way Thomas wanted it. He was afraid it would upset Jim." I glanced at Thomas's father. He was hunched over with wet eyes, looking broken. "And," I looked at Travis, who gave me permission with a nod, "he didn't want you all to know what he'd done."

Tyler's brows pulled in. "What did he do?"

I sighed. "In the spirit of full disclosure … Thomas knew if he brought Travis into the Bureau as an asset, he could keep him out of prison. He also knew he'd get a promotion."

"But I had a choice," Travis added.

Trenton frowned. "Strawberry or chocolate is a choice. Going to prison or being a pawn for the FBI isn't a fucking choice. Now, your family is in danger, Trav. How could you do that?"

"Trenton," Jim said.

"You think I wanted this?" Travis said, instantly enraged. "You think I wanted any of this?"

"Boys," Jim said.

"I think Mom didn't want any of us going into Dad's line of work for a reason, and you two pissed all over it," Trenton said.

"That's enough," Jim boomed. "We have had enough heartache in this family today without making it worse. Don't dishonor your brother by arguing over his choices. What's done is done." His breath was labored. "We've got a funeral to plan."

"What do you mean a funeral?" Hollis asked. "Uncle Tommy is going to be okay, right?"

Ezra and James were looking around too, suddenly worried.

My stomach sank. "No," I said, despondent. I was a horrible human being.

The boys began to tear up, and Travis kneeled in front of them. "Uncle Tommy was in an accident."

Hollis's cheeks flushed red. "I know, but … he's in the hospital."

"He was. Now, we're going to have a funeral for him so we can say goodbye." Travis choked on the last words, cupped Hollis's shoulders, and looked away. He felt like a monster. So did I.

Hollis hugged his father, and then everyone began hugging. Camille tried to hug Trenton, but he gently raised his hand, letting her know he needed a minute.

"These Carlisis," Trenton said. "They're the ones we're hiding from?"

"Not anymore," I said. "We just received word the last of them left town during the night."

"Why?" Trenton asked. He was getting angrier.

"Because they've gotten word that I've decided against pursuing this case. Abby's father was in protective custody before the trial of some of their higher ups, but he's gone missing. The Bureau no longer has a case against them."

"You're no longer involved in the case?" Camille asked. "You're going to let them get away with it?"

I swallowed, trying hard not to feel defensive. "I'm a widow with a newborn. I have to concentrate on Stella."

Camille covered her mouth with both hands, and Trenton broke down. Soon, everyone in the room was sobbing, even the children.

Travis hugged his twins. "Let's go see your mom." He guided them out of the room, leaving me alone with his family. I watched him with my mouth open, pleading with my eyes for him to stay. He wiped his eyes. "I'll be back."

I rocked Stella. She was already content and asleep, but I was really just comforting myself.

"This is bullshit," Trenton cried. "It's fucking bullshit!" he yelled.

Camille hugged him, but then he slipped away from her grasp, wiping his eyes and staring at the floor. I watched the Maddoxes hit every state of grief within minutes and more than once.

"Liis," Ellie said, kneeling in front of me.

I shook my head, letting her know that, although appreciated, I wasn't receptive to sympathy. I didn't deserve it, and that would just be another item on the list to hate me for later.

Travis returned. Jessica and James snuggled with their Uncle Trenton. "She's finally sleeping," he said. "When she wakes up, I'm going to take her to see Carter. Agent Davies, Wren, and Blevins will escort you home."

"So that's it?" Trenton asked. "We're free to go?"

"You're free to go," Travis said.

"I'll get Dad," Camille said. She seemed in a daze, unable to process the last twenty-four hours.

I could see that Trenton wanted to spit an insult at his brother, but he remembered Travis's twins were on each side of him. He kissed Jessica and James on the forehead and then stood, gesturing for Olive to come with him.

"Shep," Travis began.

"Yes. We'll take the twins," he said without hesitation.

"Thanks," Travis said.

Shepley nodded, helping America herd the kids and fold blankets. After Trenton had left with Jim, Camille, and Olive, Shepley and America followed with their boys, Jessica and James, and Jack and Deana. One by one, our numbers dwindled, and then it was just Travis and me with Stella and our protection detail.

Travis watched the last of his family leave and then rubbed his face with one hand. "Fucking hell, that was awful." He retreated into the waiting room and sat, leaning back against the cushions of the couch and lacing his fingers behind his neck.

"Well," Val said, joining him. "The worst of it is over."

"No, it's not over," Travis snapped. "The worst is looking them in the face and telling them I lied … again. Trenton's definitely going to take a swing, and I'm going to let him do it."

"I'm hoping they'll be so happy that they'll forget what we've done. Otherwise, they'll never speak to us again," I said.

"Yeah, they will," Travis said.

I craned my neck at him. "Would you?"

He looked down and frowned. "I don't know what I'd do."

# CHAPTER NINETEEN

## FALYN

AS SOON AS WE ARRIVED AT JIM'S, we all showered and changed, and then reconvened back downstairs. My phone had been buzzing for the last hour, but I already knew who it was. Peter Lacy had received his first response from me that morning, telling him if he didn't stop contacting me, I would file a complaint with the Estes Park Police Department. Somehow, that only entertained him more.

Taylor and Tyler were in a daze, sitting at the dining room table staring at their clasped hands. I put my phone on silent and shoved it in my back pocket. I didn't want to turn it off in case Travis and Abby or Liis needed anything, but a part of me seriously weighed that against the possibility of Taylor discovering Peter was still trying to contact me. In his current state of mind, I didn't know how he would react. I definitely didn't want a scene in front of Alyssa.

Jim was asleep in his bedroom, Alyssa was on watch in the living room, and the kids were upstairs watching a movie, leaving the four of us to grieve alone. I wanted to hold Taylor, to touch him. He was my husband, for God's sake, but pride kept my hands in my lap. We had been living by my rules since I'd left, rules I felt needed to be followed as a lesson for Taylor to learn. It wasn't fair to send mixed signals in order to comfort him.

The house was quiet, only the occasional creaking of the walls from the foundation settling. I tried not to think about Alyssa being in the next room, but it was impossible. It was easier to let my mind worry about things I could somewhat control. The coffeepot beeped, and everyone suddenly awakened from their motionless state.

"I'll get it," Ellie said, standing. She returned with a tray of mugs and the pot of coffee, setting down each cup and then filling it.

Tyler drank his black, but I knew to search for cream and sugar for Taylor. As I opened each cabinet, I noticed items in strange places, and then I paused, seeing an ice tray next to the spices. I pulled it out, and water sloshed, startling me.

"Oh!" I cried.

Alyssa jogged in. "Everything all right?" she asked, already knowing the answer.

I flung the water from my hands and then wiped the excess on my pants. "I didn't realize Jim was keeping the ice trays in the cabinet."

Alyssa wrinkled her nose. "Pardon?"

"Nothing," I said, refilling the tray and placing it in the freezer.

Alyssa nodded, turning for the living room, but then she paused. "I admit that I asked for this assignment."

I stared at her. "I'm … not really sure how to respond to that."

"I've been curious about Hollis for a while but especially after you left Taylor."

My face twisted into disgust. "You've been keeping tabs on us?"

She shrugged, unapologetic. "You have my son."

"*My* son," I said. "I've raised him. I've sat up with him countless nights pressing a cold cloth to his forehead when he was sick. I've made him breakfast every morning, his birthday cakes every year, and rocked him to sleep every night until he was six. I was there for his first day of school and when he kicked a soccer ball into his first goal. He's *my* son."

"He is," Alyssa said. "In every sense of the word."

"Then why did you want to be here?"

"Curiosity, mostly. The rest is sentiment."

I fidgeted, suddenly nervous about her intentions. "Are you going to tell him who you are?"

"No," Alyssa said. She looked down. "Especially not now. It would be inappropriate to drop that on him when he's grieving his uncle."

Even with no sleep and her long hair pinned back, she had barely aged since the last time I'd seen her. Her long, straight dark hair and doe eyes reminded me of Cher when she was married to Sonny, with the exception of killer curves which made her look more like an actress who played an agent on TV than a real one. Without chasing around children and having only herself to take care of, she had aged far better than I had. It was easy to feel threatened as I stood there in lounge pants, an oversized T-shirt, ten years of marital baggage, and crow's feet around my eyes. Alyssa was a supermodel who could steal my husband and a kick-ass FBI agent who could steal my son. The inferiority I felt was crushing.

I glanced back at Taylor, who turned his head, pretending he hadn't been watching. I wasn't sure if he was listening or staring at Alyssa.

"I don't begrudge you moments with Hollis," I said. "I've often wondered how you did it, how you just walked away and didn't look back. It's just …"

"Confusing," Alyssa said, finishing my sentence. "I understand. And I don't want to make this week any more difficult for you. I've seen the way he looks at you. I couldn't win him over if I tried. I just … wanted to see him."

"Hollis?" I asked. I couldn't help it. The words just came tumbling out of my mouth, and my cheeks instantly caught fire.

"Of course, Hollis. Who else?"

I glanced at Taylor to see if he was watching. He turned away, caught again. I wanted to pack my things and get on the first plane back to Colorado. Embarrassment normally made me ragey, but I couldn't even muster enough dignity to get angry.

"Oh. No," Alyssa said. "No, no, no. You misunderstand. Completely. Totally."

I crossed my arms, feeling absolutely insane. I was actually *indignant* that she wasn't interested in Taylor.

She noticed my irritation and sighed. "Let me rephrase. Taylor was never an option. It was always you. I knew it then. I know it now."

It was a strange feeling to have someone so threatening offer me so much comfort.

Alyssa paused and then crept up the hallway. She walked quietly up to the front door and then pressed her ear against the wood. She listened for a moment and then rolled her eyes, yanking open the door. Olive jerked to a stop, waiting for permission to come in. Alyssa opened the door the rest of the way and then closed and locked the door behind her.

"I'm sorry," Olive said. "I'm not used to it being locked."

Alyssa gestured for her to go ahead and then returned to her spot in the living room. I watched Olive hug Taylor, Tyler, and Ellie, and then she walked toward me. Years ago, I stopped wondering when my heart would stop pounding in my chest when she was around. She threw her arms around me, and I hugged her, flattening her hair against the back of her head. I knew exactly how Alyssa felt, and I had no excuse to make her feel anything but welcome. Hollis was her son, too. Just because she'd walked away didn't mean she didn't love him.

"Coffee?" I asked Olive, bringing the sugar and creamer to the table.

She shook her head and followed me. "I just had my second cup before coming over."

"How's your mom?" I asked, sitting next to Taylor. "Is she ready for you to move into the dorms?"

Olive shook her head and smiled, snickering. "Not at all. She's such a baby."

I playfully poked her. "Cut her some slack. It's a big deal." My phone buzzed. I checked it and put it away.

"I told her about Thomas. She's going to bring Jim a casserole later," Olive said.

"That's sweet," I said. I used my finger to brush away a strand of hair that had fallen into her face. She was a young woman now, creeping closer every day to the age I was when I brought her into the world. She was working at a local grocery store as a cashier like she had every summer since she was fifteen, but this would be her last before college.

Taylor took a sip. "Thank you, baby." He tensed when he realized what he'd said, but I covered his hand with mine. The rules seemed trivial now, the terms of endearment, the living apart until I'd felt Taylor had done his time and felt sufficiently kicked while he was down. He could have lost his job and gone to jail, and I wanted to punish him more. My heart sank. I was wrong. I'd been wrong.

"Taylor," I began, but my phone buzzed. I checked it and again put it away.

"Is that the kids?" Taylor asked.

"No," I said simply.

His gaze fell to my back pocket. "It's him, isn't it?"

"Is it weird that I'm mad at him?" Tyler blurted out, looking at his twin.

"Mad at who?" Taylor asked.

"Thomas. I'm fucking pissed. I keep thinking that if he were here, I would punch him in his lying fucking face."

Taylor shook his head.

"I feel like that's weird," Tyler said. "Like I shouldn't feel that way, but I do." His bottom lip trembled. "And then I remember he's not here, and he's not going to be here. But I'd still punch him, and then I'd hug him until he wouldn't let me hug him anymore."

Ellie rubbed Tyler's back. "That's not weird. This is all very confusing. Feelings aren't wrong. Whatever you're feeling is exactly what you should feel."

I smiled at my sister-in-law. She'd gone from drunken pill popper to a meditating, full-lotus-posing soccer mom. She'd worked so hard to get sober and had spent a fortune in rehabilitation before Gavin came along. She was not only sober, but she was beginning to sound like her therapist, and I loved it.

"Falyn?" Olive said.

Without fail, when she said my name, my heart would sing. Because of Taylor, I was able to be involved in her life more than I ever thought possible. She was our flower girl at our wedding, she babysat Hollis and Hadley when we visited, and now, she was sitting next to me, my mirror image, looking at me for advice. I rested my chin on the heel of my hand and looked at her with a smile. "Yes, love?"

"When do you think the funeral will be? I should ask for the day off. I want to be there."

"I'll ask Papa when he wakes up. We're going to have to decide a lot of things today, so he should get some rest."

She picked at her nails, nodding absently. "Yes, ma'am."

I looked to Taylor, wishing I could thank him for that moment, and every moment with Olive before that one. I'd been wrong, and it was time to admit it to both of us. My phone buzzed again. I didn't check it this time.

Taylor looked down to the source of the noise. His shoulders sagged. "Is that who I think it is?"

I hesitated. "I … don't know who it is."

"Falyn," Taylor said, sounding tired. "Is it him?"

"Who?" Tyler asked.

"Peter Lacy," Taylor said.

"The mayor's son?" Ellie asked, surprised.

"She didn't give him her number, and she doesn't respond," Taylor said.

"I did this morning," I said. Taylor looked devastated. "I told him if he didn't stop, I was going to file a complaint with the police department."

"And he's still trying to contact you?" Ellie asked.

"Yes," I said, annoyed.

"You did?" Taylor asked. "You told him that?"

I turned to him. "I told you. I want nothing to do with him."

Taylor managed a small half smile. He didn't lose his temper. He didn't punch at the air or scream or slam doors. Maybe it was because he was emotionally exhausted, but I'd asked him to do better, and he had. "I wish I could do better by you. That's what you deserve."

The shocked expressions across the table prompted me to reach for his hand. His vulnerability at that moment was so incredibly moving.

He looked down at my hand on his and blinked, seeming surprised.

"Will you sit on the porch with me?" I asked.

He stared at me for a moment like I'd spoken in a foreign language, and then he nodded, finally processing my request. "Yeah. I mean yes. Of course."

Taylor's chair grated against the floor when he pushed it back to stand. I kept his hand in mine while we walked to the front door. He didn't try to pull away, but he was on autopilot, letting me lead him outside. We sat down on the top step and listened to the birds whistling, the wind pushing through the leaves on the trees, and watched the cars drive by. It was a beautiful, sunny summer day. It should have been pouring rain from gray skies, but instead, the storm was inside. Taylor's cheeks were wet from silent tears, and I felt myself growing desperate.

"I know this is probably the worst time for this, but I have to. I'm going to say something that I wanted to say the other night, so I don't want you to think there is any other reason for this than me telling you of a decision I've already made," I said.

"Falyn." He waited several seconds before speaking again. I was afraid he would tell me to shut up because he didn't want to hear anything from me. That anything I had to say would be of little importance to him that day, and I couldn't be mad because he would be right. "If you tell me you want a divorce right now, I'm warning you … I might just walk into the street and lay there."

I couldn't help but smile, but it faded. "I don't want a divorce."

His eyes met mine, and he really saw me for the first time in hours. "You don't?"

I shook my head. "I love you. And you're right. We should work on this together, not apart. It's not doing anyone any favors, particularly the kids, and …"

"I think I'm hearing you say that when we get home, we're not separated anymore." He waited, cautiously optimistic.

"I'm saying we're not separated anymore."

"Anymore? You mean now?"

"Yes."

"As in right now?" he asked, still unsure.

"If that's okay with you. I don't mean to assume."

He closed his eyes and rested his head in his hands, leaning forward almost onto his toes.

"Be careful," I said, holding him back by the arm.

He puffed out a cry, and then he pulled me into his arms. Soon, he began to sob, and I held him. The muscles in my back began to burn, but I didn't dare move. If he needed me, I would sit in that position for the rest of the day, holding him.

His shoulders stopped shaking, and he took in two deep breaths, pulling back and wiping his eyes. I'd never seen him in so much pain. Not even the night I left. "I do love you," he said with a faltering breath. "And I'm going to be better. I can't lose you, too. It'll break me, Falyn … I might already be broken."

I leaned over to kiss his cheek and then the corner of his mouth. He stiffened, unsure what to do, worried to do the wrong thing. I pressed my lips against his, once and then again. The third time I parted my lips, he kissed me back, holding each side of my face. We hadn't touched in months, and once we started, we couldn't stop. We were crying and kissing, hugging and making promises, and it felt right.

Taylor held his forehead to mine, breathing hard, relieved but once again cautious. "Is this for now? Is it going to be different when we get back to Colorado and go home to the same problems?"

"We'll be working on the same problems, but it will be different."

He nodded, a tear dripping from the tip of his nose. "It will. I promise."

# CHAPTER TWENTY

## ELLIE

I SWIPED LEFT ON MY EREADER DISPLAY, turning the page, and then adjusting my body when Tyler stirred. He'd been asleep on my right thigh for two hours, and Gavin on my left for three. I wasn't sure why I moved. Trying to adjust after one of my boys did to make them more comfortable usually just made them uncomfortable, and they would shift again. For whatever reason, I thought I'd know what would make them more comfortable than they did, and I was almost always wrong. It was in part a control issue and maternal instinct. I needed to feel I was helping to make them comfortable, when in reality if I'd just sat still, they could have done it themselves.

I skimmed down the page, absorbing ideas about coping with death, helping others to cope with death, and the comfort in the belief held by a Ph.D. that our energies move on to the next life. I wasn't sure if that made me a transcendental new age fruit loop, but it made me feel better, and as far as I was concerned, that was my purpose—to exist and heal wounds in the healthiest way I could.

I'd been grappling with finding peace in Thomas's death, in the lies, and in the danger we'd been put in. I tried not to think about Gavin's picture being one in the more than a dozen photographs scattered on the passenger seat of the vehicle carrying three mafia hitmen, or that his picture had likely been spattered and stained by their blood. The same dark red in color as Gavin's, and not long ago surging through veins of a man who was once a boy; whose only difference from me was a series of bad choices, spurned by childhood experiences marred by his parents' bad choices: a cycle that was never broken.

My heart ached for the men who would have murdered my child without a second thought, and that was unnerving as well. I'd given up anger, and with that release, I found myself without the tool I needed to hate. I could hate them, but it was difficult when I'd spent so many years viewing adults as children and studying the origin of their actions. I'd never considered that in my discipline to view the world in a new way, I would struggle with having expected emotions that would have come so easily to me a decade earlier.

Still, those men I couldn't hate weren't imaginary. They'd come to Eakins with guns and a very real threat to our family. It was easy to blame Thomas and Travis for bringing them there, but that would require placing the blame on someone else's choice. Thomas and Travis might have made their own choices based on the Carlisis, but they were on the right side of this. Their only other choice was to allow the Carlisis to avenge Benny's death. I was a person who detested violence, but sitting in a room with my sleeping husband and son, I realized there truly was a time for everything.

The only solution was to stand and fight.

That recognition both devastated and empowered me, as each new understanding did. I swiped the page again, feeling my cheeks burn with the tears that had begun to spill over. I sniffed and wiped my nose, waking my husband.

He saw my face and sat up, tucking a stray strand that had fallen from my bun behind my ear. "Elle," he said, barely above a whisper. "What is it?"

"Just reading a sad part," I said.

He smiled. He teased me often that I was the only person he knew who cried over non-fiction, but growth was rattling, and I often had to leave the bruised pieces of me behind, no matter how attached I'd become to them.

"What part is that?" he asked, settling in next to me.

"That Thomas and Travis's choice was reasonable, and it must have been so hard for them. They've been walking this earth so conflicted."

Tyler thought about my words and then sighed. "Probably."

"It's hard to see the light in circumstances like this, even if you're holding the candle."

Tyler chuckled and then turned to me. "Did you read that?"

"No."

"Your brain amazes me. Your thoughts are poetry."

I breathed out a laugh. "Sometimes, I guess. It's important to find strength in pain."

Tyler kissed my cheek and then reached for our son. Gavin was the perfect balance of Tyler and me—at peace when he was angry, wearing pale, soft skin encompassing a kind, brave spirit, and an analytical mind. I ran my fingers over the short cut he insisted upon to look more like his daddy, making his lids flutter. His warm russet eyes embraced the dark. Just like us, he would live through his worst before being his best, and I both dreaded and welcomed the challenge. I'd spent a lot of time earning the right to be his mother.

"He's been sleeping for a long time," Tyler said.

"I don't think he got a lot of sleep at the hospital. He needs it. His body will wake when it's rested."

We heard footsteps pass our door, walking down the hallway to the top of the stairs. Once they'd descended, Jim's muffled voice greeted them.

"He's up," Tyler said. "We should go down."

I nodded, carefully lifting Gavin's head from my lap. Tyler placed a pillow under his head, and I tucked the blankets in around him. Tyler held my hand as we made our way to the table where Jim sat with Liis and Mr. Baird, the representative from the funeral home. He'd come earlier before Jim had woken from his nap, and insisted on waiting patiently for the family to gather. Mr. Baird was tall and lanky, his ash-colored hair parted to the side and carefully gelled and combed over. He turned the page of a catalog, quietly discussing the pros and cons of oak, cedar, and pine, and the more eco-friendly bamboo or banana leaf and explaining the difference between a coffin and a casket.

Two boxes of tissue were the centerpiece of the dining table, and Camille reached over her seated husband to pull out a sheet, wiping her red-rimmed eyes. She was standing behind him, rubbing his shoulders, but it seemed to be comforting her as well.

Liis was sitting next to Jim, stoic, almost disconnected. I assumed she would handle the details as she did her job, organized and meticulous, but she was deferring to Jim for almost every decision.

"What about an urn?" Travis asked.

Jim frowned, likely imagining the cremation of Thomas's body instead of the vision Travis meant.

Liis nodded. "We could spread his remains in the backyard. He has so many stories of watching his brothers play there. I think he would like that."

"I was thinking of giving him my plot next to his mother," Jim said.

"That's sweet," I said, acknowledging the thought, but Trenton sighed, agitated.

"No, Dad," Trenton said. "You belong next to Mom. Liis is right. Thomas wouldn't want people staring at his body lying in a coffin."

"Casket," Mr. Baird corrected. "A coffin is a six or eight-sided wooden or metal burial unit that was historically used as a less expensive option. The angles provided use of fewer materials and…"

"No offense, Mr. Baird," Trenton said, "but I don't fucking care." He looked down at his watch. "Damn it. I have to get to work."

"I called in for you," Camille said.

"You did?" Trenton asked, bewildered.

"You should be here."

"Did you call in, too?" he asked.

"I can work from home." She put her hands on his forearm, their skin a masterpiece of lines and colors. "I should be here with you."

He turned, nodding and taking a deep breath. The smallest things seemed to bring everyone closer to the fact that this wasn't a bad dream. Thomas was dead, and we were going to say goodbye to him soon.

"Most of us haven't seen him since Christmas," Taylor said, holding Falyn's hand in his lap. They'd barely been able to stop touching since they'd made up earlier that day. "It would be closure for me to see him."

Everyone looked at Liis, who stumbled over her next words. "I don't think … I think in this case, an urn is preferable."

"Are you saying that because he won't look the same or because it can't be an open casket?"

I tried not to gasp, but it happened, anyway. Olive did, too.

"I think," Liis said, trading glances with Travis, "an urn is preferable."

Jim looked away, trying to gather his emotions before responding. He cleared his throat. "Let's see the urns, then."

Papers rattled while Mr. Baird gathered the casket choices and put them away. He brought out a new catalog and printouts, and Liis opened the book to the first page of options.

"I need to know," Trenton said.

"Please don't," Camille cried.

"Why can't we have an open casket?" Trenton asked.

"Olive," Falyn warned. "Go check on the kids."

"Yes, ma'am," she said, immediately turning for the stairs.

"Liis?" Trenton prompted.

"Trent," Liis said, closing her eyes. "I understand knowing is part of your grieving process, but I can't. This is too hard."

Travis walked over to her and cupped her shoulders. "It doesn't matter, Trent."

"It fucking matters. I wanna know what happened to my brother."

"He died," Travis said.

Trenton slammed his fist on the table and stood. "I know! I know he fucking died! I wanna know why! I wanna know who let that happen!"

Travis's voice was noticeably restrained. "No one. No one let it happen. It just is. We don't have to pick someone to blame, Trent …"

"Yeah, we do. Tommy is dead, Travis. He's fucking dead, and I blame the FBI. I blame him. I blame her," he said, pointing at Liis. "And I blame you." He was shaking, his eyes bloodshot and glossed over.

"Fuck you, Trent," Travis said.

Trenton rounded the table, prompting the twins to stand between them. Travis stood stoic, unflinching while Trenton thrashed about wildly. I scrambled from my chair and stood with my back to the corner, palms flat against the walls.

"Every last one of you suited up motherfuckers ...!" Trenton seethed.

"Stop!" Tyler said, gripping the collar of Trenton's shirt. "Stop, goddammit!"

"Fuck off!" Trenton said, shoving Tyler off him. He was breathing hard, pacing back and forth a few feet and glaring at Travis like he was between rounds during an MMA match.

Taylor stood in front of Travis, gesturing for his wife to step back. Falyn obeyed, pushing away from the table and walking around to the other side to stand next to me. "What do we do?" she whispered.

"Stay put," I said.

"All the damn lies," Trenton said. He pointed at Travis. "And you shot their fucking boss, and then they murdered our brother!" He took a few steps, and Taylor braced himself. "And half a goddamn day goes by before you tell us what the hell is going on? What the fuck is wrong with you, dude?" He took another step, too far into Taylor's space.

"Don't make me knock you out," Taylor said, his brow furrowed.

I closed my eyes. "Please stop," I said, my voice too weak for anyone to hear except Tyler. He glanced at me just long enough to check that I was okay.

"No one is knocking anyone out," Camille said, standing behind her husband. "Back off, Taylor."

Falyn took a step forward. "Taylor? Tell your husband to calm down. This isn't solving anything."

Camille narrowed her eyes at her sister-in-law. "You know what didn't solve anything? Putting us all in danger and lying about it. I think Trent has a right to be upset."

"Really?" Falyn said, crossing her arms. "Really, Cami? You're going to pretend you weren't on Team Thomas twenty-four hours ago?"

"Oh, shut the fuck up, Falyn," Camille said, disgusted.

"Hey!" Taylor boomed. "Don't talk to her like that. Ever."

"Then she needs to watch her tone," Trenton said.

"She's my *wife*!" Taylor said. "No one talks to her like that."

"Weren't you just yelling at Cami yesterday for the same thing?" Falyn asked. "That she was keeping secrets? Now, you're blaming Liis when she's sitting there trying to mourn her husband? Liis doesn't owe you anything, Trent."

"She owes me the truth!" he yelled.

Jim was still turning pages, trying to ignore that his family was falling apart a few feet away. It was too much for him, and too much for Liis, who couldn't find words or the will to stop them.

"Are you finished?" Travis asked.

The front door opened, and Shepley's boys barreled down the hall, barely waving to us just before they shot up the stairs. When Shepley and America came to the end of the hall to see almost everyone standing, and me backed against the wall, they froze.

"What's going on?" Shepley asked, his eyes bouncing from one person to the next.

"Why don't you ask Travis?" Trenton said, jerking his hand out and upward in Travis's general direction.

Shepley looked to Travis, seeming uncomfortable. "What's going on?"

Travis sighed, relaxing a bit. "Trenton's having another one of his outbursts."

Trenton shot Travis a dirty look.

Travis shrugged. "You told him to ask me."

America walked up to the table and pulled up a chair, unfazed by the fact that a war was about to break out. "What now? Is he pissed about Cami again?"

Camille narrowed her eyes. "Really?"

"Really," America said, picking at her thumbnail.

"I wasn't trying to hurt anyone," Camille seethed. "And if every single one of you judging me would have known from the beginning, it wouldn't have changed anything. Not a damn thing. So put away your pitchforks. I was respecting Thomas's wishes. That's all."

"America didn't mean that, Cami," Shepley said.

"Yes, I did," America deadpanned.

"Mare," Shepley chided.

America rolled her eyes and sat up. "Five people have been lying to us about a safety concern involving our entire family. Thomas, Liis, Travis, Abby, and Cami." She looked at Camille. "So don't try to snake out of the blame, Cami. Just because your husband is angry about the lies and you want to be on his side doesn't excuse you from the truth."

Camille's cheeks flushed red, and her eyes glossed over. "I didn't ask to be put in this position."

"You still had a choice."

Liis finally chimed in. "Abby only knew because I told her. And I asked her to be discreet about the information she had."

Travis looked down at Liis, surprised. "You told her?"

Several seconds passed before Liis could look Travis in the eyes. "Years ago."

His shoulders sagged. "So every time I left town and lied straight to her face about where I was going … the elaborations … she knew?"

"She was in a dark place," Liis said. "She was sure you were having an affair. She knew you were lying, she just didn't know about what. Telling her saved your marriage."

"Then why not tell me?" Travis said, fidgeting. "You let me continue lying to her?"

"If you told her, the FBI would have rescinded the agreement. She had to have a valid reason for coming up with it on her own. The information she gave you on Mick was more than a satisfactory explanation, and the Bureau knows Abby is an extremely intelligent individual."

"Don't speak analytics to me, Liis." He closed his eyes and shook his head, rubbing the back of his neck. "She's being released from the hospital today. I need to get back there."

The twins sat down, whispering about the new development. They had been lying, too, and had agonized over it for years, but Thomas and Travis's had overshadowed their secret, giving them an unexpected easy out. It reminded me of the time my sister Finley had snuck out and stole our parents' car. She had no plans. She just wanted them to notice her for once instead of catering to my cries for attention. When they realized what she'd done, they were too busy hiring an attorney to get me out of trouble for setting fire to my father's partner's vacation home to be angry with her. She didn't even get grounded. My antics made anything less than arson seem trivial.

Trenton noticed the twins were occupied and used the opportunity to rush Travis, slamming him against the wall. Seconds before their collision, Liis scooted her chair into the corner, pulling Jim and Mr. Baird with her. She had quick reflexes, just like I imagined an FBI agent to have. The other agents rushed into the room, but Travis held up one hand, signaling for them to back off.

Trenton's face was wet with tears. "Why did you have to kill Benny, Travis? Why didn't you stay with Thomas and protect him if you knew he was in danger?"

"I didn't know, Trent," Travis said, staring into his brother's eyes. "I didn't know. And even if I did, I would have stayed here to protect my family."

Trenton gripped Travis's collar and shoved him against the wall. Travis didn't even attempt to fight back, and I wondered why. "He was your family. He helped raise you, Travis. You just let him face that alone?"

"I'm sorry," Travis said sincerely. "I'm so fucking sorry, Trent. You have no idea how bad I feel about this, or how much worse I'll feel later when … It's not fair. Maybe it should've been me."

Trenton released Travis's shirt and took a few steps back.

Shepley patted his back. "It could have been you. It could've been Abby, or James, or Jess, or Ezra, or Mare. And we would've never known it was coming."

Tyler tucked his chin with a confused look on his face. "What are you saying, Shep? That what happened to Thomas was lucky for the rest of us?"

"Of course not," Shepley said.

"He's saying what happened to Thomas shouldn't have been our warning," Trenton said. "We should have all been notified and ready the moment Travis was embedded in the fucking mafia as a spy."

Tyler wrinkled his nose. "You're going to blame Travis for this? He didn't ask for this. He's just playing the hand he was dealt, man. So stow that shit before you say something else you're gonna regret."

"He's not going to regret asking questions," Shepley said. "If we had done that years ago, maybe we wouldn't be planning a funeral."

Travis seemed hurt that Shepley was taking Trenton's side. "Really?" Travis asked.

Shepley patted Trenton on the shoulder, showing his allegiance.

"You're my best friend," Travis said in disbelief.

"You're wrong on this one, Trav. We have a right to be upset about what you've done," he said.

"If you don't mind," Jim said, scooting his chair to the table again. "I've got some plans to make. If you do mind, you're going to have to leave. This funeral's not gonna plan itself."

"No," Mr. Baird said, straightening his tie with a nervous twitch in his eye. "No, it is not."

The boys sat down, and Jim looked each of them in the eye. "Not another word. I mean it."

"Yes, sir," they said in unison.

"Ladies?" Jim said, looking at America, Camille, and Falyn.

They all nodded.

It felt strange to me, even after a decade of sobriety, not to be included in the calling out of bad behavior. It was even stranger to feel proud and validated.

"Okay, then." He turned another page, and Liis pulled her chair next to his, looking over urns like nothing had happened.

# CHAPTER TWENTY-ONE

## CAMILLE

JIM CHOSE TO HAVE THE FUNERAL at the high school auditorium. The attendance would be too many people to fit into any of the small churches in Eakins. People were standing against the wall in the back and along the sides. Fellow Eastern alumni, former high school friends, and football teammates. The stage looked like a mini botanical garden, surrounded the urn with plants, sprays, and bouquets. One wreath wore a sash that said son, another father, another husband. I was sitting in the second row directly behind Liis, unable to stop watching her for any reaction. She sat stoic, and the few times she looked back to scan the crowd in disbelief, she looked uncomfortable and a bit ashamed.

Sniffling and muffled conversation filled the silence, the acoustics amplifying the crowd's pain. It was unbelievable how many knew and cared about Thomas. Even his FBI colleagues were present, taking up the three rows behind the family. The director sat behind Travis and reached up to pat his shoulder.

Jack stood up and, with Shepley's help, carefully climbed the stairs to the stage. With folded notebook paper in hand, he stood behind the podium. The paper crackled as he unfolded it, and then he cleared his throat.

"My brother asked me to read this letter for him. I'm not convinced I can get through it myself, so please bear with me." He fished his glasses from his jacket pocket and placed them on his face, pushing them up the bridge of his nose.

"My dearest Thomas," he began, pausing for a moment before he continued, "you are my firstborn, and that means you and I spent quite a bit of time together alone before your brothers came along. We bonded in a unique way, and I'm not sure … I'm not sure how I'll move on with my life without you. But I've said that before.

"I remember the moment you were born. The first time I held you in my arms. You were a tiny giant. Your arms flailed, and you screamed, and I was both filled with pride and terrified. Raising another human being is a harrowing responsibility, but you made it easy. When your mother died, and I was overwhelmed with my own grief, you took over. And that was an easy transition for you because when the twins were born, you used to insist on being the other pair of arms to hold either Taylor or Tyler. You used to follow Trenton around with a Kleenex, and you orbited Travis like he would break at any moment. I've never seen a young boy fawn over babies the way you did, and I was looking forward to watching you do that with your daughter.

"When you were eleven, I took you hunting. We'd shot guns before, and you were pretty good at it, but that particular morning was rainy and cold, and you decided you'd wait in the truck. I trudged out to my favorite spot and wiped the rain out of my eyes for two hours, chilled all the way to the bone, wishing you were bearing that miserable, foggy morning with me. I didn't see a single doe. And then I heard a shot, and then another. I gathered my gear and ran back to the truck as fast as I could, nearly slipping in the mud when I stopped to see you inspecting your kill. I'll be damned if you didn't get your first buck that year—a twelve-point, nearly dry and warm while I'd been sitting in the freezing rain. I should have known then that you knew what you were doing; that you had your mother's intuition and not just her eyes.

"When Diane passed, you never asked me what to do, you just knew, as if she were whispering in your ear. You rocked Travis to sleep, you calmed Trenton, and you dressed the twins in matching outfits like your mother used to. You combed their hair and made sure they were clean for school, no matter how many times you had to scrub them before you led them onto the bus. You took care of everyone else, and then you went and did what you wanted to do, and I can't be prouder, son. I really can't.

"I wish we could have had one more evening at the dining table with a hand of cards, talking about the world and how amazed you are by the mother of your child. I'd do anything to listen to you talk about your future and your job, even if you couldn't tell us everything. I don't know why this happened to you, the most careful of us, the surest of his footing, the most prepared. You were the strongest. But thinking about you finally able to hug your mom's neck again gives me comfort in a way I can't describe. I know her death was hardest on you, not because of the burden you embraced, but because out of all the boys, you'd loved your mother the longest. You never let that get in the way of what she'd asked you to do, though, to take care of your brothers. You never let her down, not even now. I would give anything to take your place so you can be here with your wife and raise your daughter because I know you'd be a damn good father, just as you were a good son. I'm going to miss you as much as I've missed your mother, and I know just how much that's going to hurt.

"Thank you for keeping our family together and safe until the end, and thank you for ignoring everything and everyone else—even yourself—to do what was right. I knew you long enough to know you don't make a decision without good reason, and this is no different. I've adored you since your first breath. You were a good boy, and a fine man, and this family will rise up again to be our very best in your honor."

Jack pressed his lips together and then folded the paper, tucking it into his jacket pocket. He took off his glasses, and Shepley walked him across the stage as the tune of one of Thomas's favorite songs began humming through the speakers.

Jack sat next to his brother, and they comforted each other while the music played. Even Abby and Travis were crying. Abby hugged Liis, while Travis rocked Stella, touching his cheek to her forehead, tears dripping from the tip of his nose. I intertwined my fingers with my husband's trembling hand, squeezing hard. He wiped his cheeks, sucking in a breath between quiet sobs. As I scanned the faces of our family, we looked so broken, so lost. My breath faltered, watching a local pastor take the stage. He would attempt to offer comfort and pray for our loss, but nothing would take away the pain. Not even God. I looked at Trenton, watching him let his tough-guy persona fall away in front of a huge crowd without a second thought. It was heartbreaking to watch men fall apart—men who could face anything else without flinching. Now, pain flooded in with their every breath, and I sat in the midst of Thomas's brothers, wishing I could take their pain away, wishing mine would somehow disappear. It was too much to process. The music only made it hurt worse, so I decided to feel nothing, the way I did when I was little and my father was hitting my mother.

Several cars were parked in the drive, spilling out down both sides of the street in front of Jim Maddox's home, just as I'd pictured. As the news of Thomas's death spread, more people would arrive, bringing casseroles and sweet memories.

I swallowed, bracing myself for condolences. Jim was the father who would bury his first-born. Liis was the widow. I was the sister-in-law and the ex-girlfriend. I felt like my grief ran deeper than Falyn's or Abby's, and that spawned guilt. My stomach sank, and my nose burned. There was nothing I wanted to do less than walk into the house and play the part of supporting wife and sister-in-law and ignore that Thomas was also my first love, that we had shared a bed more than once, and we had almost moved in together. He had loved me, and I would have to pretend none of that existed out of respect for his wife and my husband.

Trenton squeezed my hand. "I know," he said simply. With two words, he set my mind at ease, expressing both understanding and unconditional love. He'd forgiven me the night before for my lies and omissions. It wasn't okay, he pointed out, but it was understandable, and he loved me anyway.

A black sea of friends and extended family milled about the house, trudging over the carpet Diane had chosen, through the rooms Thomas had once played in, and where they were once a complete family that death hadn't touched. This was why Diane had made Jim walk away from the police force. This was why she made him promise not to let the kids follow in his footsteps. Once Death took Diane in its arms, Jim and the boys have all been waiting for it to come for them. It became real then, a tangible thing, because it didn't just happen to someone else. It happened to *her*. Their everything, their sunshine, their constant. And then she was a memory that faded with each passing day. Trenton had said he's struggled to remember the sound of her voice and the exact color of her eyes. The moment she'd passed, they had seen Death, and Death had seen them.

Taylor and Tyler were sitting around the dining table in front of homemade dishes and a stack of clean plates. Their wives sat next to them, attempting to help them carry the pain. Because it wasn't going away. It would never go away. No matter how many times they yelled, threw punches, or lost their tempter, they couldn't win.

Ironically, Travis was taking it the best. He was making sure the brothers had water or beer, and that they were comfortable with the number on the thermostat. Trenton and Shepley were still angry with Travis, and the twins were still on his side, but they couldn't fight one another today. They needed each other to get through it.

Abby stood out from the rest in a muted blue dress, sitting in the corner where Liis had been a few days before, glaringly without Carter. I watched as she fussed with her dress, tugging at the too-tight parts and pulling at the square neckline to cover the bulging breasts of a new mother.

"You look beautiful," I assured her.

She rolled her eyes. "Thank you. It's tighter than I thought it'd be, but I didn't really have anything for the occasion."

"It's perfect," I said. "I have a lot of black. You should have called."

"Nothing in your closet is going to fit me right now," she said.

"I'm actually a little surprised Travis isn't scrambling over here to keep you covered."

Travis had been known for complaining when Abby wore something too revealing or too tight, aware of his own jealousy. In the beginning, he was trying to be proactive to avoid a fight. But after they were married, something changed, and Travis wasn't as sensitive. Still, Travis unaffected by the overabundance of cleavage was serious progress.

"Good for you," I said, crossing my arms and sitting back. The somber faces in the room reminded me why we were gathered at Jim's, and the sickness that had settled in my stomach in the last week had returned. It wasn't just grief. Something was off, and I couldn't quite figure it out. Travis and Liis were leaning on each other quite a bit, and Abby—though typically stoic—didn't seem as affected by Thomas' death. "Abby," I said. "If you knew something else ... about Thomas ... you'd tell us, right?"

Abby sighed. "When I left the hospital without my son, I cried for a full hour. I didn't want to, but I had to, so I did. I left him there alone to come here to be with family. And I'll go straight back to the hospital when this is over. I've done that every day for nearly a week. Hold my son, careful of the wires and tubing attached to him. Worry, enjoy my time with him, feel guilty being away from the twins, and then tell him goodbye, cry, and leave."

I waited for her to make her point, but she didn't seem to have one. I took that as her way of telling me my question was inappropriate, and she was just going to talk about what she wanted.

"He's doing better, though?" I asked.

"Getting stronger every day. We're hoping he can come home next week."

"You're a good mom. I know it's hard."

"Having your heart split into three pieces, walking around vulnerable outside my body? Some days it's torture. There are no words to describe how frightening, wonderful, awful, and exhausting it is. Worrying seems like second nature. It's a part of me because I love them so much, even before they were born, that if something bad happened to them, it would be worse than death. I hear about children dying, and I find myself apathetic because if I think about it too much, I'll break down. People say it's every parent's worst nightmare. It's not a nightmare. You wake up from nightmares."

"Motherhood sounds ... lovely," I said.

"You'll see," Abby said, wiping her wet cheeks.

I wrinkled my nose. "I'm not sure I want to."

Travis walked toward us, having just said goodbye to someone on the phone. He tapped the display and dropped the sleek tech into his suit pocket. "NICU says he just had lunch. He's an animal ... Hey, Cami."

"Hey," I said.

"Where's Trent?" he asked.

"I think I saw him go into the living room," Abby said.

"Straight to Dad," Travis said, sitting down with us. He picked at a hangnail on his thumb. "He's always been a daddy's boy."

"Don't pretend you aren't. That you all aren't," Abby smirked.

"Not Thomas," Travis said. He seemed to catch himself before saying anything more. Abby grabbed his hand and calmed him with a shushing noise she might make to her children. "It will be over soon," she whispered.

I sunk back into my seat, the muscles in my face feeling tired, my eyes raw, and my sinuses congested. Trenton had placed tissues and trash cans in every room, and the twins were making sure to empty and replace the trash bags regularly. I blew my nose, making a horrid sound, and tossed it into the can next to me, hugging the box of Kleenex to my waist. We all had different currency on different days. In an airport, I saw people hunting for a chair close to outlets or choosing to sit on the floor. Today, people congregated next to the booze or the tissues.

I held onto the thin cardboard box like a lifeline. It was the only thing to hold. Trenton was in the living room comforting Jim, and I was at odds with my sisters-in-law, still pissed they had taken sides. I guess I had, too, but it was inevitable. We would choose when it came to the brothers and Shepley fighting, except Ellie Peace-and-Love. She remained disgustingly neutral, while Falyn was pissed at Trenton, as was Abby. Trenton and Shepley were angry with Travis. Even though everyone was civil during the funeral, I couldn't help but wonder what would go down afterward. I planned a quick escape so Trenton wouldn't say or do anything else he'd regret later.

"It's not going to be over," I muttered. "Not if he's gone."

Abby craned her neck at me, and I could tell she was holding her tongue.

"He doesn't feel gone," I said, feeling my eyes fill with tears. I looked at her. "Is he really gone?"

Abby glanced around before she spoke. "Cami, I'm just going to tell you this once. Whatever you're doing, stop. If anyone heard you … it could be very upsetting to a lot of people."

"I need to know," I begged, feeling my lips tremble.

The wheels began to turn, and then Abby faced me, suddenly angry. "What do you mean he doesn't *feel* gone? His future wife is sitting next to Jim. You're not it," she hissed.

"Pidge," Travis warned.

I was taken aback by her sudden vitriol. "I still care about him. What happened between us wasn't just erased because we went in different directions," I said.

Abby seemed to be increasingly concerned about the volume of my voice. "I'm sure this is confusing for you, but you didn't just go in different directions, Cami. You married his brother. He moved on. You're not the grieving widow, as much as you want to be."

"Abby," Travis said.

She sat back in her seat, crossing her arms. "I knew she was going to make today about her. She's appropriated Jim, Trenton's miserable over their infertility, and now, she wants everyone to acknowledge that she loved Thomas first."

"I would love for you to visit more," I said.

"You don't live here," Abby said, indignant. "You've got balls welcoming me to Jim's home. I've been in this family longer than you have."

"I'm not making Trent miserable. He wants a baby just as much as I do," I said, ignoring her response to touch on one of her original points.

"But he seems to live life between pregnancy tests, unless he's trying to show you how miserable he is."

"I did love Thomas," I said finally.

"He's marrying Liis," Abby snapped. "I'm sure you feel you have a right to feel like you've lost just as much as she has, but she's in there holding his daughter. Have you even once gone to her to express your sympathies?"

I stuttered over my words. I wasn't expecting a full-on attack. I wasn't sure where Abby's contempt was coming from, but it had been building up for a long time. "I just didn't … I don't want to make her feel awkward."

"If you think for one second that Liis sees you as anything but Thomas's sister-in-law, you're wrong. I promise you there is nothing to feel awkward over."

She couldn't have said things more hurtful. I pressed my lips together and looked down, covering my nose with a tissue.

"Baby," Travis said, cupping his wife's shoulders. "Ease up."

"Cami?" Trenton said, walking toward us.

"Oh, fuck," Travis whispered.

He kneeled in front of me, waiting for me to speak. "You need a hug, baby doll?"

I wiped my nose and eyes and looked up with a small smile. "It's just sad," I said.

Trenton combed one side of my hair back with his fingers. "Yeah. C'mon. Dad's asking for you."

I stood, leaving Travis and Abby alone. She had never spoken to me that way before, and my mind was already racing for excuses. She'd just had a baby, her hormones were out of control, Carter was at the hospital alone while she was here to mourn Thomas and support Travis. Maybe she didn't mean any of it. Maybe she was lashing out. But it wasn't like Abby to lose her cool, especially without provocation.

Trenton guided me to the living room, and I looked over my shoulder at Abby. She already looked ashamed. Travis was comforting her, but their expressions were different from everyone else's in the room. My eyes drifted to the urn on a shelf, the one we were told held Thomas's ashes, hoping to God they were keeping something from me and that my instinct was right. As Jim came into view, I held my breath. He was hunched over, the bags under his eyes swollen and weighing down the rest of his face. Surely, if it were all a cover-up, they would tell him. They wouldn't let him think his son was dead.

Jim's ice water was nearly full, so I picked the tall glass off the side table next to his recliner and prompted him to take a drink. He took a sip and then handed it back. "Thanks, sis."

I sat on the floor next to him, rubbing his knee. "Hungry?"

The casserole dishes that filled nearly every inch of the dining table had barely been touched. A week before, the Maddox boys would have torn through it all, but the only people eating were the kids. Everyone else lumbered around like the walking dead with a wine glass or tumbler in their hands.

Jim shook his head. "No, thanks. You doing okay? You need anything? I haven't seen you in a while."

I smiled, not feeling so much like the monster Abby had made me out to be just moments before. I took care of Dad, and I could see that he was comforted when I was around. He knew I would take care of him. Abby could say what she wanted, and maybe part of it was true, but I was a Maddox, and the only thing that mattered to me was the way Jim and Trenton saw me.

I nodded and stood, watching as extended family cleared an area of the couch closest to Jim. Liis sat in a folded chair on the other side, holding her sleeping newborn. Stella was beautiful—one-half Liis, with her almond-shaped eyes, dark, straight hair, and pouty lips, and one-half Thomas. Her eyes still had a sheen of blue, but beneath I could tell she would have hazel green eyes like her father.

Trenton squeezed my hand, noticing that I was staring at the baby. Part of me felt obligated to look away and spare his feelings, but another demanded that I experience my feelings honestly so I could grieve like anyone else.

"She's beautiful," I said to my husband.

"Yes, she is."

"It was a beautiful service," a cousin said to Liis. The elderly woman patted Stella's back, her fingers lingering on the navy and gray dress. "She looks so pretty."

"Thank you," Liis said, holding Stella close to her chest. I'd never seen folded dress socks or Mary Janes so tiny, and her diaper was covered with frilled, navy blue bloomers.

Val approached Liis, leaning down to whisper in her ear. Liis' eyes widened a bit, and then she relaxed, even managing a small smile. Val flashed her a quick glance of a text message, and then tears fell down Liis's cheeks.

Travis and Abby came straight over, and they decided to take the conversation into the next room, helping Liis gather the baby's things before scurrying off to talk.

"That was … odd …" Trenton said.

I grabbed my husband's hand, pulled him to stand, and then walked down the hall and out the back door. Jim had decided to wait until everyone left before spreading Thomas's ashes and warned he would likely wait until just before the boys left. He was in no hurry to do something so final and needed a few days to breathe after the funeral.

"What is it?" Trenton asked.

I didn't stop until we were under the shade tree in the farthest corner of the backyard, near the fence. The boys had carved their initials into the bark; the only difference was the middle letter. The grass was bare in some places, already dehydrated from the Illinois heat. The temperatures were hovering in the mid to high nineties, and the buzzing of the cicadas took the place of the birds. It was too hot to sing, too hot to move. The only breeze felt more like a heater blowing on us than a reprieve. But there we were, outside in a black dress and suit. Beads of sweat had already formed along Trenton's hairline.

"Something's not right," I said.

"I know."

"You know?"

Trenton loosened his tie. "Something's off. Travis is acting weird. Abby and Dad are acting weird."

"Do you think he knows?" I asked.

"Knows what?"

"The reason why Travis is acting so weird. He knew the twins were hotshots. He knew about Travis and Thomas. Maybe he senses something is off, too."

Trenton shook his head. "I dunno. Maybe."

"They wouldn't …" I hesitated. "You don't think they would …"

"Lie again?" Trenton muttered. "Yeah, I do."

I tucked my chin and wrinkled my nose, feeling silly for even saying it aloud. "But not about … I mean, you don't think Thomas is alive somewhere, getting updates about his grieving family."

"No," Trenton said. "They wouldn't do that to Dad. I know you want him to be alive. I do, too. They've lied, but they wouldn't do that."

"You heard them at the hospital. Liis isn't going to testify. Mick is missing, so he's unable to testify. The Carlisis were seen leaving town. Maybe this was all to keep anyone else from getting killed."

I could see in Trenton's eyes that he wanted to believe my theory, but even after revealing the truth about Thomas and Travis, to think they were capable of causing our family so much agony was farfetched at best.

"Dad isn't in great health. Travis wouldn't risk it."

"Would Dad want him to?" I asked.

Trenton mulled it over. "Yeah. He probably would."

"Would Thomas and Travis know that?"

Trenton's eyes bounced from one point on the ground to another. "Yeah, but …" He sighed, at his limit. "I can't hope for that, Cami, c'mon! If it's not true and Tommy is gone, I'll lose him all over again."

"Keep your voice down," I said, reaching for him.

"Why?"

"Because if it's true, this is all to show the Carlisis that they don't have to threaten our family anymore. If it's true, then someone is still watching."

# CHAPTER TWENTY-TWO

## ABBY

I READJUSTED AGAINST THE HARD WOOD of the NICU nursery rocking chair, thanking the nurse when she brought a folded blanket to cushion me. Carter had a few neighbors, meaning we'd made friends with two sets of new parents. Scott and Jennifer's daughter Harper Ann was born five days ago, and she was experiencing a setback. She'd been struggling hour to hour for the last twelve hours. Jason and Amanda's son Jake had been born two days after Carter. We were afraid he wasn't going to make it, but he'd recovered and was nearly as big as our son was. Carter was nursing consistently and gaining weight, so he'd be able to move to the step-down unit soon, and then we'd be able to take him home.

"Morning," Scott said, passing me to greet Harper Ann. Even though the couples had children in the NICU, Travis had insisted on a full background check. Scott was a former Marine; a half-inch thick, long, curved scar left a crevice just above his ear toward the back of his head, disrupting his silver hair, a scar from a head wound he'd survived in Afghanistan. Travis felt better leaving us alone when Scott was there, and lately, that was a lot.

I nodded to him, patting Carter's back. Carter let out a strong burp, and Scott and I chuckled.

Scott scrubbed his hands in the sink and then leaned over Harper Ann's bed. "Hi, baby." She stirred, and a wide grin spread across Scott's face. "Mommy's on her way up. Yes, she is. She's talking to Gramma and the doctor. She can't wait to see you. She talked about you last night until she fell asleep."

I rocked Carter, turning to smell his hair. Dark, wispy sprouts covered his head, and I loved to feel them against my cheek. It was a new experience, nuzzling one baby at a time instead of two. Jessica and James were my first try at motherhood, and they were so much work that I didn't have many instances to just sit and enjoy them. Carter was quiet for the most part and loved to be held. We snuggled every day, and the nurses said he'd fuss just before I arrived, seeming to know I would be there soon. Once he was in my arms, we were both content.

I hummed to him, trying to imprint the memory in my brain; his smell, how small his diapered tush felt in my hand, the length and softness of his fingers. The shape of his fingernails. The way his lashes fell against his cheeks when he slept. The sound he made when he breathed. He would be bigger tomorrow. I didn't want to forget.

"Well, hi there," Shelly said, greeting Travis.

I felt my eyes widen, and I tried not to wake Carter in my excitement while I watched the nurse help Travis with his sterile gown. I leaned forward as my husband bent over to kiss me. He pecked my lips and then rushed over to the sink to scrub his hands. He seemed animated. He nodded to Scott and then returned to me, holding out his hands for our son.

I giggled. "Did you miss him?"

"Gimme," he said.

We traded places, and Travis cradled Carter. No matter how much Carter grew every day, he still looked tiny in Travis's enormous arms.

Travis pushed back gently with his toes, rocking our son while gazing down at him.

"You've been gone three days this time," I said. "Don't forget, Lena isn't here to help."

"Tying up loose ends," he said.

"You have good news?"

He looked up at me. "It's done."

I crossed my arms across my middle, hesitant to hope. "What's done? Like permanent done or investigation is done so we start the trial process."

"A few of them will go to trial."

"And the rest?"

"It was the last raid, Pidge. There aren't any Carlisis left. The rest are soldiers. Grunts. They're being held without bail. They'll be in the system for a year before they're sentenced, and then they'll spend thirty years in prison by the time they serve for every count."

"And Mick?" I asked, feeling my throat tighten.

"Immunity, as we promised. As long as he stays away."

I nodded, satisfied. "And now?"

Travis cleared his throat. He was getting a little emotional. It had been five weeks since the funeral. Liis had been staying with us, and it was difficult watching her wait.

"He's coming home."

"Today?"

Travis nodded.

"Does Liis know?"

"I thought we'd let him surprise her."

My hand flew up to my mouth. "And your dad? What about the twins?"

"They're on their way home."

They were just here two weeks before, visiting more often to check on Jim. The funeral had taken a toll on him. He'd lost weight and had grown more frail every day. Travis's smile faded as he watched our sleeping son, the burden of the truth on his mind. He was here, but he was a million miles away, worrying about his father's and brothers' reactions.

"They'll understand," I said, kneeling in front of Travis.

"No, they won't," he said, not taking his eyes off Carter. "They'll hate us."

"Maybe for a while, but they'll get over it. They have to."

Travis looked up at me with tears in his eyes. "Was it worth it?"

"It probably seems all for nothing now that everything is fine, but before, when we weren't sure? It happened exactly the way we'd hoped. They backed off. It bought us time to form a plan without being targeted." I touched his arm. "It was a good plan. Difficult from start to finish, but it worked."

Travis nodded and then returned his gaze to our son. "We have to go soon. He's on his way."

"On his way here? Now?"

"He hasn't seen Stella since she was two days old, Pidge. He can't wait any longer."

I couldn't argue with that. "When?"

Travis looked up at the clock on the wall. "Two hours."

"Oh, my God. He's really coming home."

"He's really coming home."

Liis was standing over Carter's crib, her daughter surrounded by blues and greens. Stella had been using Carter's nursery while they were staying with us. I was glad. Stella's presence made my son's room feel less empty.

Liis tucked her dark hair behind her ear. It was six inches shorter than the last time I'd seen her, just a couple of hours before.

"You cut your hair," I whispered, feeling stupid for stating the obvious.

She turned to me flatting the strands against her head with her palm. "Yeah." Her eyes filled with tears.

"What's wrong?" I asked. I'd never seen Liis cry until she arrived at Jim's to tell us all the news. Now, it seemed she cried every time she spoke. "You don't like it?"

"I just," she sniffed. "I wasn't thinking. I'll look so different when Thomas sees me. Stella will look so different. If I'd kept it the same, it wouldn't be so shocking for him."

"He'll love it," I said, reassuring her. "He will. You don't look that different. He'll notice, but he'll love it."

She turned toward the crib. "Maybe it will grow out by the time he comes home."

"I hope not," I said. She looked at me. "Your hair grows slow."

She breathed out a laugh. "True."

I gestured for her to follow me to the living room, and she complied, looking back at Stella once more before padding to the hallway. She swiped the baby monitor receiver off the dresser and then closed the door behind her, leaving it open a crack. Val was in the kitchen, the potato chip sack crinkling as she fished inside it. Agent Hyde was standing by a living room window, always on alert.

"Chill, Hyde," I said. "You're making me nervous." Her dark eyes narrowed, and then she returned to her watch. She pulled the curtain back and then shifted her stance, readying to act. I realized she wasn't just her usual overcautious self. "What is it?"

"I don't know," Hyde said.

Travis checked his phone and then patted Hyde on the back. "Calm down. We've got a team headed this way."

"Why?" Hyde asked.

Travis shrugged. "Got some news they want to tell us in person, I guess."

Hyde and Liis traded glances, and Liis took a step toward Travis. "Is it Thomas? Is it over? How did your trip go?"

"Trip went well. Maybe they're coming to congratulate me."

Travis's ability to lie had increased tenfold during his time with the FBI. The second year of our marriage, the guilt of lying to me was all over his face, but he got better at it. Just before I told him I knew the truth, I could barely discern a meeting from a raid. He had no choice but to learn quickly. Most undercover agents were away from home for months at a time, if not longer. Travis was hiding in plain sight. He'd already been offered a position with Benny, so he just had to say yes. The Carlisis knew that he would come home to Eakins often, but the downside was he also knew Travis had family—and how to control him.

Travis had been careful, but we knew it was only a matter of time before they found out. But the years passed, and Travis seemed to be untouchable. Soon, he was one of Benny's most trusted men, going from bodyguard, to shaking down local clubs, to advisor. The FBI watched with excitement as Travis climbed the ladder of one of the largest, most dangerous crime families in the nation. Travis got a promotion from within the FBI as well. Five years after his recruitment, Travis went from asset to agent, and five years later, Thomas was sure they'd gained enough evidence to nail Benny. He didn't factor in Benny's wife, Giada. She was a paranoid woman, and she didn't trust Travis. That was when the Carlisis learned the truth, and everything after that happened very fast. Thomas called to inform me that they'd lost contact with Travis, and it was very likely his cover had been blown. That night, Thomas said Travis was taken to an unknown location, but they would find him soon. The next night was our anniversary; the night Benny and a few of his men were killed. It could have been Travis. We were lucky that time, and I wasn't sure how much longer my luck would hold out.

I'd handed him intel on my father, and in return, Travis promised to never lie to me again. He looked me in the eye the night he came home, his eye swollen, his brow and lip cut, and told me he was okay, and I chose to believe him. It took him being run off the road and nearly murdered to admit that he'd been the one to pull the trigger.

Lying was the hardest habit to break, especially when we believed we were protecting those we loved.

Now, he was standing in our kitchen, skirting around the questions Liis and Agent Hyde were asking. I watched him speak half-truths without blinking an eye, and I wondered just how much he knew that I didn't. How many times he'd been able to keep secrets because I didn't want to believe he had any.

"Congratulate you for the trip?" Liis asked. "So it's done, then?"

"The only suspect we're missing is Giada. We can't connect her directly … yet … but we will."

"Giada Carlisi?" Val asked. "So we're not done. Because Giada has her own people, and the Bureau killed her husband and sons. She's a crazy bitch."

"We're done," Travis said.

"What about Giulia? Vittoria? Her bodyguard Chiara? What about Angelo's new wife?" Val said, her tone bordering accusatory.

"Angelo got married? When?" I asked. He was an uncompromising bachelor, married to the family. He was known to assault his girlfriends, and only one had stuck around more than a year. We had so many pictures of her battered body; I wondered how long she would stay. Then she disappeared. I wasn't sure if I should fear the woman who had finally tamed him or fear for her.

"We're currently unable to locate Coco," Travis said.

"Since when?" Val asked, seeming concerned.

"Since yesterday."

"Coco is Angelo's wife?" I asked.

Travis nodded, but he didn't look at me, a telltale sign he wasn't being completely honest.

"Then we're not finished," Val snapped. "Any loose ends equals unfinished. They are the wives of the Carlisis, and Chiara is a known hitman for Giada. What? They aren't dangerous because they're women? Tell me you're not that stupid."

Travis bristled. "We have it covered, Val."

"It's all or nothing," Val said, pointing at him. "Those words came from your mouth, Maddox."

"I know what I said."

"Then *why* are you being so careless now? *Why* would you … oh." Recognition flashed in her eyes, and she realized the rush. Thomas was in a hurry to get home, and no one could argue with that. Not even the director.

Liis covered her mouth, her eyes glossing over.

Agent Hyde put her hand on her holster, inching back from the kitchen window curtain with two fingers. "Incoming," she said.

Liis tried to run for the door, but Travis stopped her.

"Just wait," he said.

Agent Hyde relaxed. "It's not us."

Travis's brows pulled together. "Who is it?"

Hyde nodded toward the door. After two knocks, Trenton pushed through, leading Camille in by the hand. They instantly knew something was up, gazing around to the strange positions of everyone in the room.

"Fuck," Travis said, glancing out the window, and then tried to herd his brother out the door. "You have to go."

"What the hell?" Trenton said, slinking away from Travis's grasp. "Hi to you, too, spunk trumpet."

"Seriously, Trent," Travis said. "You can't be here right now."

"Why not?" Camille asked.

"We're having a family meeting," I said.

"We're not family?" Trenton asked, offended.

Travis sighed, and then raised both arms, pointing eight fingers at the door. "You have to leave, Trent! Now! We'll explain later, but for now …."

Something outside caught Hyde's attention, and she held up a finger. "Everyone quiet. Incoming."

Travis rolled his eyes and pulled Trenton to the side. "Whatever you see in a few seconds, just … try not to freak out. Let Liis have her moment."

"What do you mean?" Trenton asked.

"Just keep your fucking mouth shut for once," Travis growled.

"What's going on?" Camille asked me.

"You keep it together, too. This was supposed to be for Liis."

We waited behind the sofa, staring toward the door. Liis stood in the middle of the room holding the baby monitor in her trembling hand. The door opened, and Thomas stood in a white button-down shirt and navy slacks, freshly showered and shaven. He was breathing hard from running up our long drive. He stepped through the threshold, a wide grin on his face. Liis ran, throwing her arms around him, sobbing.

Trenton's knees buckled. Camille and Travis held him up for a few seconds before letting him fall to his knees.

Camille kneeled next to her husband. "I knew it, baby!" she said with a smile on her face. She kissed his cheek, rubbing his arm with her hand with excitement.

Trenton shook his head slowly, his mouth hanging open. "What the hell is going on, Travis?"

"We'll explain later," Travis said, watching his oldest brother with a smile.

Trenton looked up at Travis. "There's an *explanation*?" He stood and took a breath, preparing to throw a tantrum. Before a sound came from his mouth, Travis grabbed Trenton's shirt with both fists, dragging him into the kitchen. Camille and I followed, trying to calm them both in hushed tones.

Travis shoved Trenton's back against the refrigerator.

"Don't you fucking start," Travis said. "I know this was hard on you and unbelievably unfair, but Liis has sacrificed the most in all of this, and you're not going to ruin this for her. Do you understand me?"

Trenton tensed as if he might make a move but then took a deep breath. His eyes filled with tears, and betrayal replaced the anger. "You lied to us? He was alive this whole time, and you lied to us? Dad's health has gone down the shitter. How could you do that?"

Travis clenched his jaw and then released Trenton. "I didn't want to. If there were any other way, we wouldn't have done it. We had no choice, Trenton. The Carlisis left us alone long enough to form a plan, and it worked. We set a trap and staged a raid. We've brought them all in. Whoever's not in jail without bail is dead. Our family is safe."

Trenton shook his head, and then he walked out to the living room, waiting for Thomas and Liis to finish their moment.

Thomas looked at Trenton. "I hope one of these days you'll forgive me. Forgive us. I'm truly sorry for what I've put you through."

Trenton stomped over to his brother and squeezed him tight. Once they let go, he stormed out of the house to his truck. Camille was still standing still, stunned. She walked over to him, gently touched his cheek, and then reared back, slapping him hard. Thomas closed his eyes tight for a second and then met her eyes.

"I deserve that," he said.

"Yes, you do," she said, walking over to Travis.

I stood between them. "I don't care if he deserves it. If you hit my husband, I will slap you into next week."

Camille glared at me, then at Travis, and then followed her husband outside, slamming the door behind her. Stella wailed, and just as Liis turned to get her, Thomas held up his hand. "I'll do it." We followed him to the nursery, watching him from the doorway. Liis stood in front of us just a few steps, still wiping tears from her cheeks.

"Hi," Thomas said, his voice soothing and hushed.

Stella immediately stopped crying, looking up at her dad.

"Do you remember me?" Thomas asked. "Can I pick you up?" He reached in and lifted her into the air, taking a look at her while she stared at him. "You've grown so much. Practically a young lady now," he said, hugging her to him. He sniffed once, and Liis hugged them both.

Travis closed the door, kissing my forehead.

"Should we follow Trenton?" Val asked. "Make sure he doesn't tell the family?"

Travis shook his head, hugging me to his side. "He won't. He knows he wasn't supposed to be here."

Val was unhappy. "You think Giada won't do something drastic when she finds out Thomas isn't dead, after all? She's going to come for him. She's going to come for all of you."

"We'll be ready," Travis said.

Val narrowed her eyes. "You insane son of a bitch. You put your family through all that, and now, you're using Thomas as bait?"

I glared at Val. "That's one hell of an accusation." I looked at my husband, waiting for him to deny it. He didn't. "Travis. Tell me it's not true."

"You couldn't get a direct connection with Giada or the wives, so you're luring them in. You're hoping they take another shot at Thomas? Or Liis? Are you out of your damn mind?" Val seethed.

"Travis," I said, unable to say anything else.

"I—" he began, but I turned on my heels to find something to clean in the kitchen. The decision had already been made. I could hear him following closely behind. "Baby," he said. I stopped at the sink, and he grabbed my arm.

"Faking Thomas's death was enough, don't you think? Now, you're intentionally putting us all at risk? What if they don't go for Thomas? Or Liis? What if they come for you? What if they come for James or Jess?" I seethed.

"They won't."

"How do you know, Travis?"

"I … Pidge, please just trust me."

"How can I trust you if you're not being honest?" I turned on the sink and then turned it back off, flipping around to face him. "When were you going to tell me? After our house was sprayed with gunfire?"

"No," he said, stumbling over his words. I hadn't been angry with him for a long time, and he was unprepared for my reaction. "But I know who their target will be. We just have to find out when, and that should be soon."

"Your dad lost Thomas once. What do you think it will do to him if he loses him again?"

"He won't."

"How do you know?" I yelled, throwing the plate in my hand to the floor. It shattered, prompting Val, Hyde, Thomas, and Liis to rush in.

Travis breathed hard out of his nose. He glanced at Thomas, and then back at me. He was holding back, keeping secrets he didn't choose to keep. I could see the agony and conflict swirling in his eyes.

"It was my idea," Thomas blurted out. "It was my way of coming home early and drawing Giada and the wives out at the same time."

"If something goes wrong," I began.

"It won't," Travis said.

"Don't" I yelled, closing my eyes, "talk to me." I glared up at my husband. "Don't say another word unless it's the complete truth."

Travis opened his mouth to speak but then closed it, thinking twice. That only made me angrier, so I turned to grab the broom, hearing Thomas, Liis, and the agents leave the room.

"I love you, Abby. You have to know that. Our family's safety is my first priority. That's the truth." He took the broom and dustpan away from me. The glass scraped against the tile floor as he swept up my mess.

"You know I have your back, but Travis ... this is a terrible plan. It feels rushed because Thomas wanted to come home."

"It's not rushed, trust me," he grumbled, bending over to sweep up the glass. "They've been working on this since Thomas was well enough to stand."

"Even Liis?"

"Even Liis."

"Despite the likelihood of sounding like an insolent child, I'm still going to ask. Why does Liis get to know about these things and I don't?"

Travis stood, opened the cabinet, and let the glass fall into the trashcan. "She has higher security clearance than you do."

I frowned. "So now your honesty with your wife is based on security clearance? Are you fucking kidding me right now?"

"Baby," he said, reaching for me.

I stepped back.

He let his arms fall to his sides in frustration. "This is almost over. Can you be patient just a little longer?"

"Then what? You're lying to me about the next case?"

Travis sighed, walking away from me, and then coming back. "I'm sorry. I'm sorry that this is our life. The alternative is worse."

"Have you even asked them, Travis? Have you asked them to let you go? You've served your time. You've helped them close one of their biggest cases in the history of the Bureau. Enough. It's not a life sentence." Travis stared at me, unable to respond. "You don't want to leave."

"I love my job, Pidge. When I think about going back and being a personal trainer or having a nine-to-five in some cubicle, it makes me sick to my stomach."

"You love your job? More than you love your wife? Your children? Your brothers? Your dad? How many times have you lied to my face? How many times have you put us in danger? I ignored it all because it was part of a deal that would keep you out of prison, but can't you at least *ask*?"

"I suddenly realize how Dad must have felt when Mom asked him to quit the police department."

I arched an eyebrow. "But he did it."

"She was on her deathbed, Pidge," he said dismissively.

I reached over to grab his shirt. "If anything happens to our kids because of your need to play cops and robbers, so help me God, Travis."

"What? You'll leave? You're going to leave me because I love my job?"

"That's not it, and you know it! Don't you dare twist my words!" Fighting with him was almost an out-of-body experience. We hadn't argued like this since college.

"I'm not twisting your words! I'm afraid, Pidge. You've left me before for a very similar reason."

"And look. You went and did it anyway. Worked out for you. Now, you're hoping I'll keep turning a blind eye, but I won't. Liis chose this, but we didn't. *I* didn't! I don't want this for our kids anymore. I don't want to raise Carter alone while you're off fighting crime instead of being a father."

He pointed at the floor. "I'm a good father, Abby."

"You are. But you're choosing to keep working a job that takes you away, sometimes for weeks at a time."

"Okay," he said, lost in thought. "What if I work out of an office here? In Illinois?"

"Away from the glamorous organized crime unit?"

"I could get transferred. Liis knows people in the Chicago office."

"No more undercover work?"

"Just regular ol' investigating."

I thought about it for a few moments. "After this is over, you promise you'll put in for a transfer?"

"I promise."

I nodded slowly, still not sure what my decision was.

Travis walked over to me and wrapped me in his arms, kissing my hair. "Don't get mad at me. It freaks me the fuck out."

I pressed my cheek against his chest, wondering if what just happened was compromising or giving in.

# CHAPTER TWENTY-THREE

## AMERICA

"CAN YOU STIR THE GRAVY for me, baby?" Shepley asked, putting on oven mitts.

With a wooden spoon, I stirred the brown liquid in the pan, turning to smile at Jim, Jack, and Deana. Shepley's parents had visited Jim every day since the funeral; sometimes, they would stay for dinner, sometimes not. When Shepley wasn't exhausted after work, we would join them. Tonight, Shepley was making his famous meatloaf, Deana's recipe—that was, of course, also her late sister's, Diane's. Eating was comforting, but especially when the dish reminded him of his wife's cooking.

Shepley closed the oven. "Almost done."

"Smells good," Jim called from the dining room.

My cell phone buzzed, and I fished it out of the back pocket of my shorts. It was a text from Abby.

*We'll be at Jim's soon. Meet us there.*

I tapped out a reply.

*Already here. Cooking dinner.*

*Oh, good. Text me when you're finished. We'll wait.*

*For what?*

It took her a bit longer to respond.

*Until dinner is over.*

*There's enough for everyone but suit yourself.*

*Trust me. It's best if everyone eats first.*

*And what's that supposed to mean?*

*See you soon.*

I huffed, stuffing my phone back into my pocket.

Shepley glided by, plucking my phone out again and placing it on the counter. "How many times have I told you? Cell phones emit radiation. Do you want colon cancer? Don't put them in your pockets."

"Does anyone *want* colon cancer? What kind of question is that? First, I can't eat Cheetos, then I have to replace water bottles with glass containers because the bottles heated in the car causes cancer, and now, I can't put my phone in my pocket. You realize the sun causes cancer, right? Should we become cave dwellers?"

"Which is why I keep buying you that organic sunscreen," Shepley said, kissing my cheek.

"You're such a soccer mom," I grumbled.

"I'll take it," he said, leaving me for the dining room table.

I teased him, but I knew he feared going through the same thing his Uncle Jim and his mom had when they lost Diane. Once we had Ezra, he began reading about everything that could kill us and started forbidding us from eating certain things. He did it out of love, and of course, he was right, but pretending to be annoyed softened the frightening reality. We were getting older, and a few of our friends had already been diagnosed. Sometimes, it felt like the whole world was dying.

The front door swung open, and Taylor walked through, holding one of his kids in each arm. Falyn was behind him, carrying the luggage.

"Hey!" Shepley, Jim, and Jack said in unison. Shepley helped Jim to stand, and they bear hugged Taylor and the kids, then Falyn, with Tyler, Ellie, and Gavin not far behind.

"Oh, my God!" Taylor yelled. "It smells amazing in here!"

I turned the stove fire to low and wiped my hand on my apron, leaving the kitchen to hug the family. After everyone had said their hellos, Jim glanced around the room. "Where's Trenton?"

Tyler shrugged. "He hasn't been by today? I thought he'd be here. That's what he said earlier."

"I'll text him," Taylor said, pulling his phone from his back pocket.

I smirked at Shepley, gesturing to Taylor, and he rolled his eyes.

"I'm not married to Taylor, am I?" he said.

Everyone turned to my husband, and I snorted.

Taylor raised an eyebrow. "Eh?"

"Nothing," Shepley grumbled.

Falyn glanced around the room. "Is Olive not coming for dinner?"

"They're on vacation this week," Jim said.

Falyn's face fell. "Oh."

Jim looked at his watch. "They should be getting home later this evening."

Falyn's eyes brightened. "Oh! Well, that's … I'm really glad. I've missed her."

Jim nodded in understanding. We all knew Falyn looked forward to seeing Olive when she was in town, even if Olive had no idea she was actually part of the family instead of just Trenton's best friend.

We chatted about their flight from Colorado and Taylor and Tyler's new jobs at State Farm Insurance. Shepley couldn't resist making a joke about the State Farm khakis commercial. Ellie reminisced about working for the *MountainEar* magazine in Estes, and Falyn and the kids had just unpacked the last box back at home with Taylor.

The oven door creaked as Shepley opened it to pull out the meatloaf pan, I mashed the potatoes, and Ellie and Falyn set up the card table for the kids. Dining chairs scraped against the tile as the adults sat down at the dining table to eat.

Jim looked around. "Hasn't Trenton gotten home yet? Is Travis still out of town?"

I touched his arm. "We texted Trent. I'm pretty sure Travis is flying home today."

Jim shifted in his seat, uncomfortable.

Jack patted his brother's back. "They're fine, Jim."

I tried not to grimace. Thomas's death had taken a toll on Jim. His clothes were hanging off him, purple half-moons hung under his tired eyes, and he looked more frail than ever. He was constantly asking about the boys, calling each one every day to check on them if they didn't call him first. Most of them already knew to call during their lunch break to set his mind at ease.

Taylor checked his phone, chewing. "He texted back. He's at home. He can't make dinner tonight."

"Really?" I said, surprised. That wasn't like Trenton. He was at Jim's for dinner every night, even before the funeral.

Agent Wren approached the table.

"Wren," Tyler said between bites. "Have a seat. Have some meatloaf; it's my mom's recipe. Best damn meatloaf you've ever had, I promise you that."

"I don't know why we're cooking," Falyn said. "There are still stacks of casseroles in the freezer."

"Because your dad wanted Diane's meatloaf," Shepley said. "And what Jim wants, Jim gets."

Jim managed a smile, pushing his glasses up the bridge of his nose. Camille had bought him suspenders a few days before, and although Jim wasn't a fan, I thought he looked adorable.

Agent Wren touched his earpiece. "Yes."

"Yes, what?" I asked. "Who is that?"

Agent Wren ignored me, returning to his post in the living room. I glared at him, far beyond irritated with the secrecy. *What else didn't we know?* I glanced at my husband. "Why is he still here?"

"Who? Wren?" Shepley asked.

"What was that about? Are we"—I glanced back at the kids and then leaned in—"still in danger? Have we heard an update on where Travis is with the Carlisi case?"

Jim shook his head, picking at his plate.

"Not hungry?" Deana asked.

"It's very good," Jim said, looking apologetic. "I feel full pretty fast these days. No appetite, I suppose."

"Just try," Deana said. "It's Diane's," she lilted. "God, I miss her. I think she could've cheered you up."

"She could've," Jim said with a short chuckle. His smile faded. "She's with Tommy, now."

We finished dinner, and I served dessert—just a simple yellow sheet cake with chocolate frosting. The kids made the few pieces that were left disappear.

The front door swung open. "Hi, Maddoxes!" Olive said, appearing at the mouth of the hallway with her bright smile. She had a new bronze tan from her trip, making her teeth appear whiter and her freckles blend in. Her hair was even blonder than before, and Falyn beamed the moment she set eyes on her.

"Olive!" Falyn said, rushing over to hug her tight. She held her out at arm's length. "Holy crap, you look amazing. How was vacation?"

"It was good. Sort of sad. Mom acts like it's our last one. I keep telling her we'll have plenty, but she's a wreck." Olive pulled at the frayed edges of her shorts. She was wearing a white tank top and a flowing, short-sleeved kimono-esque top. We marveled at what a beautiful young woman she'd grown into. Woe to boys at Eastern who paid any attention to her—the Maddoxes would eat them for lunch. She'd already given up bringing home any boys to Trenton in high school. He was just too scary for any teenage boy to handle.

The twins and their wives had just finished cleaning off the table, and Jessica, James, and Ezra were nearly finished loading the dishwasher when everyone grew silent. The younger kids were just bugging us to play outside in the sprinkler when Wren began looking out the window and speaking in hushed tones into his earpiece.

"Keep the kids inside for now," Wren said to Shepley.

I helped him herd the kids into the kitchen, away from any window facing the street.

"Has Trenton changed his mind?" Taylor asked, frowning. He checked his phone again, and then set it on the counter.

A car engine grew louder outside, and I pulled Eli and Emerson closer.

"I've been instructed to ask you all to remain calm," Wren said. He glanced at Jessica and James. "We've got incoming."

"What the hell does that mean?" Shepley asked.

"Travis and Liis are in the drive," Wren said, irritated that he'd had to explain that much.

We all relaxed, waiting for a signal from Wren. None of us knew what was going on, but we were so used to being kept in the dark, it didn't seem so abnormal anymore to wait for something to happen.

The front door opened, and Travis, Abby, and Liis walked in, followed by Agent Hyde and Val. The door closed, and the moment Travis stepped into the kitchen, he was apologizing.

"Just, please hear me out. This is going to be difficult, and at first, you won't understand, but you will."

"What's going on, Trav—" Shepley began, and then Thomas stepped out from behind Agent Hyde.

A collective gasp filled the room.

Jim immediately began to whimper, and then he hobbled to his son, falling into Thomas's arms. The kids began to wail, and Hollis ran over, hugging his Papa and Uncle Thomas. Ellie and Falyn both covered their mouths, their cheeks wet with tears.

"You lied?" Shepley cried, consoling his parents.

"Why?" Tyler choked out.

"I don't care why," Taylor said, rushing to hug his brother. Tyler did the same, and then we all crowded around Thomas, hugging him and sobbing.

The living room was quiet except for the hushed humming of the ceiling fan and the hiss of the sprinkler outside. We comforted the kids and promised to explain later, sending them upstairs to play. They were hesitant but knew the grown-ups needed to sort it all out.

Olive remained downstairs, standing in the corner bouncing a fussy Stella and patting her back. Falyn stood next to her, trying to help. The rest of us were either on the couch or in dining chairs pulled from the table. Everyone's eyes were red and puffy from sobbing; Deana was still sniffing and pulling tissues from the box.

Thomas sat in a chair next to his dad, holding his hand. Jim was smiling; his relief permeated the room. The shock and relief from the others had faded, leaving the brothers confused and angry. Thomas looked prepared for anything, and I could tell he was sorry for the pain he'd caused before he'd ever said a word.

"You knew about this?" Shepley asked Travis.

"Yes," Travis said.

"Who else?" Taylor asked.

"I knew," Liis said.

The brothers' faces contorted in anger.

Tyler's face flashed red, one eye squinting. "You looked my dad straight in the eye, knowing his health, and told him his son had died?"

Liis nodded.

"She didn't want to," Travis said. "We didn't have a choice. There were too many people who could possibly make a mistake, and we were being watched. Closely."

"There had to be another way," Ellie said.

"There wasn't," Thomas answered. He squeezed Jim's hand. "I wish there was. I wish I didn't have to miss the first month of Stella's life, but we knew if we staged my death and Liis announced she wasn't going to pursue the case, that coupled with Mick's disappearance might cause them to back off."

"You did all of this for a *might*?" Tyler fumed.

"We had to act quickly. Hitmen were on their way to my house. They had already run Travis off the road thinking it was Abby. We needed to buy time. Maybe if we had more time to form a better plan, we could have thought of something better. Maybe moved you all to a safe house, but we didn't. They were in position to hit every one of you. Once they caught wind of my death, they backed off."

"Why didn't you fake Travis's death?" I asked.

Abby shot me a look. "Because he killed the men that came after him and walked away in front of a crowd of people."

"You knew about this, too, didn't you?" I said, seething. I'd never been so angry at Abby before.

"Yes," Thomas said. "And the agents we've been using for security and the director. That's it. No one else."

We all looked at one another, shaking our heads in disbelief. No one seemed sure how to feel—whether to be happy Thomas was alive or angry that they had put us through so much hell.

Wren touched his earpiece and looked out the window. "Sir," he began. Thomas stood and smiled. "It's Trent and Cami." He helped Jim up, and they walked outside to greet them. The rest of us followed.

Cami was standing outside the passenger side of her Toyota Tacoma, holding the door open and leaning in, trying to coax

Trenton out. She paused, turning to see us all staring at them. She walked up to Thomas and then hugged him, closing her eyes. I glanced at Liis. Olive was standing behind her, still holding Stella. It wasn't hard to understand their strange predicament, but for fuck's sake, I'd expect Camille to show some restraint.

"Okay," I said, approaching them. I pushed Thomas back, and he looked relieved. "You owe us a better explanation. You owe us an apology. All of you," I said, pointing at Travis, Abby, Liis, and the agents.

Thomas gestured to his colleagues. "Could you give us a minute?"

"Sir," Wren began.

"Please," Thomas said. It wasn't a request, and the agents understood and obeyed.

Camille tucked her silver hair behind her ear. "He's … It took me a long time to talk him into coming here. The only reason he agreed was so that we could check on Dad."

Thomas nodded, and Travis brought Jim forward. Trenton stepped out of the truck and walked over, trying his best not to look at anyone else but his father.

"You okay?" Trenton said.

Jim reached out to Trenton. Once he got a good grip on his shirt, he yanked him in for a hug. "You stop this. He's your brother. You may not understand why he did what he did, but you don't have to. That's not what's important." He released Trenton and looked around at his family. "What's important is that you have each other. I've said it a hundred damn times. Together, you boys are capable of anything. But you can't let those bastards tear us apart. That's what they tried to do with guns. Don't let 'em do it with lies."

Trenton couldn't bring his gaze up from the ground. Jim hooked his arm around Trenton's neck. "I'm okay, now that I know he's okay. Now, I need to know you're all okay. Hug your brother. Tell him you love him."

Trenton didn't move.

"Now, goddamnit," Jim commanded.

Trenton blinked, and then his eyes trailed up from the ground to Thomas.

"I'm truly sorry," Thomas said, his eyes glossing over. "You have to know I would never purposely hurt any of you. I had to take a bullet and leave my newborn daughter for five weeks to keep everyone safe, and by God, I did it. Because I love you. I'm sorry I got into this. If I could go back and change it, I would."

Trenton stared at his brother for a while and then looked at Travis.

"Trent," Travis said, shaking his head. He held out his hands. "I'm sorry, man. If we had another choice, I woulda taken it."

Trenton stumbled a few steps and then hugged his brothers. The twins joined in, too. A tear toppled over Jim's cheek, and the wives were a blubbering mess. An arm shot out from the huddle and grabbed Shepley, pulling him in, too. I covered my mouth, half crying and half laughing.

In the next moment, one of the brothers grunted, and Thomas flew out from the group holding his midsection. Travis and the twins separated, and Trenton went for Thomas.

"No!" Camille cried. "Trenton, stop!"

"That's your one," Thomas said, dodging a second swing from Trenton.

The twins looked at each other and smiled, flanking Thomas and attacking. Travis jumped in to fend off the twins from his oldest brother, and the once-hugging pile of Maddox boys was now swinging and bleeding with smiles on their faces.

"Oh! Lord!" Deana said, looking away.

Shepley held up his hands, trying to make them stop while ducking swings and dodging fists.

"Stop!" Ellie screamed.

"Taylor! Stop it!" Falyn said.

Taylor looked at his wife for half a second, only to get nailed by Travis in the jaw.

Falyn cupped her hand over her mouth, and Abby shook her head in disbelief. "You're idiots," Abby grumbled.

Tyler swung and hit Travis square in the mouth, and blood spattered Abby from forehead to waist. She simultaneously jumped, closed her eyes, and held her hands up, her fingers splayed.

Travis looked at Tyler. "That's your one." He licked the blood off his lip, unbuttoned his shirt, and handed it to his wife. "Just like old times."

I rolled my eyes. "Oh, gross."

The brothers finally slowed, standing with their hands on their hips, panting.

Jim shook his head, and Abby grinned, wiping the blood from her face. "Oh, those Maddox boys."

# CHAPTER TWENTY-FOUR

## THOMAS

ONE SIDE OF MY BUTTON-DOWN had been untucked during the brawl, so I pulled up the bottom hem and wiped the blood from my knuckles before reaching for my dad. I cupped his cheeks and looked into his eyes. He'd been crying happy tears since I'd walked into the house, and now, we were standing on the front lawn.

My brothers and I were covered in blood, dirt, and grass stains like when we were kids, playing outside and either fighting someone else or one another.

"I'm sorry I put you through that," I said.

Dad puffed out a breath. "You don't owe me an apology, son. You did what you thought was the best for the family." He put a hand on my shoulder. "I'm just glad you're home."

I brought him in for a hug, surprised at how much weight he'd lost since the last time I'd seen him. He coughed and then wheezed, letting me go to hold his fist to his mouth.

"Maddox," Val said, rushing toward me. "Headquarters just called. They found Lena. She's dead."

"What?" Abby shrieked. Tears spilled over her cheeks, and she grabbed Travis's shirt. "Our Lena?" She let him go and took a step back.

Travis held his wife. "She was undercover," he said, numb. "It happens."

"It *happens*?" she seethed. "She's dead, Travis! What happened?" Abby's eyes danced while she put together what information she had. "Her full name. Cocolina," she whispered.

She glared at Travis, her eyes wild. "Lena is Coco? The one you said the other day you'd lost her location?"

"We needed intel," Travis said, still processing the news. He looked at Val. "Did she go quickly?"

"Blunt force trauma and a gunshot wound to the head," Val said. She peeked at Abby and then continued, addressing only me. "We have reason to believe it was Chiara."

"Chiara is Mrs. Carlisi's bodyguard, right? Gi … Giada's?" Abby asked. "Why would you send her to the Carlisis, Travis?"

Travis's expression sagged. "It was her new assignment."

"You married her off to that monster?" Abby cried.

Travis looked at me, desperate. I nodded, and he spoke. "Her assignment was to gain the attention of Angelo Carlisi and to infiltrate the family. That's how we knew we would be safe once Thomas got home. She's been keeping tabs on them."

Abby's mouth hung open. "Lena was his new wife? Are you insane? He's an animal!"

"Was an animal," I said. "He's dead."

Abby jerked away from Travis, and he reached for her, but she pulled away again. Travis sighed. "She was his type, Abby. She spoke the language. She was the one."

"Well, now she's dead," Abby groaned. She looked down and away, unable to look Travis in the eyes.

"Did you not hear me?" Val snapped. "Giada and Chiara have been spotted in Eakins. Everyone needs to get inside."

I nodded. "Let's go. Everyone in—"

Dad narrowed his eyes, looking at the road, and then he lunged for me. "Everyone down!"

A slew of bullets pelted the front of the house, the vehicles, shattering the windows. Wren was already outside, aiming his handgun at the black Lincoln passing by. Hyde stood next to him, emptying her semi-automatic pistol's magazine before kneeling down to reload.

I scanned the yard, seeing my family on the ground. "Everyone all right?" I yelled. I looked at Dad, and he nodded. I patted him on the shoulder. "Once a cop …"

"Always a cop," Dad grunted, pushing himself up off the ground.

Stella began to wail, and Liis shrieked. "Olive?" Liis peeled our daughter from the pocket Olive had made between her body and the ground.

Falyn screamed, and rushed over, falling to her knees and grabbing at Olive's limp body. "Olive?"

One side of Stella's face and body was drenched from the crimson pool she'd been lying in on the ground. I reached down to touch Olive's neck to feel a weak pulse, growing more faint with every passing second. I held my wife and daughter close, glancing back at Val and Wren, who were on alert.

"Ew?" Trenton said, crawling over.

"Is Stella okay?" Olive whispered.

"Of course, she's okay, baby, you saved her," Trenton said. "That's what Maddoxes do."

Olive managed a small smile and then her face relaxed as if she fell asleep.

Falyn shook her. "Olive?" she cried.

Trenton sat back on his knees, touching his palm to his forehead. He looked up at me, and when I shook my head, he fell forward, holding Olive's ankles. "Oh, God, no. Please no. Please no!"

Camille sat next to Trenton, tears streaming down her face. She touched his back, not knowing what else to do.

"Someone call a fucking ambulance!" Falyn screamed. "Why are you just standing there? Do something!"

"She's gone," Liis said, sniffing.

Taylor sat behind Falyn, holding his wife while she rocked Olive and brushed back her daughter's stained hair. She let out a combination of a groan, growl, and scream, a sound of utter rage and devastation, one I was sure only a mother who had lost a child could make.

Ellie covered her mouth and then ran inside. Tyler followed her.

I gestured to Val. "Check on the kids."

Val nodded and jumped over the stairs to the porch, yanked open the door, and ran inside.

"Everyone inside!" Wren called. "They're coming back!"

Liis ran in with Stella, bringing Abby with her.

"Travis!" Abby called, but he stood next to me, pulling out his sidearm and getting in position.

"No!" Falyn wailed when Taylor tried to pull her away. "*No!*" Taylor struggled to pick up his wife and Olive's lifeless body, attempting to carry them both inside.

"Leave her," I commanded.

"Fuck you!" Falyn spat.

"I'll stay," Trenton said, looking down at his best friend.

Camille nodded, holding Trenton's hand and then Olive's, closing her eyes, pressing fresh tears down her face.

Taylor finally pulled Falyn away, wrestling her inside as she kicked and flailed, reaching for her daughter.

The Lincoln raced toward us. Chiara sat in the passenger seat, aiming a semi-automatic rifle. Vittoria, now a Carlisi widow, was behind the wheel. As the car came closer, I reached for my sidearm, but it was gone. Dad stepped out in front of me, holding up my gun and aiming it at the Lincoln.

"Dad, get down!" I yelled just as Chiara squeezed the trigger.

Bullets sprayed the yard and house again, but Dad continued to walk forward, shooting at the Lincoln once, twice, and a third time. One of his bullets hit the tire, and the Lincoln swerved, hit the drainage ditch, and cartwheeled into a boat and truck in the neighbor's yard across the street. The engine caught fire, and we stood, watching it burn.

Dad fell to his knees, and Travis and I yelled his name at the same time. As the fire burned in the background, we helped our Dad to the ground. I pressed my hands against the red circles growing larger than my palms and spreading across his shirt. He'd been hit twice in the chest, once in the abdomen.

My gaze met Travis's. He looked as panicked as I felt.

The rest of the family filtered outside, spread out and watching the chaos in disbelief. Trenton crawled over to Dad, and I realized he'd been shot in the calf. Falyn fell on her knees beside Olive, cradling her once again in her arms, her cries piercing the air as she suffered unbearable pain. Camille sobbed next to Trenton, Travis, and I. The twins came outside and rushed over.

Val was on the radio reporting the scene and requesting ambulances and the fire department. Hyde ran to the Lincoln, but the heat forced her back. She ran into the neighbor's home to see if anyone had been hurt and soon came outside waving both arms, signaling the house was clear.

"The ambulance is coming, Dad, hang in there," I choked out.

Dad smiled. "I'm pretty tired. And I'd really like to see your mom."

Travis let out a breath, his bottom lip trembling. Trenton used the heels of his hands to wipe his eyes, and the twins stood by, quietly crying.

Dad reached up to touch my cheek. "Stay together. Love one another. I mean it, damn it."

One side of my mouth curled up, and I felt a hot tear slide over my mouth and down to my jawline. "We love you, Dad."

"We love you," Travis said.

"Love you," Trenton whimpered.

"We love you," the twins said in unison.

"I love you," Camille cried.

"Thank you for being our dad," Abby said, managing a smile.

His gaze drifted to each of us, and then he whispered, "My heart is full." A single tear formed in the corner of Dad's eye, and fell away, running down his temple and pooling in his ear. He exhaled for the last time, and he stared into oblivion.

The summer breeze carried the plume of black smoke drifting up from the Carlisi's Lincoln into the yard, filling the neighborhood. Sirens wailed, matching the pitch of Falyn's cries, but the roar of the fire stifled both. The heat danced from the flames, creating waves in the air like an afternoon under the desert sun. It looked more like a war zone than the site of my childhood home, the grass soaking up the blood of the old and young.

Camille tore her shirt and tied it around Trenton's leg, but he barely noticed, holding Dad's hand to his lips. "Is he gone?"

I looked down, coughing out a sob, and my brothers did the same. My bloody fingers pressed against Dad's wrist, the absence of his pulse the only stillness amid the chaos surrounding us. He was gone.

# CHAPTER TWENTY-FIVE

## JIM

"JIM?" DIANE CALLED FROM THE KITCHEN. She was holding open the door of the icebox, frowning and looking beautiful in a black sweater and brown suede skirt with big, black buttons. "I think … I think we're going to have to call a repairman."

I couldn't help but smile, watching the two lines between her brows deepen. "What makes you say that, love?"

"Well, it's not that cold, and …" She opened the milk, took a sniff, and her face twisted. "Yep. Spoiled."

I chuckled.

"It's not funny! We just bought this house. How are we going to afford a repairman? What if he says we'll need a new icebox?"

"Then I'll work extra hours, and we'll buy a new icebox."

She closed the door and sighed, perching her hand on her hip. "James," she said. She only called me that when she was grumpy with me. "You can't just work extra hours and buy a new icebox. They're at least two fifty, and…"

"Honey," I said, walking across the kitchen to take her into my arms. "I'll take care of it."

"Good, because there's something else."

I raised an eyebrow.

"I'm pregnant."

I took her in my arms, squeezing tight, probably too tight, feeling happy tears well up in my eyes.

"Is that okay?" she asked close to my ear.

I let her go, chuckling and wiping my eye. "Is it *okay*? Like we can take it back?"

She jutted out her bottom lip.

"Mrs. Maddox," I said, slowly shaking my head. "A baby is way better than a busted icebox."

I sat in the back row of the auditorium, watching my sons prepare to say their goodbyes to me. Olive's funeral was the day before, and they all looked weary and heartbroken. I wanted nothing more than to hold them and help them through their heartbreak, but it was the one time I couldn't be there for them.

Thomas stepped forward, clasping his hands in front of him after straightening his black tie. *Of course, he has it memorized,* I thought, smiling. I knew after he graduated from Eastern that he'd moved to the East Coast to join a government agency before moving to California. It wasn't until I met Liis that I knew it was the FBI. I was never angry. It made sense for Thomas to want to protect everyone else. My only regret was that I didn't make it clearer that he didn't have to hide it from me, but at the time, I wanted him to tell me when he was ready, on his own terms.

"I met Jim Maddox when he was just twenty-one. The details are fuzzy for me, but he's told me more than once that it's a five-way tie for the second-best day of his life … second only to the day he married Mom. I learned many things from my dad. How to be a good husband, a good father, and that no matter how many times I make a mistake, it's never too late to start over. He let me believe I was protecting him, but really, he was protecting me. We could always count on him to have our backs, even when he was busting our butts to keep us from being complete heathens. We held the utmost respect for our father because he carried himself with respect. We loved him because he emitted love. He was a content man, a peaceful man, and he was our hero, right up to the last seconds of his life, and I can say with utmost certainty"—Thomas cleared his throat—"there was never a moment when I didn't feel loved by him."

He stepped back to stand with his brothers and Shepley, and then stood tall, his feet shoulder-length apart, his hands clasped in front him, a special agent of the FBI even when tears were trickling down his cheeks.

Liis, Falyn, Ellie, Camille, and Abby sat in the front row with America, empty seats between them. Jack and Deana sat in the row behind, along with two more rows of members of the police department in their dress blues.

The rest of the seats were filled with family and friends, neighbors and my brothers from Kappa Sigma, who were still left. People who'd passed in and out of my life for different reasons, at different times. All people who'd made a mark on my life, and who I'd carry with me into eternity.

Diane walked into the living room, holding Thomas' hand, her belly full with our next two children. Her eyes flashed with excitement. "Do you smell that, Tommy?"

"It's yucky," he said, wrinkling his nose.

I stood up from my recliner and walked across the room in my socks, bending over to grab Thomas. "*Yucky?* What do you mean yucky?" I growled, tickling him. He arched his back, cackling and kicking to get away. "Daddy worked all weekend on the paint and carpet!" I finally let him loose. I thought he'd run away, and I was prepared to chase him, but instead, he hugged my leg. I patted his back as Diane took in a deep breath through her nose.

Diane shook her head, looking at my hard work in awe. "You're amazing, Mr. Maddox."

"New icebox, new couch … now new carpet and paint? We'll have a whole new house about the time we're ready to sell."

Diane playfully jabbed her elbow into my side. "We're never selling this house."

Thomas made a show of waving his chubby little hand in front of his nose. "'Cause it's stinky."

"No, it's wonderful. That's the smell of new paint and carpet, and Daddy"—she paused as I leaned over her belly to peck her lips—"even put all the furniture back while we were at the grocery store."

"Oh!" I said, heading to the driveway with a start. I popped the trunk and loaded my arms with brown paper sacks and brought them into the house. As I walked into the kitchen, I blew away the leafy celery stems that were poking out the top and tickling my face. Diane giggled at my funny faces as I set the groceries on the counter. She dipped her hands into the sacks to unload the fresh vegetables. "Two more," I said jogging back to the car. I lifted the remaining sacks, slammed the trunk shut, and walked back in, whistling. I was glad the carpet and paint were finished, and we could enjoy my last night before work. I'd just celebrated my second anniversary at Eakins PD. We didn't get many Sunday nights together, and now, we could relax in our practically new living room.

I walked through the mouth of the hall into the kitchen, frozen mid-step. Thomas and Diane were staring at the puddle on the linoleum, stunned.

For half a second, I worried about broken glass, but then I recognized that her water had broken. The doctor had to break her water during Thomas's delivery, so I was surprised to see her standing there in her bare feet, wiggling her toes and grossed out by the liquid on the floor. She hadn't even complained of any contractions.

She grunted, and her knees bent. She reached for the icebox to steady herself. "Jim?" she said, her voice shrill.

"Okay. Babies are coming. Don't panic. Going to get the bag, and I'll be right back." I sprinted up the stairs, and just as I hooked my hand around the strap, I heard Diane moan. I bounded down the stairs three at a time, nearly breaking my ankle as I landed at the bottom.

"Oh!" Diane shrieked, holding out her free hand.

Thomas was sopping up the water with a towel.

"Good job, son. You ready to meet your new little sisters or brothers?"

Thomas grinned wide as I picked him up in one arm. I supported Diane's weight, holding her to my side with my free arms, and dipped my head so she could hook her elbow behind my neck. I walked sideways out to the car, helping Diane in. Thomas stood up in the center of the bench seat, stroking his mom's hair while she breathed.

"Shit! The keys!"

"The dining table," she said, her voice low and controlled. She began her Lamaze, and I turned on my heels, sprinting into the house, swiping the keys, and then returning to the car. I slid in behind the wheel of our green 1970 Chevelle, and I yanked the gear into reverse. I stretched my arm across the top of the bench seat behind Thomas and Diane, and I turned around watching behind me as I stomped on the gas.

Diane caught Thomas when he jerked forward as I braked and stared at me with wide eyes. "Get us there in one piece, Daddy," she said.

I nodded, a little embarrassed. I was a cop. Panic wasn't supposed to be possible for me, but I'd been nervous for four and a half months, knowing Diane was going to deliver twins. So many things could go wrong with a single birth, never mind two.

Diane leaned over, grabbed her belly with both hands, and moaned.

I pulled the gear into drive, and we raced toward the hospital.

Thomas slipped his arms around Trenton's shoulders while Taylor stood behind his twin at the podium. Tyler repositioned the microphone's thin, silver neck, tapping the foam cover before gesturing for Taylor to start. Taylor shot Tyler a look like that was not what they had agreed to, but he stepped up and bent down.

"Dad was the best assistant coach in the league. He had a busy schedule with weird hours, but I don't remember him ever missing a game. He didn't so much coach as carry the ball bags for Mom and cheer from the dugout. Everyone said we had the best parents. When Mom died, no one said that anymore, but to us, they were still perfect. When Dad stopped missing Mom so much, he picked right up where he left off. He coached our team"—he paused, breathing out a small laugh—"we didn't win as many games"—the congregation laughed—"but we loved him, and he took us out for ice cream after every game, win or lose. He packed our lunches, drove us to football practice, and attended all of our games. When Dad was around, I was never scared, whether it was because he knew the right thing to do, or because he had my back. He was the toughest man I've ever known, and my brothers are damn tough. I know if he had to go out, protecting his family is the way he'd want it to be." Taylor touched his knuckle to his nose. "We couldn't've had a better dad, and that's the truth. The same for our wives. And my kids couldn't've had a better Papa. I wish we lived closer so they could have gotten to know each other better, but the time he spent with them, he made it count. That's what I want everyone to remember about Jim Maddox. He made his life count."

Tyler hugged his brother, and then he opened a piece of paper. His lips trembled, and he looked out at the crowd and then back down at his paper a few times before he spoke. He cleared his throat and then took a deep breath. Taylor put a hand on his shoulder, and Thomas did the same, then Travis and Trenton added their strength for their brother as well.

Tyler's lips formed into an "o," and he breathed out. "I love my Dad," he said, his voice breaking. He swallowed and then shook his head. Thomas patted him on the shoulder for encouragement. "He had to divide his time between five sons and his wife, but I never felt like I had to wait for his attention. We weren't rich, but I don't remember wanting for anything. I remember when Mom died; I wondered if he would get remarried because he'd always said there would never be another woman like our mom. When Travis left for college, I asked him if he'd reconsider, thinking maybe he was just concentrating on his kids. He said the only woman he'd ever love was waiting for him in Heaven. I'm just … I love my dad, and I'm sad he's gone, but I'm happy for them that they're together now. They've been waiting a long time to be together again, and it comforts my heart to know they're somewhere right now, unable to keep their hands off each other, grossing out all of your passed friends and relatives the way they used to do to us." The crowd chuckled. "They never spent more than a shift apart from the time they met until Mom died, and I know Dad never got over it. So Dad, I'm glad … I'm so happy that you're with Mom now. I know she's telling you how proud she is of how well you took care of us, because you did."

"Run!" Diane screamed, pulling her white ball cap with the blue bill off her head, waving it in a big circle, side-skipping toward first base. "Run, run, run, run!"

Taylor dropped the bat and took off, running away from the tee post as fast as his short legs could take him. He finally made it to the white square, jumping up and down when he realized he'd gotten there before the ball.

Diane jumped with him, whooping and hollering and carrying on, giving him a high-five. Taylor beamed like it was the best day of his life. Diane reset, clapping as she jogged back toward the next batter. Thomas tossed her a new ball from the dugout, and she set it on the tee, telling Craig Porter to keep his eye on the ball and swing through. It was our last out, the last inning, and we were two runs down. Craig reared back, and as he swung, Diane leaned back, narrowly avoiding a bat to the face. The ball bounced off the tee, not reaching halfway between home base and the pitcher's mound, but she yelled at him to go.

"Run! Yes! Run, Craigers! Run your little heart out! Taylor, go!" she said when she realized her son hadn't started running yet.

Taylor took off, but the shortstop had picked up the ball and tossed it to second base. Without thinking, Taylor hopped right over him and kept running, standing on the base, pulling down his cap like he was the god of T-ball.

"Yes! Those are my boys!" she cheered, pointing at the two on base. "Get ya some!"

Tyler stepped up to the plate, looking mean and intimidating even though it was just him and the ball tee.

"All right, son," Diane said, leaning over to grab her knees. She had a big wad of pink gum in her mouth, chewing it like it had made her mad. "You got this. Relax. Stare at that ball and swing your little heart out." She clapped three times, taking a few steps back. Tyler was our best batter.

Tyler took a breath, wiggled his hips, and swung. He hit the tee, and the ball bounced behind him. He frowned, disappointed in himself.

Diane patted his backside once. "C'mon now, none of that. Shake it off. This is it. This time, you've got it."

Tyler nodded and hit the bat against each of his little cleats. He bent forward, got in position, and then swung, launching it past the pitcher's mound. It bounced, zipping between the second and third base, and the shortstop chased after it.

"Go, go, go!" Diane said, waving her hat. "Go to second!" When Taylor paused at third, she gestured him to come to her. "Home, baby! Home, home, home! Keep going, Craig, don't stop! Go home, Taylor!"

Taylor slid into home and then stood. Diane grabbed him and held him close, yelling for Craig, who ran past home seconds later.

The third baseman caught the ball from the shortstop, and then he hurled the ball to the catcher.

"Book it, Maddox!" Diane barked.

Tyler put into high gear and slid into home. When the dust cleared, the umpire crossed his arms and then held them out to his sides. "Safe!"

I yelled, running toward home, and the team followed me out. We crowded around Diane, everyone hugging her, cheering and laughing. The parents stood up, clapping for Diane's Little Dodgers. Diane yelped, and she fell over, hugging the boys and cackling as they piled on top of her.

Once the celebration of winning their last tournament was over, and the boys and their parents waved goodbye, I hugged my wife tight. "You're fierce," I said. "Matt's Mustangs didn't know what hit 'em."

She smirked, arching an eyebrow. "I told you they would underestimate me."

"And they did. You handled a whole team pretty good, coach. Great season."

"Thanks," she said, pecking my cheek. She rubbed my whiskers with her knuckles. "I hope you like the idea of me and a team of boys."

I chuckled, confused. "What do you mean?"

She picked up the bag of t-balls and swung it over her shoulders. "I'm pregnant."

I stood, my mouth hanging open as she walked to the car. I looked down at the twins. "Really?"

"Really!" she yelled back. She put her thumb and pinky in her mouth and blew out an ear-piercing whistle. "Load up!"

Thomas, Taylor, and Tyler took off after their mom.

I blew out a breath, my cheeks filling and then puffing out the air. I nodded once. "Okay, then." The boys carried their bats and gloves, and I carried everything else, pulling down my Little Dodger's ball cap. "Let's do this."

Trenton broke off from Thomas, Travis, Taylor, Tyler, and Shepley, limping to the podium for his turn. It was our family's third funeral in six weeks, and the purple under his eyes and his sagging shoulders told a story of sleepless nights and grief. The paper crinkled as he unfolded the words he'd written down just days after I'd left him. It was full of eraser marks, pencil smudges, and dried tears.

"Dad." He sighed. "When I sat down to write this letter, I tried to think about the many moments you were a good dad, and the hundreds of times we laughed or that just stuck out to me, but all I can think about … is that I'm so sad that you're gone and how much I'm going to miss you. I'm going to miss your advice. You knew everything about everything, and you always knew the right words to say—whether I was hurting or trying to make a decision. Even when I was making the wrong one. You never"—he shook his head and pressed his lips together, trying to hold in his tears—"judged us. You accepted and loved us for who we were, even when who we were was hard to love. And you were that way to everyone. Our wives called you dad, and it was real to them. Olive … called you Papa, and she meant it, and I'm glad to know that wherever you are, you're together. I'm going to miss you telling stories about Mom. I felt closer to her no matter how many years passed by because when you talked about her, you talked like she was still here. I'm glad you can finally be with her again. I'm going to miss so many things about you, Dad. I couldn't name them all. But we're all lucky that we had you for the time that we did. Everyone who crossed your path was better for it, and they were forever changed. And now, we'll be forever changed because you're gone."

"Stay out of the street," Thomas said to his identical younger brothers.

The twins' toy fire engines were flying four feet above the sidewalk two blocks from our house, intermittently crashing into each other without spinning out of control into space. Trenton's tiny hand was in mine as he waddled next to me, his diaper crinkling as he walked, even under corduroy pants and pajama leggings. He was bundled up like an Eskimo baby, his nose and cheeks red from the icy wind. Thomas herded the twins back to the center of the sidewalk, shoving Taylor's knit cap down over his ears.

I zipped up my coat, shivering under three layers, wondering how Diane was so happily dragging me along by the hand in just a stretched-out sweater and acid-wash maternity jeans. Her puffy nose was red, but she insisted she was on the brink of sweating.

"It's just the next street!" she said, encouraging the boys not to stop in front of us.

"Trenton, I can't see you when you're just below me, so if you stop in front of Mommy, we'll both go down with the ship," she said, shooing him with her hands. "There!" she said, pointing at a long driveway. "Thirty-seven hundred! Can you believe it?"

A practically new conversion van sat with a For Sale sign in the front windshield; its red paint barely visible under three feet of snow.

I gulped. Our current van that barely fit our family of six still wasn't paid off. "It looks new. Are you sure that's the right price?"

She clapped her hands. "I know! It's like Heaven just plopped it right in front of us!"

Her perfect smile and the deep dimple in her left cheek melted me every time, making it impossible to tell her anything but yes. "Well, let's get their number, and I'll make an appointment to take it for a test drive."

Diane clapped her hands once, holding them at her chest. "Really?"

I shook my head once. "If it's what you want."

She jumped, and then held her belly, looking down. "See? Didn't I tell you? Everything is going to be all right, little T."

"Mommy," Trenton said, tugging on her jeans.

Diane slowly maneuvered her body to kneel, always sure to get eye-level with whichever son wanted her attention. Trenton was holding her index finger, and she lifted it to her mouth, kissing his pudgy hand. "Yes, sir?"

"I like the car."

"You like the car?" she asked. She looked up at me. "Hear that, Daddy? Trenton wants the car."

"Then we have to get the car," I said, shrugging.

Trenton and Diane flashed matching smiles with matching dimples.

"Did you hear that?" she squealed. "Daddy's going to get you the car! Good choice, Trenton!"

Trenton threw his arms around his mom's neck and squeezed. "Love you, Mommy."

"And I love you." Diane pressed a wet kiss on Trenton's cherub cheek, and he wiped it off, although he was more than happy to get a kiss from his mother. She was a goddess in their eyes, capable of anything. I spent the majority of every day trying my damnedest to deserve her.

I helped her stand, watching her lean, a bit off balance.

"Easy." I gently took her chin between my thumb and index finger. "I don't know what I would do without you."

She winked. "Keep saying yes and you'll never have to find out."

The boys hugged one another, and after some discussion, Travis stepped forward. He gripped each side of the podium, looking down. It took him a long time to speak. Even from behind, I could see Abby cover her mouth, hurting for both of them. My youngest son clenched his teeth, and then his eyes scanned the crowd.

"I've thought about what I would say. I really … I don't know what to say because there are no words for this. None. Thomas is right. You always made us feel loved, Dad. Even the times when we were unlovable. Taylor and Tyler are right. You were the strongest of us. You always made us feel safe. And like Trent said … you spoke about Mom so often that I can't help but be happy that you're finally with her again. You wanted that more than life, but you loved us enough to stick around for as long as you did, and I'm so thankful for that. Some people thought you were a fool for holding onto someone who was never coming back, but you knew different. You knew you would be the one going back to her. I …" He sighed. "My brothers have told me stories about the other kids saying they wished they had our parents. If I could choose to do it all over again or have different parents for the rest of my life, I would choose you. I would choose her. Just so I could spend the time with you that I had." A single tear fell, and he sniffed once. "I would, and there are no words for how much that means to me. There are no words for how beautiful your love was, and that it had an effect on your children long after Mom died. The love you showed us will stay with us long after today."

My brows pulled together, and I shifted uncomfortably in the chair stationed beside my wife's hospital bed that we'd bought the same day we called hospice. Diane was holding Travis in both arms, tubing coming from her hand, hugging him for the last time. She held her tears until Thomas took him out into the hall.

She covered her mouth, and her tired, sunken eyes looked at me for answers I didn't have. "He won't remember me," she whispered with a ragged voice. Her body had been worn by chemo and radiation, her scarf covering her bald head. She had fought hard for as long as she could, only saying enough when the doctors said she only had a few more days with the boys.

"He'll remember you. I won't let him forget."

Her bottom lip trembled, and she covered her eyes, nodding. "I'm so sorry."

I took her hand and pressed my lips against her bony knuckles. "You have nothing to be sorry for, my love. You did everything you could."

She closed her eyes. "I'm afraid."

"You can be afraid. I'll hold you 'til it's over."

"I don't want it to be over."

"I know," I said. I crawled into bed next to her, letting her lay her head on my chest. She settled in. It took everything I had to stay strong for her. She had been strong for the boys and me all these years. I owed her that.

Diane nodded her head, and with tears streaming down her face, she rested her cheek on my chest. "I love you, Diane. I love you. I love you. I love you." I held my wife until her breathing evened out and then touched my cheek to her forehead when more time passed between breaths. "I love you," I whispered. "I love you. I love you. I love you."

When she exhaled for the last time, I watched the nurse, Becky, check Diane's pulse by the wrist and then use the stethoscope. Becky pulled the earpieces from her ears and offered an apologetic smile. "She's gone, Jim."

I sucked in a breath and wailed. I knew my sons were just outside the door, but I'd never felt so much pain in my life, and I wasn't strong enough to hold it in. I held Diane's face gently in my hands and kissed her cheek. "I love you." I kissed her again, my tears wetting her face. "I love you. I love you. I love you." I buried my face in her neck and sobbed.

Travis stepped back from the podium, and the boys hugged one another before walking off the stage in a line led by Thomas. The song Diane and I danced to at our wedding played as the boys filled the empty seats next to their wives. Trenton leaned over, his entire body shaking. Camille and Taylor both touched his back. Camille whispered in his ear, and he leaned his head against her chin.

Part of me wanted to stay, to watch over them and guide them, but something too strong to ignore was pulling me back; something I hadn't been able to ignore over four decades before. A delicate hand touched my shoulder, and I turned, seeing my beloved wife's face. She sat next to me and took my hands in hers.

My eyes glossed over. "I've been waiting for you."

She watched the pastor speak for a few moments and then turned to me, a peaceful smile on her face and tears in her eyes. "Ditto."

"I did my best."

I interlaced my fingers in hers, and she squeezed my hand. "You were perfect. I knew you could do it."

I lifted her hand to my lips and closed my eyes. A peace came over me that I hadn't felt since before she'd died. She stood up, pulling me toward the double doors in the back of the auditorium.

"I love you. I love you. I love you," she said, reaching behind her. She pushed the door, wearing the smile I'd fallen in love with, walking backward. She looked the way she had before she got sick; the happy, tough-as-nails, stunningly beautiful woman I remembered. I couldn't take my eyes off her, just as I couldn't then. I'd missed shamelessly staring at her, but I glanced over my shoulder one last time at my sons.

Diane hugged my arm and rested her head against my shoulder. "They're going to be fine."

"I know."

I kissed her temple, and we continued through the doors. Our past was now and now was in the past. Just as she'd promised, we were together again, in a moment of no sickness or pain—only love. And when love was real, so was forever.

THE END.

# ACKNOWLEDGMENTS

A Beautiful Funeral is probably the most difficult book I've had to write. It was more than just emotional, it was keeping the various family members and timelines straight, along with incorporating all of their careers and personalities. So many people contributed to helping me make this book what it is.

Jessica Landers is the admin for the MacPack, a McGuire fan group on Facebook. Not only does she keep it interesting, positive, and fun for everyone, but she also helped me in research for each character and the timelines, and stepped up when I needed a temporary assistant. Thank you for everything you do, Jess, but most of all for being a trusted friend for more than two years. People have come and gone, but you've remained. Ride or die, girlfriend.

Thank you to Michelle Chu for beta reading a very early version of A Beautiful Funeral and asking questions I know all the diehard fans would want answered.

Thank you to Nina Moore for taking time to make incredible teasers and graphics for marketing. You do an incredible job and I am so thankful for you!

The packaging of a book is very important to me, and I knew that the cover had to be exceptionally beautiful to offset the anxiety of the title. Hang Le provided the "quiet beauty" I asked for in the most perfect way. Thank you, Hang, for making an amazing cover that made everyone gasp as much as the title—hard to do.

Thank you to Ben Creech and Fiona Lorne for helping with the firefighting information, and thank you to Georgia Cates for helping with obstetric /preemie info.

A big thanks to Fiona Lorne, Jenny Sims, and Pam Huff for answering my call for help, and for jumping in to edit this novel when I experienced scheduling conflicts. Thank you to Jovana Shirley for editing the description on-the-spot, and for formatting.

Thank you to my agent Kevan Lyon for sticking with me through a particularly rocky first year back to self-publishing. The bright side is that our many conversations provided a quick and dirty introduction, and you are one of the most patient and professional women in the business! Another thanks to my foreign agent Taryn Fagerness for all of her hard work this year as well.

Thank you to my husband and children for always forgiving me when I work too much or too late, and sleep in too long.

Thanks to author Andrea Joan for keeping me sane while writing this novel, for being a loyal, trusted friend, a wise consultant, confident, and comedian. I'm not sure when it happened, but you are one of my very best friends, and I treasure you.

A special thanks to my personal assistant Deanna Pyles and family. Not only was Deanna a cheerleader and beta read this novel numerous times in its many forms, she kept me hydrated and fed while I edited this novel. She also moved her family sixteen hours away from the place they were all born and raised to help my husband and I grow our businesses. That's love, and I love you for being so brave and trusting.

# ABOUT THE AUTHOR

JAMIE MCGUIRE was born in Tulsa, Oklahoma. She attended Northern Oklahoma College, the University of Central Oklahoma, and Autry Technology Center where she graduated with a degree in Radiography.

Jamie paved the way for the New Adult genre with the international bestseller *Beautiful Disaster*. Her follow-up novel, *Walking Disaster*, debuted at #1 on the *New York Times*, *USA Today*, and *Wall Street Journal* bestseller lists. *Beautiful Oblivion*, book one of the Maddox Brothers series, also topped the *New York Times* bestseller list, debuting at #1. In 2015, books two and three of the Maddox Brothers series, *Beautiful Redemption* and *Beautiful Sacrifice*, respectively, also topped the *New York Times,* as well as a Beautiful series novella, *Something Beautiful. Beautiful Burn*, book four hit the New York Times in February 2016.

Novels also written by Jamie McGuire include: apocalyptic thriller and 2014 UtopYA Best Dystopian Book of the Year, *Red Hill*; the Providence series, a young adult paranormal romance trilogy; *Apolonia*, a dark sci-fi romance; and several novellas, including *A Beautiful Wedding, Among Monsters*, *Happenstance: A Novella Series,* and *Sins of the Innocent.*

Jamie is the first indie author in history to strike a print deal with retail giant Wal-Mart. Her self-published novel, Beautiful Redemption hit Wal-Mart shelves in September, 2015.

Jamie lives in Steamboat Springs, Colorado with her husband, Jeff, and their three children.

Find Jamie at www.jamiemcguire.com or on Facebook, Twitter, Google +, Tsu, Snapchat, and Instagram.

Upcoming works from Jamie include *All the Little Lights* (2017), a YA romance, and the Other Lives series, a Maddox Brothers spinoff centering around the complicated lives of Trex, the Alpine hotshots, and other crew that protect the public and property from wildland fires. *Trex*, book one of the series, will release in fall 2017.